THE FALLEN

With stories by
Marie Morin
Jaide Fox
Kimberly Zant
Celeste Anwar

Paranormal Romance

New Concepts   Georgia

Be sure to check out our website for the very best in fiction at fantastic prices!

When you visit our webpage, you can:

* Read excerpts of currently available books
* View cover art of upcoming books and current releases
* Find out more about the talented artists who capture the magic of the writer's imagination on the covers
* Order books from our backlist
* Find out the latest NCP and author news--including any upcoming book signings by your favorite NCP author
* Read author bios and reviews of our books
* Get NCP submission guidelines
* And so much more!

We offer a 20% discount on all new Trade Paperback releases ordered from our website!

Be sure to visit our webpage to find the best deals in e-books and paperbacks! To find out about our new releases as soon as they are available, please be sure to sign up for our newsletter (http://www.newconceptspublishing.com/newsletter.htm) or join our reader group (http://groups.yahoo.com/group/new_concepts_pub/join)!

The newsletter is available by double opt in only and our customer information is *never* shared!

Visit our webpage at:
www.newconceptspublishing.com

The Fallen is an original publication of NCP. This work has never before appeared in book form. This work is a novel. Any similarity to actual persons or events is purely coincidental.

New Concepts Publishing
5202 Humphreys Rd.
Lake Park, GA 31636

ISBN 1-58608-698-7
© copyright August 2005, Marie Morin, Jaide Fox, Kimberly Zant, Celeste Anwar

Cover art (c) copyright 2005 Eliza Black

NCP books are available at special quantity discounts for bulk purchases for sales promotions, premiums, fund raising, or educational use. For details, write, email, or phone New Concepts Publishing, 5202 Humphreys Rd., Lake Park, GA 31636; Ph. 229-257-0367, Fax 229-219-1097; orders@newconceptspublishing.com.

First NCP Paperback Printing: 2005

TABLE OF CONTENTS

THE BEGINNING

In the beginning, when the star dust of an exploding sun sprinkled the world with the seeds of life, *they* were among the first to crawl from the primordial soup, emerging as chameleon-like creatures, able to change shape and color at will to protect themselves from the predators that emerged along side them. Like the salamander, they could heal the most grievous wounds with amazing speed and grow new appendages when necessary. This gift for rapid cell regeneration, they used to give themselves an even stronger advantage over the beasts that would prey upon them, the development of wings to glide high above the tangle of vegetation that had sprouted from the soil, where death lay behind every frond and leaf. Eventually they developed the ability for true flight.

These endowments gained them the right to life when others perished and eventually, over time, *they* emerged as the Elumi, evolving into the dominant, intelligent species of their world.

When the first, ape-like creatures that were man's ancestors emerged and began their struggle to cultivate and dominate nature, the Elumi had already conquered the known world and its skies, and their gifts had led them to see what no other eyes could see--the gateway to a world that coexisted with the primitive, violent Earth, beyond the destructive forces of nature, beyond the reach of time, beyond the tedious struggles of mankind, who were multiplying and polluting the world the Elumi had dominated for ages.

For a time, the Elumi and mankind lived side by side and the Elumi enjoyed the awe with which these weaker creatures viewed them, calling them gods, angels, demons, fairies--and endowing these God-like beings with many powers the Elumi didn't actually possess. For a time, the Elumi fought the boredom of their existence with these intelligent beasts, amused themselves with these savage, pseudo-intelligent creatures, but there was little sport in it when all was said and done and in time they grew more annoyed than amused and the Elumi passed beyond the gate, away from the distraction of these lesser beings to pursue their own course.

Their gifts had made them virtually immortal, resulting in a notable lack of fear of death, which encouraged their natural aggressiveness. With no reason to progress beyond that stage they found most compatible with their warlike dispositions, they simply did not. The strongest and most aggressive carved out kingdoms for themselves, twelve in all. Twelve kingdoms dwindled to four as the ages passed and one by one they fell to a mightier foe.

Many ages of mankind passed in the world below them while the remaining kingdoms contented themselves with merely squabbling over boundaries and incursions into the other kingdoms from time to time to count coup or to take a particularly appealing prize, but the time came when they grew restless. The time came when the petty disputes erupted once more into all out war when King Braeden of Nardu threatened the balance of power by seeking to ally himself to the kingdom of Marceena by marriage to the Princess Leia.

Wily King Edric, father of Princess Leia, did not oppose the match, but did not approve it either since he was well aware that King Braeden wanted his kingdom far more than his daughter. He allowed the courtship and bided his time while he considered how he might turn the situation to his own advantage and add the Kingdom of Nardu to his own holdings under his rule.

The threat was enough to alarm both King Sorecet of Garyn and King Gozal of Tearra and although they were fast enemies, they began to negotiate the possibility of joining forces to oppose the army they feared would rise against them the moment King Braeden and King Edic settled their differences.

And thus it came about that the wars in the land of Pearthen, high Earth, spilled over into the lower world of mankind once more.

FALLEN ANGEL

By
Marie Morin

Chapter One

"It's been two frigging years," Kylee said angrily. "You mean to say you've got nothing? How could you have nothing?"

She could see that the detective sitting across from her was holding onto his patience only with a strenuous effort, but she didn't care. Snatching a drawer open, he hefted a file fully six inches thick from it and plopped it down on the top of his desk.

"We've got a whole lot of nothing," he said tightly. "We've followed every lead, but we ran out of leads more than a year ago. So, unless you have something new...?"

Her stomach tightened as she stared at him, trying to gather up the nerve to put her plan into action.

She'd never considered herself a coward--still didn't. The plan that had slowly evolved in her mind wasn't the product of a sane person of bravery, but one insane with grief and the need for vengeance. But she was not so far off the deep end to feel no fear of something she had every reason to fear.

"I've--I decided to smoke him out. I'd like your help if you're willing to help me, but I'll do it anyway," she said quickly before she lost her nerve.

Detective Strand gave her a patronizing look that made her long to slap him. "If you'll pardon me saying so, that would be plain out stupid. You'll only end up getting yourself killed."

"You know it was her...." She stopped. She couldn't bring herself to say 'pimp', not about her baby sister. Drug dealer sounded almost as bad. The truth was the bastard had gotten her little sister hooked and used her and then killed her when she tried to get out because she knew too much about him. "...boyfriend that killed her," she finished, feeling ill even to use that description, although it was less offensive to her sister's memory.

"We *think* it was him, and that means exactly zero, because we haven't found anything to link him to the murder aside from the fact that he was her pimp. It could just as easily have been one of her johns."

Kylee winced at the word pimp. How dare the bastard sit in judgment on poor Stacy! She hadn't been much more than kid, easy prey for the sonofabitch that had used her, but she could see it in his face. As far as he was concerned, Stacy was nothing but trash, a whore and a junky and undeserving of life--or his valuable time. White faced, Kylee got to her feet. "Well, how about I do your job for you? If I get a confession for you on tape, do you think you could put the bastard away? Or does it take more than two hands for you to find your ass?"

Detective Strand was beet red when he shoved his own chair back and surged to his feet. "I'm going to *pretend* I didn't hear that," he growled. "If you're so damned determined to go out and get yourself killed, I don't see how I can stop you, but if you do anything illegal, you're the one that's going to end up in jail, *Ms.* Griffin!"

"It's a hell of a lot safer to run in law abiding citizens, isn't it? Especially if it's a woman half your size!"

His eyes narrowed. "I put my life on the line every day," he growled, "not that people like you appreciate it."

"It's your *job*, Detective! If you didn't like the job description, you shouldn't have taken the job to start with. I don't *have* to appreciate your half ass service. I pay the taxes that support you! The biggest problem I see with that is that I don't have anything to do with hiring and firing. I just get to pay taxes through the nose and listen to excuses whenever I actually need you!" Grabbing her purse up,

Kylee stalked from his office before he could fall dead in a fit of suppressed rage.

She was still so furious when she left the precinct that she merely stood on the sidewalk for a time, staring at nothing in particular while people walked by her, jostling her. Finally, she moved to the curb and hailed a taxi to take her back to the room she was renting.

She hated the city. There were too many people, too many cars, and too many opportunities for corrupt and/or incompetent cops and outright criminals.

She was still seething when she reached the shabby room she'd rented. She was also terrified. All she really wanted to do was to tuck her tail between her legs and high tail it back for home where she could feel safe and untainted.

She was hardly a saint, but the filthy things that happened in the dark corners of the city made her feel unclean just from proximity.

She couldn't just go home knowing the bastard that had butchered her little sister was still going about life as usual, making money off of the bright eyed young girls that flocked to the city for adventure and ended up as carcasses on a slab in the morgue, picked clean, sucked dry.

She'd spent a solid year hoping to hear he'd been caught, hoping to hear he'd been found dead--anything that would make her feel that justice had caught up with him and he wasn't able to prey on anybody else's little sister.

She was never going to be able to put this behind her as long as she had the mental picture of his grinning face next to her sister's cold, dead one.

She didn't want to die, though, and she had very little confidence that she could carry out her scheme. She wasn't street smart. She'd seen plenty of violence, even in the small city where she lived, but although she'd been a 'wild' teenager she hadn't dealt with the drug scene and certainly not prostitution. She hadn't rubbed elbows with users, or dealers, or women that had been forced to make their living in such a way.

She was going to stick out like a--victim just waiting to be pounced on. She might as well strap a sign to her ass.

After taking a hot shower to try to calm her frayed nerves, she lay down on the bed, hoping she could force mind and body to rest. If she was going to be out half the night, she needed to have her wits about her.

* * * *

Kylee had spent nearly a year training in self-defense. She had a bottle of pepper spray in one pocket and a tape recorder in her bra and she still felt naked, completely defenseless, and scared totally shitless as she made her way down the dimly lit streets where her sister had lived and died.

How could Stacy, five feet nothing and, maybe, ninety pounds soaking wet have gotten up the nerve to come to such a dangerous place to start with? How could she have *lived* here, she wondered? Were drugs that powerful? Did they distort reality that much? Even if they did, Stacy would have had to have been bombed out of her mind all the time not to notice how dangerous the area was even for a two hundred pound gorilla, much less a speck like Stacy.

Knots of hookers waited on just about every corner. They gave her suspicious, aggressive glances whenever she passed them. Derelicts dotted the landscape, swigging from bottles, lying in the gutters, squatted behind the dubious concealment of trash dumpsters that over flowed everywhere, or staggering along the sidewalk. 'Pimp mobiles' passed along the street at intervals, creeping along so that the 'ladies' could get a good look at them and stay on their toes.

She was almost relieved when she saw the sign she'd been looking for, the bar slash pool hall where Enrico, Stacy's former boyfriend, was known to hang out. Girding herself, without waiting to think it over, she grabbed the door handle and stepped inside.

Her lungs seemed to collapse in her chest like deflated balloons. Her heart put on brakes.

There were probably two dozen of the lowest looking low lifes she'd ever seen hovering around the pool tables, slouched in bench seats in front of rickety tables, and standing along the walls. A few of them glanced toward the door when it opened and did a double take.

Kylee ignored them, raking her gaze over the assemblage in a desperate attempt to see if she could identify Stacy's killer.

One of the guys that had glanced her way elbowed a man standing in the shadows. The guy looked up, took a step forward.

Kylee's heart slammed into her chest wall as it surged to life again.

Whatever doubts she'd entertained that she would recognize him vanished.

Whatever doubts she'd had that he would instantly know she was Stacy's sister disappeared, as well.

He looked like he'd seen a ghost.

It was all she'd come to do.

Stepping from the bar, she walked as briskly as her shaky legs would allow in the direction from which she'd come, resisting the temptation to break into a run. She had just reached the first intersection when she heard a shout behind her.

Glancing back, she saw that Enrico had barreled out the door of the bar. Kicking her heels off, Kylee sprinted down the next block. She'd left the rental car on the street at the next intersection. "Please, God! Don't let it be stripped down to a shell before I can get to it!" she muttered under her breath, dodging a man that tried to block her path. He caught her anyway, swinging her around. She dug for the pepper spray and filled his face full.

Screaming, he released her to rub his eyes and she leapt away, her feet pounding against the pavement in time to her heart beat. She slowed enough to dig for her keys when she saw the car. She could tell from the sounds behind her, though, that Enrico was gaining on her.

Reaching the car, she shoved the key in the hole after scraping paint off the door all the way around the hole. Diving inside, she slammed the lock down and shoved the key into the ignition. Luck was with her. The engine turned over at the first try.

Someone grabbed the door handle, wrenching on it. Kylee turned to see Enrico glaring at her through the window. "I know what you did and I'm going to see you fry for it!" she screamed at him, flicking him a bird.

It was probably one of the more ill advised impulses she'd had, and given in to.

He slammed his hand against the window so hard she was surprised it didn't shatter. Screaming, she jerked the car in gear and stepped on the gas just as he slammed his fist against the window again. That time the glass did shatter and he grabbed a fist full of her shirt, tearing it half off of her as the car's momentum yanked him off balance. He rolled away from the wheels as she jerked the car into the street, narrowly missing another car.

She ran the red light at the next intersection, almost hitting a second car as she glanced in her rearview mirror to check on Enrico. To her horror, she saw him leap to his feet, run around to the driver's side of the car and yank the driver out.

"Oh shit!"

She turned at the next intersection, whipping the wheel around the corner at the last minute. The car fishtailed. She fought for control and managed to get the car straightened out. When she got to the next corner, she turned again, glancing in the mirror to see if the car Enrico was now driving had managed to make the turn. The sound of grinding metal reached her as he sideswiped a parked car.

She didn't wait to see if he made the next turn, zigzagging through the city in an attempt to lose him. Driven by sheer terror, it was a while before she realized that she was moving deeper and deeper into no man's land.

She found herself in a 'ghost' town, an area of the city that contained nothing but run down, or falling down, buildings. About the time she realized she hadn't seen a soul in several blocks the car Enrico was driving barreled out of an alley, slamming into the rear of her car and sending it spinning completely out of control.

Chapter Two

Fortunately for Kylee, the car's momentum had slowed considerably before the car struck the pile of debris that finally brought the spinning to a stop. She hadn't had the chance to fasten her seatbelt. The abrupt stop slammed her down on the seat hard enough it stunned her for many moments.

By the time she'd recovered enough to begin trying to struggle upright, Enrico was already reaching through her window to unlock her door. In a state of shock, completely disoriented, Kylee was dragged from the car like a rubber doll, unable even to find her voice to scream. He lifted her from the ground by her throat.

Instinct kicked in when her air was cut off by his grip and her own weight, and Kylee began clawing at the hand holding her.

"You listen good, *Putta*. You mess with Enrico, he cut your pretty throat like your *Putta* sister. You got that?"

Not on the fucking recorder, Kylee thought dimly as darkness circled her like vultures, realizing she hadn't had enough presence of mind to turn it on.

He shook her when she didn't answer, though how he thought she could with the grip he had on her throat she couldn't imagine.

Close by, an explosion of sound, like something huge hitting the roof of one of the buildings surrounding the alley, made him jerk in reaction. Dropping her to the ground, he whirled around sharply, his head tilted toward the roofs as he searched for any sign of a threat. Gasping like an asthmatic, Kylee fought to drag air into her lungs and get to her feet at the same time.

A clanging from somewhere nearby, like someone banging on a metal pipe, echoed hollowly through the alley. A duller pounding, like running feet, accentuated the frantic clanging.

"What the fuck is that?" Enrico demanded, sounding further enraged that anyone would dare interrupt his assault and battery.

Kylee didn't answer. She didn't figure he was expecting one. Instead, she struggled to reach the tiny recorder to switch it on. The impact had shifted it from the middle of her bra to the outside of the left cup. "The cops know you killed my sister. *I* know you killed my sister," Kylee managed finally.

Enrico barely glanced at her. He was too busy tracking the sounds above them that continued unabated. "Yeah? Well, I tell you the same ting I tole de cops, prove it, *Putta*."

"I've got your DNA under my fingernails and all over the fucking car!" Kylee screamed at him. "If it matches the DNA they found on her ...."

He grabbed her by the throat again, cutting her off midsentence. Before he could choke the life out of her, something landed on the hood of the car so hard the car bounced. Enrico's eyes nearly bulged from their sockets. "*Madre de dios*!"

Releasing her abruptly, he tore off toward the car he'd left running, leapt into the front seat and peeled off.

Feeling the hair on the back of her neck standing on end, Kylee, on the ground once more, turned to see what had scared the thug off. Two--*something's* were struggling on the hood of the car. As she gaped, the one on top, almost as if he sensed her gaze, lifted his head and looked straight at her. His face was contorted into a mask of rage. His eyes glowed an eerie iridescent green--almost like the eyes of a nocturnal animal.

In spite of the strange eyes, he looked just like a man--except for the great wings sprouting from his back.

The distraction cost him. The man--creature--beneath him, clubbed him on the side of his head with his fist. The one on top tumbled from the hood of the car, taking the other creature with him. Abruptly, they broke apart and shot skyward, disappearing into the darkness of the night sky.

From high above her, Kylee heard the clanging again. It stopped suddenly. A strange whistling noise followed.

Frowning, Kylee stared up at the sky, wondering what the hell it was. Slowly, she got to her feet, moving toward the front of her car to look at the crushed hood. An object struck the ground beside the car, little more than a foot from where she'd been sitting only moments before. She leaned around the hood to look. A broad bladed sword lay in the dirt and gravel next to the front wheel.

Sirens screamed with a suddenness that made her jerk all over. Flashing blue, white, and red lights rounded the corner of the alley before the vehicles did. Without quite knowing why, Kylee moved around the car and pushed the sword under the edge out of sight just as the two police vehicles slid to a stop roughly a car length from hers.

Detective Strand disgorged from the unmarked car, surveying her and the car with an expression of disgust. As he shut his door, two more patrol cars pulled in behind the first two. Catching the eyes of the drivers, he made a circular motion in the air. The two cars backed up and shot off in the direction Enrico had disappeared.

The two cops riding in the patrol car got out and followed Detective Strand, waving their flashlights along the ground and studying the interesting donut Kylee had cut with rubber into the pavement.

"Satisfied?" Detective Strand commented as he reached her.

"Actually, yes," Kylee said, dragging the recorder out of her bra and handing it to him.

He played it back, frowning. "That's not a confession," he said dryly, handing the device back to her when he'd listened.

Dismay filled Kylee. "He confessed to me just before that. He said he would cut my throat like he had--my sister's," Kylee finished, struggling against the wobble in her chin.

"He said, she said. Granted you're a lot more credible witness, but the DA ain't going to go for it, I can tell you that. It's too weak."

"What about DNA? His DNA is all over the car and under my nails."

He gave her a look. "Even if it matches what we found on her, it won't prove anything. He was her pimp and her lover. She wasn't raped, Ms. Griffin. The sex was consensual and any lawyer would shoot down DNA evidence on that alone," he said almost kindly.

He moved closer and looked her over. "We can file assault and battery charges on him."

"How long would he be in jail?"

He shrugged. "A while. Several years anyway."

Kylee fought the urge to burst into tears again. "My sister was only eighteen! He deprived her of the rest of her life."

"You can get him off the streets for a little while, anyway."

She didn't want him off the streets for a little while. She wanted him off permanently.

The detective frowned when she said nothing, glancing toward the hood of the car. After a moment, he moved around her to study it better. Feeling weak kneed, Kylee moved around the car door, which was still standing open and collapsed in the seat.

"This happen when he slammed into you?"

Kylee put her head in her hands. She hadn't had the chance to assimilate what she'd seen. She still didn't know *what* she'd seen, but she wasn't so shook up that she didn't know better than to say anything about it. The cops would think she'd gone off the deep end.

"I don't know. Everything happened so fast."

And then the sword dropped out of the sky. Her heart accelerated at that thought. It was proof--but of what? The rest of the story didn't sound any better in her mind. When she glanced toward the other cops and saw they'd moved off, she leaned over, grabbed the sword from beneath the car and very carefully slipped it under the car seat.

Detective Strand was looking at her when she looked up again. She stared back at him guiltily. "What's this blue stuff?"

Relieved that he hadn't noticed what she'd been doing, Kylee lifted up slightly. She still couldn't see what he was talking about, though, and got up, moving around to the front of the car. The detective had dabbed a finger in the blue liquid smeared all over the hood of the car. He sniffed it, shook his head, rubbed it between two fingers. "It ain't paint."

It didn't look like blood either, at least not of the human variety, but the image of the two creatures struggling on top of the car instantly filled her mind--along with the pounding on the roof of the building, the clanging of metal, the sword falling out of the sky. The man/creature on bottom had had a sword clutched in his fist, she remembered, the fist he'd slammed into his opponent's head.

Blood, she realized, feeling shock go through her again, a coldness. She shivered, glancing up at the buildings that surrounded them.

The sound of an approaching vehicle caught her attention and she turned to see an ambulance pulling up. Detective Strand moved around the car. "Here, let's get you checked out. When they're done with you at the hospital, I'll need to get a statement from you."

Kylee didn't try to argue. The shock had begun wearing off and the pain level was rising. She didn't think there was anything wrong with her aside from bruising, but that was enough to make her hurt all over.

A wrecker arrived to tow the car as she was helped into the ambulance and consternation filled her. Realizing there was nothing she could do about the situation at the moment, she tried to put it from her mind. The techs helped, poking and prodding as they checked her vitals. They made her lie down on the gurney, strapping her in for the trip to the hospital. She didn't protest about that either, but she felt absurd. She wasn't hurt--not really.

She was cold though, bone deep. They covered her with blankets and kept checking her blood pressure.

They wanted her to stay overnight at the hospital. She refused. An officer drove her back to her room and parked outside. Enrico had slipped through their fingers.

Kylee thought it highly doubtful that he could've found out where she was staying but she said nothing, dragging herself inside, checking the room and then collapsing gratefully on the hard lumpy mattress. The pain medication they'd given her worked like a charm. Inside of thirty minutes she was out like a light and didn't dream once, at least none that she could remember.

* * * *

Gabriel stared down at the sleeping woman with a mixture of curiosity and irritation. She'd taken his sword. He had no idea why, but she'd hidden it from him. He'd searched the room while she slept and found nothing.

He needed to get it back. Otherwise, he was going to be trying to defend himself with nothing more than his bare hands the next time he encountered the Marceenaian scum he'd fought earlier.

A wave of dizziness washed over him. Steadying himself, he looked down at his side, frowning at the gashes along his torso and thigh. They were still bleeding sluggishly and surprise flickered through him. The wounds must be deeper than he'd thought or they would have closed by now.

He had not shifted, even though it was unlawful that Elumi walk among the humans in any form that set them apart from them. He'd needed his wings to follow the woman. He knew the sword must have landed close to where he and his enemy had landed on her vehicle, because they'd no more than engaged again when his sword had been knocked from his grip. When the humans had finally cleared out, however, giving him the chance to look for his blade, it had been gone.

She was the only one there when he'd lost it. It only stood to reason that she would've been the one who had taken it.

He still couldn't figure out *why* she'd taken it. His sword carried the heraldry of his house and his overlord, but she was human, not Elumi. She could have no interest in their war, would not have any reason to consider him an enemy.

Darkness began to crowd close to his vision as he stood staring down at her, wondering how he was to retrieve the weapon when he was forbidden direct contact with humans, the females in particular since they presented a danger to the Elumi male that human males didn't. For a moment, Gabriel thought it was a trick of the light. Finally, he realized with more than a touch of amazement that his injuries had weakened him far more than he'd thought possible.

Concentrating, he tried belatedly to shift. The effort availed him nothing at all in his weakened state, but it cost him. Darkness came down over him like a thick curtain. His last awareness of anything at all was astonishment as he felt himself drifting downward.

* * * *

Kylee was wrenched from deep sleep by the blow. Instinct fought the drug in her system and she jerked upright, tensed to fight for her life. The arm that had knocked the breath out of her didn't so much as twitch, however. With the immediate threat past, the pain killer asserted dominance again, making her head swim dizzily. Her thoughts ebbed and flowed in a totally disjointed way that made it hard to put them together into a comprehensible evaluation.

Wings, she thought, looking down at the back presented to her, folded and tucked against his length. Feathered wings, pale white/gold at the tips, growing gradually darker until they were almost amber at the root--quill? A twenty foot wing span at the very least. Big bird. Huge--but there was the arm.

Catching hold of the hand, she lifted the arm with an effort. It was dead weight and heavily muscled from forearm to bicep. Golden skin, slightly paler golden hair sprinkling the top side of the arm, but it was definitely a man's arm. Angel, she wondered a little dazedly?

She shook that off, realizing it was absurd.

She shifted since the arm wasn't pinning her to the bed anymore and looked down at the head that had creamed her shoulder when he fell on her. Long wavy hair that was somewhere between light brown and golden blond covered the face.

Her arm began to ache from holding the 'log'. Anyway, she was supporting herself with one arm. She dropped the arm she was holding so that she could brush the hair out of his face. It landed bruisingly on one hip and slid off.

Gathering the hair with her fingers, she pulled it back and tucked it behind his ear. Nothing strange about the ear. The face sparked a memory. She frowned in concentration, trying to figure out why it looked familiar--but didn't.

Her heart executed a series of painful little skips when an image flashed in her mind--two winged man-like creatures trying to choke the life out of each other on the hood of her car.

She could only see half his face, and it wasn't contorted with effort and rage now.

He opened his eye.

She jumped, drawing away.

Groaning, he struggled for several moments and finally managed to roll over.

Despite her wariness, her gaze automatically skimmed his body.

The same blue substance they'd found on the hood of her car was smeared all over his torso and seeped from a deep gash in his side. Her stomach clenched in sympathetic pain at the sight of his wound. "Oh, God! It is--was--is blood."

Panic subverted the drug high again, although her head swam a little sickeningly as she glanced around the room seeking--she had no idea. Help?

The scan of the room diverted her for several moments. She *was* in her room. The door was still closed. She could see that the security chain was undisturbed and the window seemed to be intact. There was no broken glass beneath it.

Dismissing the puzzle of just how he'd gotten in for the moment, she struggled to get off the bed. He caught her wrist in a surprisingly powerful hold. She looked down at him. "It's alright," she said, prying his fingers loose from her wrist with the infinite patience of the mentally impaired, for, the moment she managed to pull one loose and reach for the next, he closed the first around her wrist again. "I just need to find something." She frowned, giving up the effort to free herself and glancing at the gash again. "You need a hospital."

"No."

His voice was deep. The notes reverberated through her in a pleasing way that completely distracted her from the meaning of the word for several moments. She frowned doubtfully. "You're sure? It looks bad to me."

"I need my weapon."

Kylee's confusion deepened. "Weapon?"

"Sword."

Her eyes narrowed as she thought that over. "It's in the car," she produced finally, settling back on her pillow and yawning.

"Where is the car?"

She puzzled over it with her eyes closed since it was too much effort to open them, but no amount of prodding produced the information he'd asked for. "Sorry. The pain killer they gave me is kicking my ass. Ask me tomorrow," she mumbled, reaching blindly for his arm to give him a reassuring pat. "I'll figure it out tomorrow."

Chapter Three

Kylee swam toward consciousness reluctantly. She'd been having one of *the* most bizarre dreams, but she couldn't quite remember what it was about.

Bird feathers, she finally realized.

That *was* weird.

Why would she be dreaming about feathers?

She opened her eyes finally, unable to either grasp the elusive dream or drift back into sleep and found herself staring at the bedside table.

The lamp was still on. She must have really been out of it by the time she'd made it back to her room. Shuddering as memories of the night before crashed in on her, she moved slowly and carefully to sit up. Her throat hurt.

Pushing up from the bed, she amended that. Her whole body hurt.

Staggering a little from the after effects of not enough sleep and too much pain killer, she winded her way to the mirror for a look at her boo-boos. Just as she'd suspected, Enrico had left an imprint of his hand on her throat. She pulled her blouse up, turning to study the bruising that wound around her waist to her back--probably from the crash.

She was lucky she'd only gotten bruises.

She froze as she faced the room again.

There was a man sprawled in her bed!

Good God! How had she gotten back to her room with a man?

Frowning, completely forgetting her aches and pains, she moved a few steps closer, peering down at him. She'd thought the bed sheets were draped across his waist. She realized on closer inspection that it was some kind of wrap.

She caught a glimpse of wing then. The sight touched off a horrendous avalanche of memories.

She hadn't seen him and then *dreamed* he was in her bed. He *was* in her bed.

Except for the wings, he looked as human as--well a *lot* better than most of the men she knew. In fact, now that she could see him really well, with a clear head, he was downright--beautiful.

He couldn't be human, though, not with those wings.

Alien?

She wasn't going for the angel thing. She didn't believe in all that supernatural stuff. Most of it was scientifically explainable, or a trick.

She studied his face for a long time, partly from pure admiration and partly because she wanted to reassure herself that he was unconscious--not dead. Seeing no sign that he was feigning sleep, she allowed her gaze to drift downward. His chest was moving slowly and evenly.

There was no gash along his side, and very little of the 'blue blood', dried or otherwise. Most of that was on the bed sheets. There was a long angry red line, however, that ran from just beneath his left pec downward in a curved line that met the waist of the thing he was wearing. It looked like a very recently healed wound. He had another, somewhat shorter wound along one thigh, barely visible through the torn fabric but noticeable because the fabric around it was stained just as the sheets were.

She stared at the sarong-like thing around his waist, wondering if he looked as human *there* as the rest of him did. After glancing at his face again to make certain he was still asleep, or unconscious, she took a step closer and caught the edge of the wrap, lifting it very carefully for a peek. There was definitely something there. She couldn't quite make it out, though. Leaning a little closer, she lifted the cloth just a tiny bit higher for a better look.

He moved. *It* moved, standing up to look at her with one dark eye like a serpent that had been disturbed.

Dropping the cloth as if she'd been burned, she jerked upright.

His eyes were not only open, he'd propped his arms behind his head.

His expression was unreadable, but she had the feeling somewhere in his mind was the question--*See anything you like?*

Her face grew hot.

"I was--uh--just checking the wound on your thigh."

His brows rose. He didn't comment on the outright lie-- the very obvious lie. His leg hadn't been anywhere near where she'd been looking--unless one counted that middle leg, which had looked way too lively to be wounded.

He sat up abruptly, threw his legs off the bed and stood. "I am curious also," he murmured, walking right up to her and taking hold of her blouse. He had her shirt unbuttoned to the waist before she recovered enough from her shock to slap his hands.

His brows rose, but he removed his hands, folding his arms over his chest "You prefer to remove it yourself?"

"I do *not!*" Kylee gasped, outraged. "I'm not just going to--to strip because you're curious."

He dropped his arms to his sides and walked around her, looking her over curiously. "I've not had the opportunity to observe a human woman so closely before. You appear much the same, though, as the Elumi women--you have not their abilities, their strength, or their skills, but physically you seem not so different--except smaller, much smaller."

Kylee turned with him, fairly certain she didn't want him behind her where she couldn't watch him. She ignored the insulting comparison. If he thought for one minute that that kind of comment was going to put her on her metal to prove herself, he was wrong. It just irritated her.

"There are superstitions about mortal women that I find intrigue me. I myself am not superstitious, but many believe these tales and I have wondered how such strange beliefs might have come about."

She should have felt far more threatened by the strange being than she was intrigued, but the reverse was true. She wondered if that was because of some primal sense that told her he was no real threat to her, or if it was her own latent superstitions about angels and the fact that he looked so much like the concept of goodness and purity.

She didn't really believe in such fairy tales on an intellectual level, but she supposed on a more primitive level she didn't disbelieve either. Rather like disputing the existence of ghosts in the daylight, but fearing the cemetery at night.

It didn't hurt that he was the next thing to naked, looked more human than not, and he was magnificent in every way--tall, blond, well proportioned, muscular, and intimidatingly handsome.

"What tales?" she prompted when he didn't finish.

He moved surprisingly fast. One moment he was merely standing before her, studying her. The next he had her pinned against his length, one arm around her body, the other clutching the back of her head. "An Elumi finding himself too weakened to heal swiftly, may draw strength from the energy a mortal woman yields in the throes of passion."

Stunned, both by the remark and his assault, Kylee could only blink at him blankly while her mind spun its wheels ineffectually.

"It is said that this can not be done, however, without the Elumi male becoming enslaved by the pleasure he finds in the woman's flesh. It is forbidden for this reason.

"I, myself, can not conceive of it. You are--tempting, though. And I am weakened by my wounds."

Those comments only succeeded in producing more disjointed and ,fractured thoughts, but rather like speed reading, key words stood out and were assimilated. He wanted sex, passion. She'd never seriously considered having sex only to try it, especially not with a stranger, a no strings, never meet again, no pretense of a relationship animal coupling.

She was a little startled to discover how much that appealed to her at the moment.

His lips were warm as they brushed experimentally along hers, more as if he were testing his interest than her resistance. When he had explored the feel of surface to surface, he caught her lips gently between his, sucking lightly first the upper and then the lower tender flesh. Heated desire instantly tautened every muscle in her body and brought every nerve ending tingling to life. Enthralled that so tame a kiss could awaken her so thoroughly, Kylee held perfectly still, waiting, expectant, holding her breath unconsciously.

He exhaled a harsh breath, his lips parting from hers fractionally. As if that had prodded her own memory of the need to breathe, Kylee released a shuddering breath, as well, dragging in the scent and taste of their mingled breaths as she inhaled deeply once more. The merging scents sent a chemical rush through her that shut down any ability to think with her rational mind. Guided solely by instincts, her hunger thoroughly roused, she bridged the slight distance that separated them, pressing her lips to his in offering and then nibbling provocatively at his lips when he didn't immediately accept.

A harder rush of anticipation and excitement filled her as he opened his mouth over hers almost crushingly, plunging his tongue into her mouth with ravening hunger, as if he'd been holding back only with an effort and she had broken the dam of his resistance.

Her head swam dizzily as she found herself twisting, falling, colliding jarringly with the mattress. Briefly, their lips parted as they landed on the bed but even as she began to float upward toward greater awareness, he sought her lips again and he kissed her more feverishly than before as he sank against her, supporting part of his weight with one arm as he sprawled half atop her.

A new level of tension and expectation invaded her at the ferocity of his kiss, the feverish need communicated by his restless quest to familiarize himself with her body by touch. His palm glided over her bare midriff, cupped one breast, massaging it through her bra, then moved downward to tug at the waistband of her trousers. The pressure eased as he probed the intricacy of the closure and surpassed it, brushing his hand along her stomach and spearing his fingers through the thatch of hair on her mound.

Her belly quivered at his touch. Warmth and moisture burgeoned within her passage as he eased his fingers lower, delving into her cleft, finding the little bud that sent keen jolts of need through her.

After only a moment, he withdrew his hand. Hooking his thumb in her trousers, he peeled both trousers and panties from her hips and down her thighs. Abandoning that pursuit when he gained the limit of his reach, he deserted her lips for the tender skin of her throat, his heated breath and lips sending shivers of delight through her as he moved lower until he was nibbling at the edges of her breasts. Lifting one hand, he pushed her blouse and bra strap from her shoulder, scooping one breast from its cup and covering the tip with his mouth.

Kylee sucked in a sharp breath as she felt the heat of his mouth close around her engorged nipple and shards of pleasure sliced through her, making every muscle in her body go taut.

Reaching down, he pushed her clothing from her thighs to her knees. Anxious to feel his skin against her own, Kylee wiggled free of the restriction. He slid a hair roughened knee between her thighs. She widened them, offering him access to her body, wanting him to touch her as he had before.

Transferring his attention from one breast to the other, he pushed her shirt and bra strap from her other shoulder, pushing the cup beneath her breast and capturing the peak lightly between his teeth as he ran his palm downward, over her belly and settled his hand between her thighs.

Fettered by the restricting fabric of her blouse and bra, Kylee clutched at him as he delved into her cleft, digging her fingers into the flesh of his upper arm and arching upward as he teased her clit with his finger. Her belly clenched spasmodically with the acuteness of the shock wave of sensation that went through her. She dragged in a shuddering breath, panting as wave after wave rolled over her until she was so taut with need she felt like a mindless mass of raw nerve endings.

"Please," she gasped desperately.

He lifted his head from her breast, nuzzling her neck as he settled between her thighs. "Gabriel," he murmured, his voice harsh with need as he probed her body, entered her slowly and paused. "Say it."

With an effort, Kylee unclenched her eyelids to look up at him. His face was taut, fierce with need and his struggle to control it. His wings were arched behind the golden halo of his long, flowing hair, dispelling any illusion of a coupling between an ordinary man and a woman. If anything the exotic aspect only made her heart pound harder with excitement. Her fingers tightened on his hard, bulging biceps. "Gabriel, please."

As if he'd merely been waiting for her to acknowledge him, to refute any possibility that she was holding the image of another in her mind, he claimed her completely in a series of thrusting sorties that plowed past clinging, resistant flesh until he'd sunk his engorged member to her depths. He hesitated then for many moments, his eyes squeezed tightly shut, his muscles trembling from tension. Sucking in a harsh breath, he caught her wrists, manacling them to the bed on either side of her head as he began to move rhythmically after a long struggle for mastery, as if he could no longer contain his need, as if his control had slipped beyond his grasp.

Wild jolts of exquisite sensation surged through her with each stroke and Kylee clenched her eyes to focus on the pleasurable tension that wound inside her. Digging her heels into the mattress, she rose to meet his driving thrusts, feeling the rise of pleasure magnified by the shift in position, feeling it intensify so rapidly that her struggles to catch her breath became sharp cries of need.

He began to shudder with his own imminent release. His rapid ascent to his pinnacle touched off an answering demand within her own body, bumping her up the scale until her body could contain the tension no more, culminating in a shattering eruption of bliss that made her cry out with the sharpness of it. Uttering a harsh growl of sound, he followed her over the edge, shaking with the force of it and finally sinking heavily against her as if the explosion had drained him of every ounce of strength he possessed.

Kylee dragged in a deep, shuddering breath, feeling perfectly limp with repletion. His weight crushed down upon her, even though he still supported some of the weight of his upper chest on his elbows. She found it surprisingly welcome for all that, relished the illusion of a lover's intimacy, of being held tightly, possessively.

She had never experienced passion that had even come close to what she'd just felt. She wondered lazily if it would be like that again, or if it was only the circumstances surrounding the situation that had intensified it beyond anything she'd ever known.

She thought very likely that that was it.

She'd nearly been killed the night before. The need to reaffirm that life would go on as before had no doubt contributed to the explosive nature of her release--residual fear and tension from the night's events sharpening the pleasure to a keen blade that had sliced through all other considerations--such as the fact that he was totally alien and unknown to her.

He roused slightly and began to nuzzle against her neck. "There is a man who claims you as his woman, Kylee?"

Surprise flickered through her and then amusement and irritation.

"Women do not *belong* to men here. If a man and woman care enough about each other to stay together, they belong to each other."

He nipped at her neck with the edge of his teeth. "But there is no man?"

"If there were, I wouldn't be here."

"Good. Then I will not have to kill one to claim you," he murmured, covering her mouth in a deep kiss before she could respond to that remark. She dismissed it as she felt him grow hard inside of her again.

He made love to her more slowly, building the tension lazily until it became a great conflagration no less intense than the feverish need he'd built in her before. In fact, as impossible as she would have thought it to so quickly and easily build a fire among the embers, he did so, and built it hotter than before.

Her second release was so powerful she was not only left weak in the aftermath, but drained of even the will to struggle to hang on to consciousness. She drifted off to never land wrapped in a fuzzy cocoon of expended bliss.

Gabriel was pacing the room when she awoke. As if he sensed her gaze on him, he turned and strode toward her. "I have dire need of my sword."

Still disoriented from sleep, it took Kylee a minute to make any sense of his remark. As memory flooded back, embarrassment joined it. She looked down at herself, more than half hoping she'd dreamed the earlier events. No such luck. She was naked from the waist down. Her bra was still under her armpits, her blouse open and a crumpled mess, and the stickiness between her thighs left her in no doubt he'd made a deposit.

Good God! She hadn't even had the presence of mind to use protection?

She didn't especially want to think about that right now, particularly since he was looking her over like he was considering dessert. Grabbing a handful of sheet, she pulled it across her lap and then quickly adjusted her bra.

Something flickered in his eyes, but he seemed to dismiss it. "The sword?"

Kylee frowned thoughtfully. "Oh!" She looked at him guiltily. "I put it under the front seat of the car."

Anger and frustration flickered across his features. "The vehicle you were in last night? It is not here."

"Uh--that's because it was towed to the police impound lot."

Chapter Four

Detective Strand glared at the lab tech in irritation, wondering if he was on something. "Too much caffeine?" he asked suspiciously.

The tech calmed himself with an effort. "I found this in the vehicle you asked me to check," he said in a voice tinged with awe as he opened the fuming cabinet and dragged out a sword nearly four feet long.

Detective Strand eyed the piece curiously. "And?"

"I carbon dated it. This piece dates back to somewhere around the stone age."

"A real antique, huh?"

The tech gaped at him speechlessly for several moments. "It *pre*-dates the metal age," he emphasized, his voice carrying a thread of hysterical laughter. "It's--it's probably the find of this century."

Detective Strand looked at him in disgust. "Which means zero. Did you find anything I can use on the damned case or not? DNA?"

Several emotions washed over the tech's face. Disappointment was one, outrage another, but at the mention of DNA, he perked up again. "That blue stuff-- you're not going to belief this shit!"

"Probably not," Detective Strand said dryly, "and unless it's got something to do with my case, I don't give a shit."

"It's blood. Not human, can't be, too many strands, but some match human--but the DNA is off the charts. I've never seen anything like it. The persons these blood samples came from are--well, they would be like super human, I suppose--except they aren't human despite the similarity of some of the markers--I don't think."

"Wait--run that by me again. Persons? There was more than one? Was either one of them that low life, Enrico?"

The tech stared at him with his jaw at half mast. "Not the blue blood--I did find his DNA--Enrico's--on the window glass, though. No doubt about it. He is the one that put his fist through it. But...."

Strand cut him off. "That's all I need to hear," he said with satisfaction. "I'll have a uniform pick that sleaze ball up.

* * * *

Kylee was still trying to think up a convincing story to tell the cops when she pushed through the doors of the precinct. She completely saw Gabriel's point about the damned sword. It was his, and it was *her* fault it was missing and therefore her responsibility to retrieve it, but she had no idea how the hell she was going to manage it.

She'd just stopped at the desk to ask if Detective Strand was in when he hailed her from across the room.

"Good! I was just about to call you. I had forensics check out the car."

Kylee felt the blood rush from her face. A wave of weakness followed it.

Strand frowned. "You ok? Come on in my office and have a seat."

She didn't really want to go to his office, but she was certainly in no condition to run, which was her first thought. By the time she'd sunk into the chair in his office, it occurred to her that she had no reason to feel guilty. She hadn't done anything wrong.

Nothing illegal, she mentally corrected.

"Feeling better?" Strand asked as he sat behind his desk.

Kylee managed a nod. She didn't feel a whole lot better, though. She felt a little nauseated in all honesty. She'd been uneasy when she'd realized she was going to have to try to get into the vehicle in the impound lot. Now she didn't know what to do.

"Good news! We got the bastard. Got his DNA all over the window. With your statement and the evidence, we can send him away for a while. I'm charging him with deadly assault. The pictures we got last night and your testimony ought to be enough to make a slam dunk."

Kylee struggled to shift gears. She'd already told the detective she didn't want Enrico sent up for assault. She wanted him charged with murder. How was she going to get evidence on him if he was locked up?

"You've caught him?" she asked finally.

"We're looking for him. It's only a matter of time. You'll need to give me contact information so that we can get you up here to testify when the time comes--I assume you're planning on going home soon?"

Kylee stared at the man. The emphasis on that last comment was clear enough. He was 'suggesting' she go home. She didn't like being ordered around, not even with subtlety. "I suppose," she said finally. "I have to take care of that rental, though, first."

Strand shrugged. "It's part of a crime scene. We'll release the car back to the agency when we're done with it."

That sounded ominous, but not nearly as unnerving as his next question. "What were you doing with a sword in your car?"

A jolt went through Kylee. She did her best to hide her reaction.

"Technically, it constitutes a concealed weapon since it was found under your seat, but the tech says it's some kind of antique."

Surprise filtered through Kylee. He was offering her an out. She'd been trying to think up a lie, but decided just to tell him the truth--or the part he might believe anyway. "I found it by the car when I got out--after Enrico took off. I don't know why I picked it up--except I could see it must be valuable and I didn't want to leave it there."

Strand frowned. "Curious thing is, the tech said it had blood on it--really strange blood. That blue stuff all over the hood--turned out to be blood."

Widening her eyes, Kylee did her very best to look shocked, appalled, and thoroughly confused. She wasn't certain how well it worked, but not well if Strand's expression was anything to go by.

"Anything you want to tell me?"

He wouldn't believe her if she did tell him. She knew that. She wouldn't have believed it herself if she hadn't been there, seen it, and then seen the--angel or whatever he was afterwards--alien, she decided. "Like what?" she hedged.

He shrugged, seeming to dismiss it. "You should consider going home as soon as possible. I doubt it's likely Enrico knows where you are, but you can't be too careful."

Kylee nodded, pushing to her feet. "About the sword...."

Strand's brows rose questioningly.

"What will happen with that?"

He shrugged. "If it doesn't have anything to do with this case--which I can't see that it does--it'll stay in the evidence room until we see if we can locate the owner-- since you said it wasn't you and you found it."

Kylee felt like kicking herself. "I did find it, though," she managed to say after a moment. "If it isn't claimed, I'd like to have it."

"Check back with me in a month or so," Strand said, getting to his feet.

Dismayed as she was, there was nothing Kylee could do but nod and leave. Gabriel grabbed her as she passed the alley beside the building, dragging her into it.

"Well?"

Kylee's heart was still in her throat. Anger swiftly overtook the fear when she saw it was Gabriel, then dipped into fear again as she stared up at him. Whatever he was, he was probably a lot more dangerous than Enrico--and he was not going to be happy about his sword.

"It isn't in the car anymore."

"I know," he responded, his lips set into a grim line.

Kylee blinked, but she wasn't going to ask him how he'd managed to find and search the car. "They've got it in there--I think. The detective said it was evidence in the crime scene and the lab had it doing their thing, then it would go into the evidence room. Or maybe it's there already?"

When Kylee nerved herself to see how he was taking the news, she discovered Gabriel had disappeared. One moment he was there and then, in the blink of an eye, gone. She hadn't heard a thing.

Confused, she looked around the alley, deserted except for her, and then frowned, wondering if she was hallucinating. Had he not been there at all?

She was still looking around in bewilderment when she noticed a strange phenomenon. The wall nearest her seemed to have turned liquid--sort of. She blinked, trying to focus her vision, certain it must be some trick of the light or her eyes. Before she could decide what it was, Gabriel stepped through it.

He was holding his sword.

Kylee felt her jaw sag to half mast.

He studied her frowningly for a moment and finally hooked a hand around the back of her neck, dragging her toward him. Kylee was too shocked even to enjoy the kiss as he dipped his head and thoroughly ravished her mouth-- *almost* too shocked. Just about the time she swayed toward him, feeling warmth flooding through her, he released her, set her away from him and--his wings appeared.

Kylee was still trying to assimilate the fact that they hadn't been there moments before when he launched himself into the sky and vanished in a matter of seconds.

"I need to lie down," she muttered, looking around the alley a little dazed.

She might have stood like a dolt in the alley longer except that it occurred to her suddenly that Gabriel had just waltzed right through the police station, collected his sword and walked out again.

She didn't want to be anywhere near the place when they realized the sword was gone. Leaving the alley, she walked briskly to the corner and hailed a cab.

Once she'd settled in the seat, she wasn't certain of where she wanted to go. She finally decided, however, that she'd just had too many shocks too closely together. Her mind was completely disordered, probably at least partly because of the medication she'd been given for pain.

Finally, she simply told the driver to take her back to the room she'd rented. She would rest, she decided, and then when she was a little clearer in her mind, she would decide what she wanted to do.

* * * *

Kylee ended up taking a two hour 'nap' and felt almost worse when she first got up than before she'd lain down. After a long hot shower, though, she'd begun to feel almost human. Wiping the steam off the bathroom mirror, she studied her bruises. A shiver skated down her spine as it sank into her just how close she'd come to dying. If Gabriel and the enemy he'd been battling hadn't landed on her car at precisely the moment they did....

She frowned at the thought of Gabriel, wondering what sort of battle was going on. Was it some sort of personal vendetta with another of his kind? Or something broader? And why had they been fighting with swords of all things?

The mystery surrounding Gabriel was almost as bizarre as--well, Gabriel. If she'd been a religious sort of person--which she wasn't--she would've been poring over a bible trying to figure out what was going on. She didn't believe he was anything close to being a deity, however, or that there was anything of any religious significance to the fight that had ended on the hood of her car. She wasn't certain what was going on, but she didn't believe that.

Alien?

She supposed if he wasn't human--and he wasn't--and if he wasn't a deity or heavenly being--which she didn't believe--there wasn't much left but alien. What sort of alien race would have the technology to travel to Earth, though, and then fight with swords? And why fight at all?

Were they fighting over who could claim the place?

Unnerving thought, but she dismissed it after a moment. If aliens were slugging it out to claim Earth, she felt fairly confident everybody would know.

He'd acknowledged that he was of another race. He'd also spoken about superstitions his people had about hers--which meant the Elumi knew about humans whether humans knew about them or not.

So maybe they'd been around a while, coming and going for whatever reason and they'd been seen in the past? It seemed pretty farfetched on one level, but what would have made people from the past believe they were seeing and sometimes interacting with God-like beings if they'd never encountered something to make them believe that?

It still confused her to think that the Elumi could have had the ability to travel to Earth for centuries and behave so--barbarically that they fought one another with swords.

Now that she thought about it, though, his clothing was very reminiscent of statuary and paintings she'd seen from way back--which meant that if she'd guessed right, they hadn't changed a lot.

It didn't take much thought to figure out the sarong. He had wings. Unless she'd been hallucinating earlier, he also had the ability to 'vanish' them. It was fairly easy to figure out why he wouldn't want to wear anything that would impede his ability to make the change.

She wondered if he could change besides that, make himself assume a completely different form.

Her eyes widened as it occurred to her to wonder if he even really looked like he had appeared to her. What if he had just made himself look like that?

She dismissed that after a moment. Why make himself look almost human but with wings? It didn't make any sense.

Realizing she'd been staring blankly at the mirror long enough the mirror had dried, she finished drying herself, combed the tangles from her wet hair and left the bathroom to search for a change of clothes.

Gabriel was lying on the bed, his arms propped behind his head.

Kylee let out a whoop, did a war dance, and fled back into the bathroom before it dawned on her that it was Gabriel. When she'd wrapped herself in her towel, she peered around the edge of the door again.

Gabriel was staring back at her, a bemused look on his face.

"You scared the hell out of me! What are you doing here?"

He came up on one elbow, studying her assessingly for several moments. "I brought food," he said finally.

Kylee glanced toward the table in one corner of the room, saw that white Styrofoam containers were stacked on it, and looked at Gabriel again. "But--I thought--you said you were just looking for your sword."

His eyes narrowed. A faint smile curled his lips. "Tonight I came to find my sheath."

"Your sheath?" Kylee repeated blankly. "I didn't see a.... Very funny!"

He came up off of the bed and began to move toward her, slowly, as if he thought she would run if he rushed her-- which she would have. She didn't feel threatened, however, and it didn't even occur to her to slam the door and lock it.

Not that that would've done her a hell of a lot of good. She knew she hadn't imagined seeing him pass through the brick wall of the police station as if it was nothing more substantial than air.

"I may have given you the wrong impression when--uh-- before," she said a little unsteadily.

He stopped when he was toe to toe with her, placing his hands on her shoulders and kneading them. "How is that?"

"Uh--well--I--uh--I think it was the drug--partly. I got carried away with the moment. I don't usually do things like that and I hardly know you--well, actually, I don't know you at all and I didn't then either, but...."

"You will," he murmured, threading one hand beneath her damp hair and pulling her closer.

Desire flooded through her as his lips skated lightly over hers and their breaths mingled. "I shouldn't," she said doubtfully, breathless with anticipation.

He nibbled at her lips. "Because?"

Chapter Five

Because, why? Kylee couldn't think of a single reason not to at the moment.

He slipped his hands down along her arms, catching her wrists, and then tugged her with him to the bed. She followed like a sleepwalker, mesmerized by the promise in his eyes. Pulling the towel from her, he tossed it aside and then removed his sarong and flung it the way of the towel.

Her breath caught in her throat as he lowered her to the bed and settled half on the bed beside her, half covering her. One hair roughened leg stroked along hers before settling between them as he supported himself on an elbow and explored her body with his gaze and his free hand. Currents of warmth and excitement eddied and flowed through her from the feel of his warm, faintly calloused fingers and palm. Through half closed lids she watched the skate of his hand as it roamed her body, gently cupping one breast, smoothing down over her midriff and belly and finally gently plucking the curls on her mound. After teasing the sensitive nether lips briefly, he moved upward once more in his exploration, tracing the curve of her hip with his large palm and long fingers, the dip of her waist, and then moving up to cup one breast again and pluck gently at the nipple that hardened and nudged against his palm.

"You are a beautiful woman, Kylee," he murmured, lifting his gaze to hers at last, "pleasing to my eyes, to my touch--to my taste." He leaned closer, until the tip of his nose brushed her skin, breathing deeply and nibbling a row of kisses along her neck and collar bone. "Now I understand why this is forbidden. There is much truth to the tales. I thought that I had supped from your lips and drank my fill. Instead, I only thirst more than before," he whispered near her ear, sending shivers of want and anticipation through her. Her belly quivered as he sucked her earlobe into his mouth.

He lifted his head after a moment, staring down at her and Kylee opened her eyes with an effort. He cupped her face in his hand. "Are you certain death, Kylee? Or salvation? My thirst for war has dimmed before my thirst for you," he murmured, leaning down and covering her mouth in a kiss of unrestrained passion, of need, of possession that made her senses reel.

The questions startled her, filled her with a nameless dread, but the heat of his kiss banished awareness of anything beyond the feel of his mouth on hers. It was drugging, depriving her of any will to resist that remained, though there was little enough of that from the moment he had looked into her eyes with desire. His taste engulfed her, entranced her as he laid siege to her senses, stroking his tongue along hers possessively, exploring the heated, keenly sensitive cavern of her mouth with a thoroughness that made her heart leap, pounding frantically, and her breath catch in her chest.

She might know little or nothing about him, but her body knew his well as her pleasure master, responding with a will all its own, a desperation to experience the ecstasy he had wrung from it before. Murmuring a sound of need, she laced her fingers through his silky hair, urging him closer, kissing him back with abandon, her mind and body already pounding with the need for full possession. Heat and moisture collected in her sex. Blood engorged the tiny capillaries in her most sensitive places, making her feel swollen and achy with a need only his touch could assuage.

He drew his knee up between her thighs. They parted in invitation before his advance, until his erection nudged against her nether lips. Skimming a hand downward along her body once more, he traced a path that went directly to her mound, parting the swollen lips with one long finger and exploring the hot wetness of her arousal. Breathing gustily into her mouth at his discovery, he broke the kiss and shifted to catch one erect nipple between his lips, plucking at it briefly before he sucked it into his mouth.

Gasping in a sharp breath, Kylee arched upward to meet the tantalizing heat of his mouth and tongue as jolt after jolt of keen sensation arrowed through her, colliding in her belly with the exquisite sensations touched off by his exploring finger along her cleft. The muscles in her belly clenched, seeking his hard, heated length, needing it with a growing desperation.

Unable to move the leg he lay against, she dragged the other one upward, bending her knee and bracing one foot against the mattress as she spread her thighs wider to accommodate his broad palm. Accepting the invitation, he shifted over her. Lifting his head from her breast, he captured her lips once more, settling his narrow hips between her thighs and surging against her so that his swollen member scraped along her tender inner thighs and butted the sensitive flesh of her sex.

Kylee sucked in a sharp breath, arching her back and spreading her thighs wider still until she felt his hardened flesh plowing along her cleft. Shifting his weight, he reached between them and aligned their bodies, pressing steadily until he had buried the head of his cock in her channel. She held her breath, held still, panting as her body slowly adjusted to his intrusion.

Dragging his lips from hers, he burrowed his face against her neck, breathing raggedly as he forced his engorged cock deeper, by agonizingly slow degrees until he filled her completely. He pushed his upper body upward then, supporting himself with his arms, studying her face as he stroked her inner passage with his heated length. Sensing his gaze, she opened her eyes with an effort. His face, taut with his own need and his efforts at self restraint sent a shaft of need through her. The muscles in her belly clenched in response, tightening around him. A look of pleasure/pain skimmed his features. He sucked in a harsh breath, holding it. A tremor went through the bulging muscles of his arms.

Releasing his breath on a hoarse groan after a moment, he lowered himself against her. Burrowing his face along her neck and slipping his hands beneath her hips, he began to move within her, stroking his flesh along hers feverishly. Kylee's gasps of pleasure became moans of desperation as her body tautened with the escalation of sensation and grew tighter still until she felt she could contain no more. And still it grew, expanding until she couldn't catch her breath, until her heart could not seem to keep pace with the flood of adrenaline through her, until her struggle to drag enough oxygen into her lungs made darkness crowd close upon the fringes of her mind.

When it burst upon her, rolling over her like a tidal wave, the sensation of release was so exquisite, she uttered sharp, keening cries she was scarcely aware of. The convulsing of her vaginal muscles in the throes of passion sent him over the edge. A deep groan seemed to be dragged from his chest as his cock jerked and convulsed, pumping his hot seed against her womb.

He settled heavily against her as the last waves of rapture rolled over him and began to dissipate. Gasping for breath, still shuddering, he nuzzled her neck, sucked a love bite just beneath her ear.

Scarcely aware of anything beyond the cloud of repletion and utter contentment that enveloped her, Kylee merely lay limp beneath his caresses, struggling to gather her senses to her once more.

Minutes passed in a haze. Finally, almost reluctantly, he pulled away from her. Settling beside her on the bed on his back, he gathered her against him, stroking her back.

Sighing, Kylee reveled in his soothing caress, feeling almost like purring with contentment. She'd begun to drift lazily, more than half tempted to relax into sleep, when he moved away from her and got out of the bed.

Roused, Kylee rolled onto her side, watching him as he strode across the room and stood examining the plates of food. A faint smile curled her lips. She was still smiling when he glanced toward her.

An answering smile gleamed in his eyes. "Hungry?"

She searched herself and discovered with a little surprise that she was. She nodded, but got up from the bed and went into the bathroom to clean up. Grabbing another towel when she'd finished, she wrapped it around herself like a sarong, tucking one corner edge in and went back into the main room. Gabriel was sprawled in the bed, eating.

She sent him a disapproving frown. "You'll have the bed full of crumbs."

He held out a hand to her. After a moment, she answered the summons, settling on the opposite side of the bed. He offered a tidbit of food. When she reached to take it, however, he closed his hand over it, shaking his head. Feeling a little shy, a little embarrassed, she leaned toward him again, opening her mouth. He placed the tidbit on her tongue.

It was chicken, fried and barely warm now, but it tasted it delicious. She chewed it, looking around for something to drink. After a moment, she got up and went to the table. Collecting the bottled drinks there and another container of food, she returned to the picnic on the bed and examined the contents, then fed him a piece of chicken.

She frowned slightly as she took another bite. "Are you-- forbidden to tell me anything about yourself?"

He looked a little surprised. After a moment, amusement gleamed in his eyes. "We are forbidden to have any congress with humans. The rest hardly matters--now."

Kylee nodded. "Where are you from?"

"My home lies in Tearra in Pearthen--high Earth--beyond the gateway."

The explanation only left Kylee more confused. "High Earth--then you're not...?" She paused. "Is it, like another dimension?"

"Clever and beautiful," he murmured approvingly, offering her another tidbit of food.

Wryly, Kylee thought she wasn't that clever. It still boggled her mind. It would've been easier to grasp another world altogether than a dimension unseen and inaccessible to humans. "Why are you here?"

His lips twisted. Anger filled his eyes. "I am banished for displeasing my king. It has always been the way of things-- to be banished from our own beautiful kingdom into the land of humans--lower Earth--as punishment--when death is not the punishment. When war erupted once more, though, the banished grew rapidly in numbers. It is much harder to please the king, much easier to fall from grace, when he is beset by enemies."

Kylee stared at him while she tried to assimilate that. It was almost as if they'd been caught in a time warp that kept them prisoner of the dark ages--or something like the dark ages of Earth.

"So--when did your people discover the gateway and learn about humans?"

He chuckled. "My people discovered the gateway long before humans evolved into an intelligent species. We evolved here on lower Earth first, built our civilization here. We passed through the gateway when the human infestation became--intolerable to us."

Kylee reddened at the insult. It didn't matter than he hadn't intended to insult her. In fact it made it worse since it made it obvious he felt humans were beneath his own race.

Or maybe species was the correct word? He had lumped all of the races of man together. *Was* he a member of another species? Or an earlier variety of human?

His blood was blue, not red, but she didn't know if that was significant or not. There was also the fact that his molecular structure seemed to differ tremendously--the wings which he could sprout at will, the staggering ability to heal wounds that would have been mortal to a human.

She shook that thought off. On a personal level, it didn't matter, really. She certainly had not been able to tell the difference in so far as their 'mating' went--unless she counted the fact that she had not had sex with anyone before that took her to such heights, but that only seemed to indicate a chemical similarity between them, not a difference.

And, in any case, there was no commitment here, or expectation of one, and no relationship. He enjoyed her body. She enjoyed his. It was as uncomplicated as that.

"So--it's a form of punishment to have to live among us?"

Something flickered in his eyes. "Nay. The punishment is to be banished from all those we know, all those things familiar to us and to live on lower Earth without even the succor of contact with humans. As I said, it is forbidden. And the only chance we have to shorten our sentence of solitude is to best an enemy of the king and win his favor once more. And so we search for others of our kind, fight our enemies here, and each hope to win the victory that will allow us to return home."

Slightly mollified, Kylee nodded, but she frowned again at one thing that was bothering her. She had been hesitant to ask for fear of insulting him, but he hadn't seemed to have any qualms about insulting her. "This war--fighting with swords--it seems very archaic to me. We did that long ago, but weapons have advanced a lot in the wars of mankind--everything has."

Instead of appearing insulted, he looked amused. "You think we are barbaric because we do not use the same weapons to kill each other that you do? Because we find it unnecessary to kill the innocent with the guilty by using weapons that kill everything in its path? You think the things that you surround yourself with are a necessary evidence of superior intelligence and advancement of civilization? The man who attacked you--he carried a blade. I have seen many that do. These things you consider the trappings of advanced civilization, they are the product of need, want, desire for change. We are content as we are, with who we are. This world seems primitive to us."

Kylee frowned, but she could certainly see his point. It was hard to convince anyone that mankind was superior when their animal side still dwelt closely to the surface and they erupted into brutal, violent behavior with regularity.

He tapped her chin. When she looked up at him, he hooked his hand behind her head and dragged her close, kissing her briefly and releasing her. Slipping from the bed, he headed into the bathroom.

He didn't close the door and, more than a little uncomfortable with such intimacy, Kylee concentrated on cleaning up the remains of their meal and disposing of it, trying not to feel domestic about the whole situation. Relieved when she heard the sound of the shower, she searched her suitcase for something to wear, wondering if he'd been teasing when he'd made that remark about her having a man.

He must have been, she decided. Or maybe it was just one of those 'lines' men fed women because they thought it was what they wanted to hear, the hint of a promise of some sort of commitment, or relationship?

Irritation surfaced. So their one night stand had turned out to be more than one. She wasn't looking for a commitment, and if she had been it would've been with someone a *little* closer to her own tribe.

Chapter Six

As unnerved as she'd been by the incident with Enrico, Kylee discovered that the moment the worst of her fear wore off, her conviction returned.

She did not want to settle for getting the bastard in jail for assaulting her. He deserved the death penalty for what he'd done to her sister. She might not be able to manage that, but she wanted him to serve life at least. A few years were probably nothing to a low life like that. He was just the sort to be involved in all sorts of things that he could use to plead his charges and jail time down. Even if that wasn't the case, he'd probably end up running his business from prison and come out as if nothing had ever happened to interrupt his life.

She'd botched the first attempt fairly badly, however, and all the careful plans she had made now belonged in the trash. She didn't think she could just pick up and start again. She supposed it had been stupid and theatrical to think she could just unnerve him by appearing and disappearing because she looked so much like Stacy.

It had unnerved him all right, but he'd known instantly exactly what she was trying to do.

So, if the chances were pretty much nil that she was going to get him to confess on tape, what was left? A trap with her as bait?

That might have some merit except that she doubted she could talk the detective into it and if she was dead she wasn't going to know if they'd got the bastard or not, which she would be if the cops weren't willing to help.

Finally, since nothing else came to mind, she decided to check and see how the case was going. If they hadn't managed to catch Enrico, maybe Strand would be willing to consider the possibility.

Go to the police station, she wondered? Or just call?

Since it occurred to her that Strand might ask her some unpleasant questions about the sword, she decided she would call and test the water.

She found his card in her purse after a brief search and settled down on the side of the bed to make the call. He picked up on the third ring. "Detective Strand."

"It's Kylee--Griffin."

"I figured you'd be on your way home." He sounded disapproving.

"I'm going in a few days. I just wanted to know if you'd caught that guy."

He was silent for several moments. "We'll find him. It's only a matter of time."

"So you haven't caught him yet?"

"Not yet--but it's only been a couple of days. He'll lay low for a little while, but he won't be able to do that long. It's bad for his business."

Kylee thought it over for several moments. "I could smoke him out."

"Don't you even think about it!" Strand growled. "You damned near got yourself killed the last time. Have you got a death wish or something?"

"Not for myself!" Kylee snapped before she thought better of it. "Look, I just want him caught, ok? I'd like to know he's in jail before I go back home. I don't want to check back in a couple of months and find out this has ended up in the damned cold case files like my sister's murder."

"Stay out of it, Ms Griffin. I mean it. This is police business and if I have to I'll run you in for interfering in a crime investigation."

Kylee grew angry. "Right! I forgot you always like to go after the easy ones. Is there another detective working on this case I could talk to?"

"It's my case," Strand growled. "But now that I have you on the phone, there's something that's been bothering me. You know anything about that sword we found in your car? The one you claimed you'd just found?"

Kylee's stomach clenched. "What about it?"

"It mysteriously vanished from the lab, that's what."

She was silent for several moments, thinking. "And you're implying...?"

"I ain't implying anything. I'm asking you if you know anything about it."

"I told you before that I didn't. I found it. It looked valuable, so I didn't just walk off and leave it lying where I found it. I figured if nothing else there would probably be a reward for the recovery," she added on sudden inspiration.

He was silent for several moments. "You don't strike me as the type to be looking for rewards."

"I don't think you're familiar with my 'type', detective." She hesitated, but when he didn't respond to that remark, she decided to just take the plunge. "Look, I was thinking about taking a walk downtown tonight to see the sights. Maybe you could suggest some points of interest?"

"Do, and I'll arrest you," Strand growled.

"For sightseeing? I didn't know that was illegal."

"You and I both know you ain't talking about sightseeing, and I ain't going for it, Griffin."

"Fine. I'm still going. I think I'll take in a game of pool. I always did like that game."

"You're going to get your fool self kill--"

She hung up before he could get the rest of it out, but that didn't change the fact that she knew he was right. The place was dangerous. Even if she didn't manage to draw Enrico out, there were so many 'bad guys' in that area the chances were still good that somebody would attack her.

She was fairly certain she couldn't count on Strand either. He might send a patrol car down and he might not. For that matter, he was liable to send someone over to her place just to watch her.

It occurred to her after a little thought that the place wouldn't be nearly as dangerous before dark. The predators mostly came out at night. Someone was bound to see her if she took a stroll though, probably somebody that knew Enrico and could make sure he got the message. She might even run across somebody that was willing to talk to her about him--maybe one of his girls.

The cabby gave her a strange look when she told him where she wanted to go.

"You sure about that?"

"Yes. I'm sure."

Shrugging, he drove her to the street she'd named. "What address?"

"You can drop me by the pool hall."

He didn't offer to wait. Consternation filled her as she watched the cab take off again as soon as she was out.

She hadn't considered she wasn't going to have any way to make a quick getaway.

Dismissing it finally, she turned and headed for the pool hall. It wasn't open for business yet and it was locked up tight. Thwarted, Kylee checked her watch and turned to scan the street.

It was late afternoon and the sun was already dipping behind the tall buildings, but the sidewalks were still virtually deserted. She didn't especially want to be caught in the area after dark, but she was determined to at least flaunt her presence if she couldn't do anything else.

Nothing, as far as she could see, would more surely piss Enrico off--that he'd threatened her and now he was the one in hiding and she wasn't intimidated.

Actually, she was, because she might be crazy, but she wasn't completely stupid.

After several minutes of indecision, she finally decided just to stroll down two blocks, cross over and come back. If she saw anyone along the way, she could try to talk to them about her sister. If not, she had a feeling she was being watched anyway and at the very least, Enrico would know she'd been strolling through his territory, looking for information about him. If she could rattle him enough, maybe he'd make a mistake bad enough the cops would actually be able to catch him.

She managed to talk to a bag lady and a wino for about three seconds each. The wino listened and then tried to bum money off of her. Digging a five out of her pocket, she waved it in front of his face. He licked his lips, studying it like it was a piece of steak, but he only managed to produce a story that was so blatantly a lie she knew he hadn't seen or heard anything about her sister.

The bag lady looked at her like she was a demon and tore off down an alley, abandoning her cart. Without stopping to consider the wisdom of it, Kylee tore off behind the woman. The only reason that she could think of that the woman had looked at her like that was because her face was familiar--which meant she would've seen Stacy if she hadn't known her.

The woman was stunningly fast. By the time Kylee managed to get around the buggy she'd abandoned, the woman was halfway down the alley to the next block. "Wait! I just wanted to ask you a few questions!"

That only seemed to spur the woman to more speed. She rounded the corner at the end of the alley and disappeared. Huffing for breath, Kylee halted when she'd rounded the corner, staring at the street, which was just about as empty as the one she'd just come from. There was no sign of the bag lady.

Catching her breath, she jogged down to the next alley and peered down it just in time to see a flash of color at the other end.

"Shit! She doubled back!" She should have known the woman wasn't just going to abandon her worldly belongings.

Wondering if there was even any point in it, Kylee ran after her, hoping the buggy would slow the woman down enough she could catch her. As she rounded the end of the alley, however, she slammed into a man. The collision stunned her. Sluggishly, self preservation kicked in and she glanced up at the man, terrified at the thought that she might have run right into Enrico.

It wasn't Enrico.

She knew instantly that he wasn't even a denizen of this neck of the woods. She didn't know how she knew, but there was just something about him--something really unnerving.

Pulling away from him abruptly, Kylee fled. She was only slightly relieved when she heard no pursuit. When she finally glanced back, she discovered the man had disappeared. Down the alley?

She looked upwards instead. She didn't see anything, but she realized the moment she did it why she'd looked up.

Somehow, although she wasn't certain exactly why, the man had reminded her of Gabriel.

A shiver skated down her spine. The 'man' he'd been fighting that first night?

Try though she might, she couldn't summon enough of an image to say for certain. The long hair meant nothing. It wasn't stylish anymore, but there were still plenty of guys that wore it long, especially in this area--except that he had been too clean and too clean cut to belong here.

Shrugging it off when she saw no sign that he was following her, she hurried down the sidewalk looking for the woman she'd been chasing. Not surprisingly, there was no sign of her. After walking along the sidewalk, peering into the alleys and doorways for a while, she finally realized that it was getting dark and more and more people were beginning to appear on the sidewalks.

Abandoning her search immediately, she hurried briskly away from the area, keeping an eye out for a cab. She had to walk nearly four blocks before she managed to hail one and by then it was fully dark. Relief surged through her when she settled in the back seat and gave the man the directions to the room she'd rented.

She wondered if she'd only imagined the guy being like Gabriel. She hadn't seen Gabriel in several days, not that she'd been expecting him or anything, but maybe it was something latent, maybe subconsciously she was looking for Gabriel?

She shook the thought off. Gabriel was probably long gone by now. He'd needed his sword. She'd helped him locate it. He'd come back for seconds--which she supposed she should have been flattered by--and that was that. Regardless of the comments he'd made that first night when they were together, he'd merely been curious. He'd said as much. Obviously, he'd enjoyed it as much as she had--poor guy. There was no telling how long it had been since he had gotten a little sexual relief.

Or even had a soul to talk to.

She could relate to loneliness. There were probably a lot of people who could, which was unreal. As many lonesome people as there were, it did look like more could get together with the other lonely ones.

That wasn't an option for Gabriel, of course. She just hoped he didn't get into trouble for spending time with her and it didn't hurt his chances of going home.

That thought so depressed her, she shied away from it, turning her mind to the woman she'd chased instead.

She might have imagined the whole thing, of course.

Poor woman! What if she hadn't known anything at all and just wondered why the kook was chasing her?

Then again, it might have been nothing except that she had seen Stacy when Stacy lived in the area. If she had recognized the resemblance, it didn't mean she knew anything about what had happened.

Maybe, she decided when she'd paid the cabby and gotten out at the hotel/apartment rentals where she was staying, she would wait a couple of days and try again. It was at least worth a shot to see if the woman knew anything about Stacy's murder.

She could always hope she'd managed to stumble onto a witness that could put the bastard away forever.

* * * *

Kylee was washing her hair when she felt a presence behind her. She let out a shriek as two arms encircled her that came out as a gurgle when the shower immediately filled her mouth with water. Choking, coughing, her eyes stinging from the shampoo, Kylee whirled to face the threat.

Her knees nearly gave out when she saw it was Gabriel.

"Damn it! You scared the *hell* out of me!" Kylee raged, so weak with relief she had to fight the urge to burst into tears.

Gabriel's smile died. He looked her over frowningly. "Why are you so fearful?"

Swallowing the lump in her throat with an effort, Kylee shook her head. "Nothing, really. My problem, not yours. I'm just a little nervous, that's all."

He caught her shoulders when she would've turned away. "It is more than that." He studied her face for several moments. "It is because of that man who attacked you? Did your--authority not catch this man?"

Ignoring the question, Kylee pulled free and moved under the showerhead to wash the soap from her hair. Gabriel, she saw when she swiped the water from her eyes, was still studying her keenly. "Not yet," she said finally, stepping out of the shower and grabbing a towel.

Stripping off his sodden sarong, he shut the water off and followed her out. "Tell me what troubles you," he demanded, grasping her shoulders.

"It's something from the past, not anything you could help me with even if you wanted to."

He frowned. "Why would you think I would *not* want to?"

Kylee stared at him in surprise. "Why would I think you would *want* to? We're strangers. And I'm human."

Shaking her head, she tried to pull away from him. His hands tightened around her shoulders. "Are you lying to me? Or trying to lie to yourself?"

Kylee swallowed with an effort, but she found she couldn't meet his penetrating gaze. "I don't know what you mean."

He shook his head slowly. "You do. I see it in your eyes when you look at me. I feel it in your touch." He shifted closer, dragging her head back and burying his face against her neck, sucking tiny love bites from her collar bone upward to one ear.

Goosebumps erupted all over her. Desire exploded inside her, a full fledged inferno of need that should never have happened--not with any man she had known less than a week--certainly not with a man of another world entirely.

When he found his way to her lips, she was lost. She met his kiss with desperate longing, wanting to believe what he'd implied--that she meant something to him, that she was more than a warm and willing body to him.

They came together tumultuously, with little preliminary, kissing and touching with feverish need. When she had wrapped herself tightly around him, he carried her to the bed, sprawling on the mattress with her and thrusting into her almost at once. She was more than ready for him. Her body already ached with the yearning to have him inside of her. Her sex was hot, wet with her longing.

Arching over her, he buried his face against her neck as he buried his cock deeply within her flesh. Sucking almost painfully at the tender flesh of her neck, he thrust and retreated with hard, powerful strokes that drove her to the brink within moments and then thrust her beyond the boundaries of endurance. She cried out as her body exploded with mind blowing bliss. Shuddering, he followed her to that wondrous plane of ecstasy.

Holding her tightly against him, he rolled when he had caught his breath so that she lay sprawled limply on top of him, her ear pressed to his heaving chest, his heart thundering comfortingly in her ear.

Minutes passed while their bodies labored to return to normal. Finally, he lifted a hand and began to stroke her back, tracing soothing circles over it. "You do not live in this place."

Kylee roused slightly. It wasn't a question, though. "No. I live in a much smaller town south of here."

"You came because of that man. He is your enemy?"

Sighing, Kylee lifted her head to look at him. "It's not the same here that it is in your world."

His lips tightened. "I do not suffer a poor understanding. I know this. I told you I was forbidden to interact with humans. I did not say I had not observed this society of yours. I have had much time to study your people. From a distance, true, but I believe I have a fair understanding nevertheless. I also understand you--now. That was no chance encounter that first time I saw you, though I had thought so at the time."

"No. I went looking for him. He killed my little sister-- more than a year ago. The police haven't got the evidence they need to arrest him, though."

She saw confusion in Gabriel's eyes. "I am not familiar with this--sister?"

Surprise went through Kylee. "The children that belong in a family--when it's a female, it's a sister. A boy would be a brother. There were only two of us, though. She was born when I was four--a fairly large age difference, actually. I'd already left home for college when she reached her teens."

He still looked confused, which surprised Kylee. He spoke English so well it hadn't occurred to her that it wasn't his first language--although it should have--and that there would be words he wasn't familiar with. She had the feeling, though, that it wasn't the word so much as the concept. His next comment confirmed her suspicion.

"This is common among you? Two offspring?"

Kylee shrugged. "I suppose. I've known a lot of people that were an only child, but I also know a lot more that have much larger families--three or four, sometimes more than that. I don't know what the national average is. It isn't like that where you're from?"

He shook his head. "Most have one. Many have none. We are very long lived people. The females only come in season twice or perhaps three times and few have taken a mate when they are first in season."

That boggled her mind--the 'in season' thing most of all, but the other comment made her wonder if it was some evolutionary thing because of their life spans. "How long lived?" she asked uneasily.

He shrugged and finally smiled wryly. "I have known no one who died of age. Most die in war--or battle of some sort anyway."

She looked at him assessingly. "How old are you?"

His gaze flickered over her face. "Far older than you."

He didn't want to tell her. She could tell from his expression that he didn't. She just wasn't certain why. Finally, she shrugged, looking away. "I don't suppose it matters."

He tucked a finger beneath her chin, tipping her head up. "It does not."

Meaning, what? He wasn't going to be around long enough for it to make any difference? She wasn't certain that that was the way he'd meant it, and yet she realized it was true.

"I will help you seek justice for the death of your sister."

Kylee glanced at him sharply, feeling a wealth of conflicting emotions. Relief, she thought, was highest, for she didn't doubt for one moment that Gabriel could manage it if no one else could. "I was trying to get his confession on tape. Unless someone else saw it and is willing to testify against him, there's no other way, because they didn't find enough physical evidence to prove it. And it has to be proven beyond a shadow of doubt. If a jury doesn't feel that there is enough evidence to prove a person did something, then they are obligated to render a verdict of 'not guilty'."

He nodded. "I will beat a confession out of him."

Kylee bit her lip. "I'm not sure that would stand up in court."

"You will record it."

"But he can say that you made him say it and it wasn't true."

Gabriel considered that for a moment. "No. I will tell him that if he does that I will come back. He will not want me to come back."

Despite her earlier amusement at his suggested solution, Kylee felt a little shiver run down her spine. Gabriel had startled the hell out of her more than once with his sudden appearances, but she had not truly been afraid of Gabriel since she had known him. She realized quite suddenly, however, that he could be very scary if he chose.

"Now," he added, slipping from the bed. "I will find food to feed you before you shrink more and make me worry that I will break you."

Kylee gave him an indignant look. "I happen to be the right weight for my height and build!" And she worked damned hard to stay that way!

He grinned at her unrepentantly. "You are perfect--as you are. I do not want you to shrink," he added, making a motion with his hands to show her he wasn't referring to her weight, but her stature.

An answering smile curled her lips despite her annoyance. He thought she was perfect! Before she could think of a comeback, he'd vanished. Shrugging, she went back into the bathroom to clean up. His sarong, still wet, still lay in the tub. Horrified at first, finally Kylee merely chuckled. Gabriel went around the next thing to naked now--and she doubted anyone would see him or that he'd care if they did. Wringing the fabric out when she'd bathed, she hung it to dry and went to look for something to wear.

Deciding not to bother with a bra since her clean laundry was running low, she pulled a T-shirt on without one and a pair of panties. She'd just pulled a pair of jeans over her hips when someone tapped at the door. Glancing toward it curiously, she adjusted her clothing and finally moved to the panel. "Who is it?"

She heard an indistinct male voice on the other side. After peering through the peephole and discovering she could see nothing more than a shoulder, she placed the security chain on the door and opened it cautiously.

The moment she unlocked the door and turned the knob, something slammed into the door so hard the chain popped loose. The force of the door slamming into her sent Kylee flying backwards. She didn't have time to do more than gasp sharply on an inhaled scream before she hit the foot of the bed a glancing blow and slammed into the floor, stunned. Before she could fully assimilate what was happening, she felt two hands digging into her arms, jerking her to her feet as if she was a rag doll.

Through a wall of wet hair, she peered at the man who had attacked her.

"You fucking cunt! I tole you to stay out of my business, *putta*! Now I got cops crawling all over my ass!" Enrico roared, shaking her so hard she thought her neck would snap.

Chapter Seven

Apparently tiring of shaking her, Enrico slapped Kylee, jerking her head sideways. Her body followed. She'd barely touched down when he grabbed her and jerked her to her feet again. His hands closed around her throat, pinching off her air. Instinct kicked in and Kylee clawed at Enrico's fingers, trying to pry them loose. There was a roaring in her ears, growing louder and louder that made it impossible to hear the curses he growled at her as he choked her and shook her like a pit bull with a terrier in its teeth. The light dimmed. Suddenly, she felt warmth at her back. An arm slid around her waist to support her. A hand reached from behind her and closed like a vice around Enrico's neck.

The fingers around her throat slackened, fell away. Still gasping for air, Kylee found herself freed of support and wilted to the floor between Enrico and Gabriel, struggling to focus her vision when blackness was crowding so close she could barely see.

Instead of slackening his grip on Enrico's through, Gabriel lifted the man clear of the floor. Enrico's eyes bulged, either from lack of oxygen, or sheer terror, or both as he looked into the face of the being that slammed him against the door he had burst through only moments before. Struggling to scream, Enrico gave up on trying to pry the fingers from his throat and began to fumble with the pockets of his pants.

"Watch out! He's got a knife!" Kylee gasped out hoarsely just as Enrico dragged a blade from his pocket, flicked it open, and shoved it to the hilt into Gabriel's mid section.

Kylee tried to scream but her bruised throat prevented more than a hoarse croak.

Gabriel exhaled on a grunt of pain, grabbing Enrico's hand in a grip that produced the distinctive, sickening crunch of breaking bones. Enrico's face contorted, though he didn't manage to force a scream out.

Wrenching the knife from Enrico's hand, Gabriel pulled it from his belly and dropped it to the floor. It bounced, landing near her and Kylee struggled to grab it, uncertain of whether she meant to make sure Enrico couldn't get it again, of if she wanted it for self-defense.

"This is the one who killed your sister?" Gabriel growled, turning to look down at Kylee.

Kylee struggled up on one arm, tried to swallow past her bruised throat and squeezed her eyes against the pain, coughing for several minutes when she choked. "Yes! He killed my sister," she managed to gasp out in a hoarse whisper finally.

Before she could say anything else, Gabriel released his grip on Enrico's throat. Even as Enrico's feet hit the floor and his legs wobbled as he tried to support himself, Gabriel whipped his sword from its scabbard. Grabbing Enrico by the hair of his head, he swung the blade.

Kylee's first inkling that Gabriel meant to mete out justice himself was the sword in his hand. "No!" she cried even as the sword descended with lightning speed, cleaving Enrico's head cleanly from his shoulders.

A fountain of red spewed from the headless body. Something heavy and moist hit the floor with a sickening thud and rolled toward Kylee. She stared at Enrico's expression of horror, his lips still moving to form a scream he could no longer utter and then the blackness she had been trying to fight off consumed her.

She had no idea how long she lay unconscious, but she awoke to frantic activity. She was seized and hauled to her feet before she could manage to open her eyes. Terror immediately assailed her and she screamed hoarsely. The effort gagged her and she choked, coughing for several moments before she could control the spasms.

"What the hell happened here?" a familiar voice growled. "Did you do this?"

Kylee opened her eyes with an effort, staring at Detective Strand blankly.

"Did you do this?" he barked the demand again, gesturing toward the floor.

Kylee's stomach rebelled when she followed his gesture, clenching so hard she thought for several moments that she would throw up. Blood had formed a huge pool beside Enrico's headless body. When she had followed the flow of the pool to her toes, she saw that she was coated with the blood.

Clutched in one hand, she saw to her horror, was Enrico's knife. She dropped it abruptly, wondering how she had come to be holding it at all. Dimly, she remembered picking it up when Gabriel had tossed it to the floor, remembered some vague thought of using it to defend herself.

"I didn't! I didn't kill him!" she managed to choke out the denial finally as someone hauled her arms behind her back, twisting them painfully and roughly binding her wrists.

Strand's face hardened. "I suppose his head just sort of popped off his shoulders? Christ almighty, this was stupid! We had him! You just had to take matters into your own hands, didn't you?"

Kylee gaped at him. "No! I didn't do this. Gabriel did it!" She glanced around the room a little frantically, searching for him, stunned to see that he was not among the people crowding the room.

Something flickered in Strand's eyes. "Gabriel?"

"Yes! Gabriel! The--uh--the Elumi. He was here. Enrico broke the door in and grabbed me by the throat and Gabriel appeared behind me...." Her voice petered to a halt when she realized what she'd said and how it sounded.

"The *angel* Gabriel," Strand said, nodding wisely. "That's good. Try a mental."

"No! Really. I'm not making this up."

He nodded at the man behind her and she was half pushed half carried from the room, her arms jerked up so high behind her she had to bend over to relieve the painful pressure. She was shoved into a waiting squad car and the door slammed firmly behind her. Righting herself with an effort, she stared out the window, too stunned to completely assimilate what was happening as she watched the chaos outside.

Lights flashed in her eyes, blinding her. A moment later, a cop climbed into the driver's seat, started the car and pulled away.

What followed was the stuff of nightmares. Fortunately, Kylee was still in a state of shock when they arrived at the police station. Cocooned by that state of unreality, she was thoroughly confused, but unable to really grasp what was going on, or to feel any real fear. The only thing she did feel was a vast weariness that further impeded her ability to think clearly.

Like a zombie, she merely moved her feet when she was led from place to place, told to sit, told to stand, told to turn.

She wasn't allowed to bathe. The blood dripped for a while and then began to dry before they'd finished taking the pictures they wanted, asking her questions, inking her fingers. When she'd been booked, she was taken at last to get cleaned up. Bathing in a communal shower, and being searched, was almost more nightmarish than wearing the blood, though. She was allowed to collapse weakly on a hard bunk for a perhaps an hour and then dragged down to an interrogation room where she spent several more hours.

After repeating her story over and over, she fell asleep in the chair.

Nobody had bothered to ask if she was hurt until she'd finally had the chance to bathe off and Strand noticed she had new bruises blooming. He wasn't sympathetic. In fact, it was pretty clear that he wasn't happy to see evidence that she might be able to claim self defense.

They didn't bother to take pictures of her bruises.

The lawyer she'd asked for didn't arrive until the police had already interrogated her for hours. She was almost sorry to see the woman, though, because the first thing she did was demand to have a doctor see her and Kylee was already so near to dropping she had to struggle to keep from bursting into tears of sheer exhaustion.

She fell asleep on the examining table and was woken to the unpleasant discovery that someone was probing her vagina. Horror filled her when she realized they were collecting a rape kit. It didn't hit her until the nurse had left with the collected 'evidence' that it was proof that she hadn't been in the room alone--maybe.

More photos followed, this time for her defense.

It was horrible that she was downright grateful when she was finally thrown into a jail cell and locked in, but all she could think about was that now, at long last, she could rest. She didn't think she actually rested though. It was more a matter of passing beyond consciousness and when she was woken again, she felt nearly as tired as she had before she'd lain down.

The institutional atmosphere, being woken at all hours without any possibility of rest, and having virtually no privacy made the experience rather like being in a hospital--except worse.

Her attorney met with her sometime during the second endless day, informing her that her arraignment had been set for the following day and arrangements couldn't be made to get her out on bail until then. Afterwards, Kylee slept some, but spent most of her time huddled in one corner on her bunk just staring at a spot on the floor.

Mentally, she wasn't in a much better state than when she'd been arrested, but she saw that she was in deep trouble. Strand was trying to charge her with first degree murder, citing the fact that she'd come to the city specifically to catch Enrico for her sister's murder and, when that fell through, had lured him to her room to murder him in cold blood.

She didn't see how he could possibly believe that, but he claimed to, and he claimed to have evidence to support it--which was a hell of a note, all things considered. She hadn't done anything to the bastard and they were willing to manufacture evidence--which they would have to do since she was innocent--yet they knew Enrico had killed her sister and he could walk because they couldn't get evidence? Some frigging justice!

What she couldn't understand was why Gabriel had abandoned her in such a callous way.

Almost as if thinking about him had conjured him, he appeared beside her bunk. She stared at him in blank disbelief for several moments before she decided he really was there. "Gabriel?"

He was frowning, studying the cell with patent disgust. "Why are you here?"

She should've been furious with him for getting her into the mess she was in, but all she could think about at first was that she desperately needed to be held. Scooting off the bunk, she threw herself against him. To her relief, he wrapped his arms around her, holding her tightly against him. At first, she feared it was a prelude to sex--which she definitely wasn't in the mood for at the moment, but he seemed to sense she just needed to be held and he didn't seem to have a problem with it. He smoothed her hair and rubbed her back soothingly.

"Why have they brought you to this place, dearling?"

"They think I killed Enrico," Kylee muttered against his chest, beginning to shake with reaction.

He pulled away from her to study her face. "Why would they believe that?"

Kylee's chin wobbled. "Because I was the only one there and I was holding his knife. Why did you leave me like that?"

He pulled her tightly against his body again. "To protect you."

"It didn't work," Kylee muttered.

Pulling away from her again, he tugged her behind him and settled on the bunk, dragging her onto his lap and cuddling her against his chest. "From my enemy, dearling," he said patiently. "The one that I had fought that first night. Somehow he tracked me to you. I am not certain that he would have tried to harm you, but I could not be certain he would not when he found me with you. Even if that had not been his intention, you could have been harmed if we had fought there. I drew him off. When I had beaten him, I returned, but you were gone."

Kylee shuddered. Abruptly, she recalled the 'man' she'd run into when she had gone to try to draw Enrico out, the one she had thought might be an Elumi like Gabriel.

The only thing she'd managed to do was to nearly get both herself and Gabriel killed, because she was certain, suddenly, that both Enrico and the Elumi had followed her back.

Stupid, stupid mistake! Why hadn't she considered that before?

She found that she didn't want to admit to Gabriel that it was all her fault they'd been attacked. Obviously, he had taken great pains when he had come to her to make certain he *wasn't* followed.

"Somebody called the police, I guess--heard the commotion. I don't know. I fainted. They were everywhere when I woke up. And I was holding the knife that--" Kylee stopped abruptly and pulled away to examine him. "He stabbed you with that knife. I saw it!"

"Yes. He did."

Kylee frowned, confused. "But--there's no sign--not at all! You're--immortal?"

He sighed gustily. "We are not immortal, but we are far more resilient than humans. We regenerate rapidly. Fighting with swords is much more than a matter of honor and skill for us. It is virtually the only way we can slay our adversaries, for if the head does not come away from the body, the body will heal itself."

Kylee settled against him again, too relieved to discover he was unharmed to want to question the how or why of it, though the knowledge left her with an uncomfortable sense of separation from him.

"We're not the same at all, are we?" she said in a small voice, realizing that that meant they would not be together, could not. She hadn't considered it before because she hadn't thought it would come to matter to her. She had wanted to believe that she could enjoy the passion they shared and there would be no strings attached, no baggage to deal with later, but she realized it hadn't happened like that at all. "You've slain an enemy warrior. I guess that means you'll be allowed to go home?"

He didn't answer, not directly, which she took to be a yes. "I will not leave you in this place."

Kylee swallowed with an effort, pushing away from him. "It's a law thing--a human thing. You wouldn't understand. I can't escape. I have to go through with this and try to clear myself. If I escaped, they'd hunt me forever."

He shook his head. Shifting on the bunk until he could lie down, he pulled her down beside him so that they were facing one another. "I understand. I will fix this. Trust me," he murmured leaning close to nibble at her lips teasingly.

Warmth flowed through her despite her certainty only minutes before that she had no desire for sex. She wrapped her arms around his neck, shifting closer, suddenly as needy of his caresses as she was of his passion.

Chapter Eight

Kylee was surprised when an officer took her from her cell to the interrogation room again. For the first time since she'd been arrested, however, she was not in shock, not scared half to death, and not exhausted. Gabriel had done far more than give her pleasure. He'd given her the comfort she needed to rest in mind and body and a sense of hope.

"My lawyer isn't here," Kylee said the moment Strand strode into the room and took a seat.

"She's on the way."

Kylee nodded and settled in her chair to wait.

"I'm considering offering you a deal."

Kylee looked him over. "I didn't think cops made the deals. I thought that had to be somebody from the DA's office."

He shrugged. "Yeah, but the deal I'm offering is to influence the DA in your favor if you'll volunteer information."

Kylee blinked. He thought she was stupid. Or maybe he thought she was still in the same totally chaotic state of mind she'd been in before and not able to think reasonably? "Let me see if I've got this straight. I give up my right to an attorney, tell you what you want to know, and you promise me absolutely nothing in return. Does that just about cover it?"

Strand's lips tightened. "I can make things a lot worse for you."

"Not unless that includes tying me to a post and horse whipping me, because that place sucks and I think I've already got the worst stinking cell you could possibly have."

"I could stick you in a cell with a girlfriend," he growled.

Kylee narrowed her eyes at him. "I'm going to tell my lawyer you threatened me."

"You can't prove it."

"I don't have to. If I tell her and then you stick me in a cell with a lesbian, you will have proved it yourself."

"I meant after you get to prison."

"I don't think you have that kind of influence, and even if you did, you're assuming you can prove the case. I know you can't, because I didn't kill that bastard."

"You were the only one in the room."

"He still outweighed me by fifty or sixty pounds besides being a man and a hell of a lot stronger than I am! And I sure as hell couldn't cut his head off with a four inch knife blade--not unless I held him down and sawed it off with the thing. You know I didn't or you wouldn't be offering me anything."

Strand shot to his feet. "Fine. I'll just send you back to your cell then. You can let me know when you're ready to cooperate."

He left then. Kylee relaxed. She'd been sitting in the room almost thirty minutes before it dawned on her that he had no intention of sending her back to her cell. He was trying to 'sweat' her, trying to unnerve her by leaving her to worry and wonder what they were planning. He'd tried that tactic the day she'd been arrested. It hadn't worked then because she was in shock and too numb to feel much of anything. It certainly wasn't going to work now.

She would've gotten up and paced except that they'd left her handcuffed to the table.

Sighing, she tried to focus on something other than her discomfort.

Gabriel had been gone when she'd woken and she wondered if he'd gone back to Pearthen. He'd said he meant to see to it that she was freed before he left, but she supposed he'd realized that there was really nothing he could do but confess to the deed and that wasn't something anybody she knew would do, especially not for a woman they hardly knew.

She thought Gabriel would have anyway, except for his own laws. He would not worry about Earth laws, she didn't think. He could allow the cops to do as they pleased and then just vanish whenever it suited him. That would not be the case with his own people, though, and lord only knew what the penalty was if they caught him. Death, she suspected, which might have been what he'd meant by that remark before--certain death or salvation.

She supposed she should be absolutely furious about the whole thing, but somehow she couldn't find it in herself to be angry with him. She was glad Enrico was dead. He'd brutally murdered her sister and, despite her horror at watching him executed, she was fiercely glad Gabriel had done it, had given her and her sister justice when the law would not.

In her mind, she had killed Enrico herself a hundred times in a hundred ways. She hadn't gone through with it. She still hoped that she could prove that she hadn't and could go on with her life, but she had decided she was not going to regret it whatever happened. In her heart, she knew she would have killed Enrico if she could have.

She was going to miss Gabriel. She understood that he didn't really belong in her world and that he must miss his own world terribly, but accepting the way things were wasn't going to make it any easier.

She loved him. It didn't matter how unreasonable it might seem to anyone else. It was one of those things one just knew even when you hadn't felt anything quite like it before. It was a joy that just seemed to envelop your whole soul when you thought about them. It was breathless anticipation whenever you thought about seeing them again, hearing their voice, just being close to them.

She hadn't known him a full week, which even she thought was crazy, but the truth was she hadn't known him a full hour when it had hit her like a ton of bricks, maybe not even a minute. It was just there. One minute he was a stranger, an alien being, and the next she'd looked deeply into his eyes, felt his touch, and everything in her had welcomed him as if she'd known him forever.

She knew she was never going to feel that way again about another living soul. She thought that distressed her far more than anything about her situation with the cops.

Strand breezed back into the room, interrupting her thoughts. "I've decided to give you one more chance to cooperate. You claimed that someone else was in the room.

Give us this guy's name and we'll see what we can do about reducing the charges against you."

Kylee stared at the man in disbelief. Finally, she merely shrugged, though. What difference would it make anyway? They were never going to find Gabriel, and it wasn't like he would object to them knowing. "His name is Gabriel."

"Don't start that guardian angel crap again!" Strand said in disgust. "We know you had sex just before Enrico was killed. We also know it wasn't Enrico and it was consensual...."

Kylee didn't even realize he'd stopped without finishing the sentence until he looked beyond her shoulder, his face going taut and pale with shock. Instinctively, she glanced around, too. "Gabriel! You came back!" she exclaimed, unable to keep the joy out of her voice.

His gaze flickered over her. There was a glint of amusement in his eyes and something else she couldn't quite define. "I gave you my word I would."

Strand, Kylee saw when she turned to look at him again was looking as if he'd seen a ghost. "How did you...? What the hell are you doing in here?"

"I came to confess. I killed the man."

Strand's jaw dropped. After a moment, he glanced around a little frantically and surged out of his seat with such force that the chair toppled over and rattled around the floor. Almost before the chair had hit the floor, someone began to pound on the door to the room which, for some mysterious reason wouldn't open.

"Why?" Strand demanded after a prolonged silence while he watched the fruitless efforts of his fellow officers to breech the door.

Gabriel knelt beside Kylee and touched the handcuffs, which promptly popped open. "Because he hurt my woman," Gabriel answered simply, tapping Kylee's chin affectionately. He glanced at the detective. "And because he threatened the life of my woman and our child."

As he rose to his full height once more, he 'displayed' his wings, arching them as he drew his sword from its scabbard along his back. "In the way of my people, I took justice for the murder of Kylee's sister, and protected my woman, as is my right."

"Gabriel," Kylee said, watching him uneasily. "You're not going to do anything, are you?"

Gabriel's gaze flickered to her, but before he could respond, the crash of shattering glass drew everyone's attention as the cops gave up on beating the door down and burst through the two way mirror instead.

"Drop the weapon! Now! Drop it!"

Gabriel tilted his head curiously at the three cops who had their pistols drawn and aimed directly at him. Grabbing Kylee by one arm, he thrust her behind him, otherwise ignoring the cops who continued to bellow, "Put it down!" "Get on the ground!" but made no attempt to come any closer.

He turned to look at Strand again. "You will release Kylee and make this go away. She did not kill the man."

"Put the weapon down and we'll talk about it."

"I will not negotiate."

"Put it down or we'll shoot!"

Gabriel looked at the cop that had spoken and smiled, slowly.

Unnerved by the look, the cop jerked on the trigger, firing off a round. The moment he began shooting, the others began shooting as well. Strand dove for the floor. Kylee screamed. The sword moved. None of the officers saw it move and yet it was directly in the path of every bullet, and every bullet hit the sword and ricocheted into the walls around the interrogation room.

When they'd run out of bullets, they merely stared at the apparition, too stunned even to consider reloading or running.

"You can not imprison me. You can not bind me with your manacles. You can not kill me with your weapons. And I will not be bound by your laws when there is a higher law which gives me the right to protect my woman with deadly force if necessary. Drop the charges against Kylee--or I will return--and you will not be pleased to see me again."

Sheathing his sword, he turned and lifted Kylee tightly against him. "This may discomfort you, dearling," he murmured. He turned to study Strand a long moment, and then simply walked through the wall.

* * * *

Strand stared at the wall for some time before he finally approached it and touched it carefully. The wall felt warm, but it was solid. Glancing around the room in search of anything that looked out of place, he came up empty. He still didn't believe what he thought he'd seen. It had to have been some cheesy magician's trick. He just had to figure out how it had been accomplished. When he turned at last to look at the officers standing on the other side of what had been an observation room, he saw that they looked as if they were coming out of a trance. The men looked at him uncomfortably, and then looked at each other.

"Did you see that?" one of the men, Jim Johnson, asked, awe in his voice.

The two men with him stared at him for a moment. "I didn't see anything. How about you, Clark?"

Clark shrugged. "I think I'll have a look at the tapes."

All four men crowded close as the tape reached the point where Strand said he'd first noticed the man. "There!" one of the men said, stabbing a finger at the screen. "Did you see that flicker?"

Strand frowned. "It could've been the light." His frown deepened when the screen filled with 'snow'. As one, they leaned closer. "I can't see him," Strand said finally.

"Because he wasn't really there," Johnson put in.

"I could go for the projection thing considering not one of us hit him a single time, but the bullets didn't just pass through. They ricocheted. Besides, how would a projected image pick Griffin out and waltz out with her? You can see her alright--right up to the point that he pushed her behind him," Jim Riker, the other man involved in the shooting, said uneasily.

"Try the tape recording," Clark suggested.

Disgust filled Strand when they'd listened to it. The tape was worse, if possible, than the video. He could hear his voice and Kylee Griffin's up until the point the man had entered the room, but even their voices were hard to distinguish afterwards. "Some kind of electrical interference. I'm going to get this down to the lab and see if they can clean it up any."

"You sure you want to do that?"

Strand paused. "Hell, yes, I'm sure. Why wouldn't I be sure?"

"We shot the shit out of that room," Clark pointed out.

"Exactly, which is why we need the tape," Strand growled.

"Except that there's nothing on the fucking tape except us shooting the hell out of the room. They're going to think we were on something to be that freaked."

Strand settled in his seat once more. "What *are* we going to do?"

"Get rid of the tape, dig the slugs out of the wall and patch them."

"We've got an escaped prisoner," Strand pointed out.

"Which you were questioning when you weren't supposed to because she'd asked for a lawyer and you didn't call the lawyer," Riker growled. "This is a hell of mess. We're all going to get canned over it."

"There wasn't any evidence tying her to the murder," Clark put in.

"She was a witness," Strand growled, infuriated to think the killer was going to slip through his fingers. He despised being outsmarted--by anybody. The bastard had admitted straight out that he'd killed that scumball.

There *was* the evidence that it had been man slaughter, not murder one, though. The girl was beat up pretty badly. Was it really worth ruining his career to get the guy on that kind of rap?

Sighing in disgust, he glanced at the other men. "I ain't having anything to do with a clean up unless everybody's in absolute agreement. I'd rather come clean now than have somebody turning on me down the road because their conscience is bothering them."

Chapter Nine

The transition wasn't really unpleasant. There was a stinging sensation all over Kylee's body and then--nothing. The unnerving thing was what Gabriel did once they'd emerged from the building.

He launched skyward. One moment they were standing in the alley, the next the building was below them and Kylee's stomach with it. She blacked out again. That time, though, she thought it was from the G's Gabriel pulled when he shot straight up into the sky.

She roused when she felt them slowing, but full awareness didn't return until Gabriel at last stopped moving. When Kylee lifted her head and looked around, she discovered that they were in the room she'd rented. It was a disaster area. Yellow tape still covered the door. Everything in the room had been turned inside out as the police searched for the murder weapon, Kylee supposed.

"We can not stay here," Gabriel said after surveying the damage. "I will take you to your home."

Kylee had a very bad feeling that the cops would be right behind them, whatever Gabriel had said and done, but the mention of home was all it took to make her yearn for the peace and familiarity of her own home. She nodded. "Yes. Please take me home!"

She wasn't certain that she could explain 'as the crow flew' directions, but she did her best. In truth, she didn't really care where he took her so long as it was a very long way away from the city, the nightmare of Enrico's summary 'execution', jail and the police.

Gabriel surprised her, again. Without any notable difficulty, he took her directly to the city where she lived. Dropping lower and flying slower then, he circled until she identified the area--not an easy task for her at night and from such a viewpoint--and found her house.

She didn't have her keys--the police still had her belongings in custody--but that wasn't an impediment to Gabriel.

As much as she enjoyed being close to him, she was relieved when he set her down at last. Wilting weakly on her couch, she stared around at the room with a stranger's eyes as Gabriel paced the room, looking it over curiously. It seemed like forever since she had been here, when, in fact, it had been no more than a month.

She wondered if she would ever get used to it again, get back into the same, dull, boring routine that she'd had before she had left.

She wondered if she would get the chance.

Dismissing it, she turned her attention to Gabriel. "Are you--will you be going home now, too?" she asked finally.

He turned to look at her in surprise. "This is home."

Kylee blinked, too stunned to think for a moment. "You're going to stay?"

He tilted his head to one side, studying her. Finally, he crossed the room and knelt beside her. His expression was piercing, fierce. "You are my woman," he said finally. "You will bear my son. I will not stay here if you do not want that, but I can not leave my son."

A knot rose in Kylee's throat. "How do you know I will bear your son?"

He placed his palm on her belly. "I know. He grows here."

Somehow, even though she had had no reason to think it, she didn't doubt what he said. She felt like crying, not because she didn't want to be the mother of his child but because his knowledge of it and his fierce protectiveness towards his child had deprived her of knowing if he wanted her or if he only stayed because of the child.

He seemed to sense her doubts. Grasping her arms, he pulled her from the couch and straightened, holding her close. "I gave my son into your keeping because I love you, Kylee," he said quietly. "Don't ever doubt that."

Kylee pulled away to look at him. "Really?"

"Truly."

A thrill of wonder surged through Kylee, a thrill that was like the best of homecomings--when one had wandered far and wide and finally found one's way home again. "I love you too. I was afraid...."

He smiled wryly. "You should not have doubted, not when I could not stay away."

Kylee blushed. "I thought that was just ... uh ... the sex."

He frowned at her. "Just?"

A smile curled the corners of her lips. "Not 'just', but just because of."

Dragging her down on the couch, he spent a leisurely hour teaching her the difference between 'just', 'just because of', and love making.

Kylee was drifting lazily in the aftermath when doubts surfaced again.

"You're going to live as human?"

"You think I can not?"

Kylee smiled at him. "I think you can do anything--if that's what you want."

"It is what I want."

Another doubt surfaced after several moments of dreamily imagining their lives together. "Your blood is different than mine. What if--there's a problem with the baby?"

"There will be no problem," he said without hesitation.

"You're sure?"

"Yes. Your blood will be the same as the infant."

Kylee frowned. "You mean the infant's will be the same as mine?"

"Nay. You will--become much the same as I."

Kylee's eyes widened. "Elumi?"

"Not precisely, but a hybrid of human and Elumi. The babe is half. It will make the changes necessary to its development."

"Oh--does that mean--will my life span be more like yours?"

He caressed her cheek. "This is why I gave my child into your keeping, dearling, to keep you with me."

The End

ARCHANGEL

By
Jaide Fox

Chapter One

Danielle Logan couldn't believe she'd finally succeeded in building the next "big thing." The "thing" that would revolutionize the world; eliminate vast amounts of pollution; connect life from one end of the world to the other in seconds ... even far reaching space travel was now a possibility.

She felt like bouncing around the room, she was so excited. Finally, she would have the respect of the scientific community, and she wouldn't have to put up with bureaucratic tic bullshit to have a good life. She would have money, lots of money, for research or whatever. The sense of achievement had her floating on cloud nine, but of course, the money aspect of her invention was a damned fine bonus.

Tamping her excitement, Danielle studied the transporter pods. She'd have to think of a less sci-fi name for them otherwise people wouldn't take them seriously.

Then again, having them linked to sci-fi might not be such a bad thing if she could get over the hump of people believing that using a transporter would turn them into a monster. It could get the system into use much quicker.

Just thinking about marketing strategies boggled her mind, but it was something she'd have to consider since she'd opted to do her experiments entirely on her own--

without help, or intervention, from established labs. It had been the only way to retain her rights. Unfortunately, most of the experimental labs had wanted her to sign away every idea she could possibly come up with years down the road-- even if she left and struck out on her own--they would see it as a violation of their rights and she'd be liable.

It'd been hard scrounging for money, but well worth the hardships she'd endured.

Once she'd worked out the kinks in her system and successfully transported simple inanimate objects like paper and pens without a hitch, she'd moved on to complex structures: DVDs; telephones; computers; fruit, KFC. When the fruit went through and tasted fine, she'd moved on to mice and then rats; a cat; a toy poodle she'd borrowed from a neighbor while she was away at work.

Okay, so it was immoral, but she'd been confident nothing would happen and she needed to test larger animals ... she wasn't an entirely bad person. This was for the good of everyone, after all, and could potentially cut down on highway deaths of animals.

Jeez, she hadn't quite thought out all the implications of the transporters, but the more she thought about it, the more excited she got.

So far her foray into living creatures was successful. The animals all checked out okay, even several months afterward. They hadn't developed cancerous cells or organ deceleration--nothing to indicate anything internal had gone haywire. She hadn't moved beyond that, though.

Now that she was nearing the end, she wanted to have the process fully documented for approval for human testing, but she hadn't managed to get approval for a Rhesus--not without showing her other tests and revealing her invention. She needed to test higher life forms, but she didn't trust anyone not to steal it. The problem was, there were so many people racing toward the same end, she felt like any day someone else would make a break through and all her work would be for nothing. She couldn't guard the house all the time if someone took it into their head to do some espionage--and as far fetched as that sounded, it was entirely probable given the monetary value of such a discovery.

She had to move forward.

Which was why she'd covered every window in her house and moved the units out of her crowded office and into the living room. She retested it. Nothing had jostled loose. All was in readiness. All she had to do now was step inside and test it out on herself.

She felt confident that there would be no problem with the process. She was ready for this. It had to be done.

She'd put consoles linked to the main computer inside both trans. pods, so she wouldn't have to worry about getting stuck. She'd have to make a small panel version in the future, maybe something like an elevator. Later.

Torn between elation and anxiety, Danielle opened the pod door and stopped. Would it be better to try it out naked or clothed? She hadn't considered that possibility before. The complex objects hadn't scrambled, so she couldn't imagine the probability was that high for it to happen to her. Still ... better safe than sorry. When she'd done a few test runs and was certain there weren't any problems, she would try it *with* clothes. Pulling off her clothes, she stepped into the small pod, hunching over the console to close the door.

She performed a vitals scan. Blood pressure, slightly elevated but in the norm. Her breathing was also elevated, but she knew that was from excitement. She was healthy and capable of traveling.

She just prayed nothing more that transporting would happen. Otherwise, the landlord would be in for a surprise next month when no rent was forthcoming.

The machine began its warm-up, cooling fans whirring softly as they picked up speed to keep the unit from overheating. A bead of sweat trickled between her breasts despite the fans, making her itch. She wiped it away, ticking off the seconds until transport. The unit hummed and released a short burst of air that ruffled her hair.

She watched the digital timer inside the unit.

Thirty seconds.

Visions of Cronenberg's The Fly danced in her head.

Twenty seconds.

Her heart rate increased. Her ear drums rumbled. Nothing to worry about. She'd be okay. The poodle had survived, hadn't it?

Ten ... nine ... eight....

Danielle clenched her hands, counting down in her head. Three ... two ... one.

Darkness engulfed her.

For a moment, she thought she'd gone blind. Then light burst all around her, mist dampened her skin. She blinked against the rush of air cooling her flesh. Light and color streamed across her vision. Abruptly, her gaze locked on an image that was traveling at almost the same speed as she, the stunned countenance of a winged man.

She shrieked.

Blackness settled over her vision again and then she was surrounded by cool, grey metal and a glass shield revealing her disarrayed living room.

Another burst of air hit her as the door hissed open, depressurizing the atmosphere inside the chamber.

Danielle's knees gave out and she collapsed in a heap on the floor, half in and half out of the receiving pod.

Her heart pounded painfully in her chest, not from excitement this time, but residual fear. Her temples throbbed. She looked around the room, dazed, willing herself to return to normal. Elation was slow in coming-- non-existent, actually.

What the hell had just happened?

After a while, she pulled herself up, feeling weak, washed out. She didn't bother to get dressed, instead she hobbled to the main computer, collapsing limply in her chair to examine the data.

She'd expected to blackout and then wakeup in the other pod across the room. She hadn't expected ... whatever *that* was.

Had she hallucinated? Had a near death experience like she'd seen proselytized a million times on TV?

She wasn't a religious person. As a scientist, it was hard for her rational mind to comprehend the fantastical, like God in his many incarnations around the world. She didn't rule it out, but neither did she truly believe in miracles. There was always some kind of explanation....

Despite that, she could've sworn she'd seen an ... angel, which was completely preposterous.

Closing her eyes, she found that she could visualize the image, recall details she hadn't been aware of her mind assimilating at the time. He had looked *exactly* like depictions she'd seen of seraphs in old books and paintings--like a human with wings. Dimly, she recalled that he'd had some kind of drapery thing covering his lower body. The image of long, wavy hair that was a very light brown with golden highlights was clearer. She remembered fair, but golden skin, bulging well defined muscles all over his chest and arms--even pierced nipples with a thin golden chain between the rings. She remembered the wings best-- palest gold tips to dark gold, shaped very like the wings of a bird and feathered. She couldn't quite envision his face, beyond the look of surprise, but she had the impression of regular, angular features--sort of Nordic and appealingly symmetrical.

How could she remember the image so vividly if she hadn't actually seen it at all? If it had been purely hallucination, wouldn't it have been all blurry and indistinct in her mind like dream images? Would she remember something as minute as the glint of light off a golden chain?

Angels didn't exist. Magic wasn't real. Cold, hard science was real, facts she could see and touch and wrap her mind around. It had to be a hallucination brought on by her mind in transience.

Shaking her discomfort over the experience, Danielle accessed the data her computer had collected and began going over it. She'd gone over it twice before she realized something was off. The transference should have only taken ten seconds at the most--enough time for the second pod to "pick up". She would have lost consciousness as her body was basically broken down and reassembled inside the other pod. Technically, she would be vaporized and dead ten seconds before the data transmitted her across the room. It was basically like an advanced fax machine.

That's what she'd always thought of it as.

But she'd been aware of something else, and the data clearly showed a delay of fifteen seconds before the receptacle had received her. She'd been transferring for twenty five seconds.

She'd seen something.

Was the mind still capable of existing even in that state, though? Was it at all possible that the soul actually existed as a separate entity within the body?

Maybe the delay was caused by the size of her body? She hadn't transported anything nearly as big before.

She didn't know, but it disturbed her greatly not knowing what had happened.

Once she'd gone over all of the data, she'd begun feeling more like herself, more the scientist than an alarmist. She put her t-shirt on and went back to the pod to run another scan. Everything was normal.

She tested the pods--every single aspect, from the casing to the console inside. Everything was in working order. The pods hadn't spontaneously changed or reset themselves. She rebooted her computer, made sure the atomic clock still functioned properly. Nothing wrong there.

She decided to resend something through the pod, to make sure it wasn't just the new location affecting it. The shoe went through fine--precisely 9.99 seconds to traverse one pod to another.

The only explanation that fit was that the human body was too complicated to transmit in less than ten seconds.

She was going to have to try it again and see if it replicated the same results the second time, she realized. She didn't have time for speculation. Even though she was tired, that wasn't unexpected. She had to believe that nothing had happened to her because the data emphatically denied that.

Uneasiness moved over her, though.

She decided to sleep on it. She was exhausted. She would rest a few hours and then test everything again. If she found no evidence to the contrary, she was going to assume it was just some sort of side effect from the process that was non-threatening and she would try the experiment again.

She found it hard to sleep. After tossing and turning for hours, she finally drifted off. The vision, naturally enough, invaded her dreams. This time, though, she wasn't startled or fearful that he represented death, far from it. In the dream, the gorgeous vision waited for her with open arms, smiled at her, set her heart to pounding with excitement when he pulled her against him and made love to her.

She was aroused when she woke and torn between the desire to burrow deeper and try to retrieve the dream and the nagging of her mind to get up and go back to work.

Work won out and she rolled out of bed with a groan and went to shower to prod her sluggish mind into awareness.

It took hours to go over everything again, but once she had, she saw the results were the same. She hadn't missed anything critical. All of her vitals were normal. Everything on the system checked out.

Her belly clenched in anxiety at the thought of testing again on herself, but she dismissed it. One thing that was definitely *not* going to sell the thing for her was any sign of doubt about using it herself.

Resolutely, Danielle stripped and got into the first pod, starting up the process once more.

Despite the mental pep talk, she was more nervous this time. Giving herself a mental kick, she willed herself to breathe slowly, forced her hands to unclench as the seconds ticked by. She resisted the urge to chew her nails or bite her bottom lip. When the rush of air came, she readied for the blackout and held her eyes open wide, as if it would somehow help her see whatever it was she'd seen before.

The sudden darkness still surprised her when it hit. The blinding light stunned her even more. She blinked, her vision blurry, unfocussed--or rather everything around her was out of focus because of the speed she was moving. Her heart beat twice. She sucked in a breath of strangely sweet air just as something slammed into her from behind, changing her trajectory instantly and smacking her face first into a blur of green mossy-like substance that turned slimy as her body smeared it.

It took Danielle several stunned moments to realize she'd stopped moving. The distinct smells and tastes of dirt and chlorophyll from the vegetation her face was burrowed against filled her mouth and nose. She struggled for breath, tensed against the pain she expected to begin filtering through to her shocked brain.

There was less than she'd expected and she did a mental inventory to see what was mangled.

She thought she might be paralyzed for a few, panicked seconds, then realized that something heavy was pinning her to the ground. Sluggishly, her perception moved beyond her own body to the world around her. The sound of wings flapping and harsh breathing caught her ears. Her hair stirred with each beat of the wings. Nearby she could hear a sizzle of electricity, similar to the sound her transporter pods made when a transference was in progress and realized with a touch of amazement that she'd been plucked from the transference stream.

With her face squished into the dirt, she couldn't see anything beyond ... dirt, though.

Abruptly, Danielle's brain threw off the effects of shock and kicked into high gear. Her mind was whirling, collecting and storing data for future use. The dirt felt like dirt, but it didn't smell like it. Nothing smelled right. Everything was ... almost sweet.

The heavy weight on her was warm. She could feel muscles flexed around her waist and knew she wasn't lying beneath a limb, not a tree limb, anyway. Fingers tightened in her hair, which explained why she couldn't move her head.

There was definitely a humanoid holding her. If she was hallucinating, it was the most vivid hallucination she'd ever thought to experience. Imagining that she was seeing things was one thing, but feeling? Smelling strange scents?

Strangely, except for those few unnerving moments when it had popped into her mind that she was paralyzed, she felt no sense of impending panic. She supposed that was because she was having to focus on dragging air into her lungs. She could almost believe something had fallen on her if not for the breathing right behind her neck and the very real feeling of a man on top of her.

She might not have had a lot of practice in the mating practices of humans, but she knew what a man's body felt like. He was heavy, hard all over. Hair roughened skin skimmed along the backs of her legs.

"Zahtifah ezeto unta," a deep, guttural voice growled behind her, pronouncing each word slowly.

Danielle tried to move her head enough to talk through her squashed open mouth. "Engwith. I sweak Engwith," she said with an effort, wondering if it was even worth it to try to communicate at this point. Surely she'd wake up in the pod at any moment?

"Zahtifah ezeto unta!" His hands tightened in her hair, making her scalp hurt and annihilating her efforts to convince herself that nothing she thought she was experiencing was real.

She'd had just about enough of that. Anger surged through her. She totally lost her cool then. Struggling until she managed to free one arm, she sent her elbow flying back to connect with hard flesh.

He grunted and loosened his hold. She bucked the instant his grip slackened, growling with the effort of trying to move him enough to gain some leverage and throw him off of her.

Finally, she managed to lift her head from the muck and cuss him. "Ow! Damn it, you asshole! Let me go."

The pressure on her backside decreased. He moved off of her, releasing her. Before she could try to follow up with her attack, or even decide if she wanted to, she was rolled onto her back, and then he was on her again, his hands pinning her wrists, his chest crushing her breasts. His face was mere inches from hers.

She gasped as the breath left her lungs and just stared, feeling her heart stick in her throat.

It was the angel.

There was no welcoming smile, no desire in his eyes the way she'd dreamed it. Aggression, not passion, tautened every line of his body. His face was a harsh mask of fury. "How did you find the gateway?"

Danielle swallowed the hard lump in her throat. "You speak English?" she asked a little weakly, her brief righteous indignation vanishing abruptly along with her spine. *Great, genius. Didn't he just ask you in English?* "What I meant to say is ... what gateway? I didn't see anything."

A muscle worked in his jaw, as if he was striving for patience ... and not succeeding very well. "Do not pretend ignorance. Twice you have passed through it."

Maybe she'd died and gone to heaven? This couldn't be happening. "Am I ... dead?"

He moved off her and tugged her roughly to her feet. "Not yet," he said through gritted teeth.

Chapter Two

Kirin snatched the woman into his arms and shot into the air. She gasped, flinging her arms tightly around his neck and clung to him with a death grip as he flew the short distance to his post.

In the many millennia since the Elumi had passed through the rift into the great beyond, the gateway had never been breached by *their* kind, the humans. That it would happen during his watch boded ill for his future as an archangel--a guardian of the borders of his king's lands. That he'd allowed the offender to escape before could mean death ... or worse, banishment to lower Earth, the realm of humans, if it were ever discovered.

Kirin could not fathom how this human had gone through, when not even all Elumi had the skills to do so. Nor could he understand, with his great speed, how he'd managed to lose her the first time she'd breached the gateway.

He might have been able to dismiss it as hallucination bred of sheer boredom if it had only been the one time, but twice? He had been too stunned even to react the first time and when she had disappeared almost as quickly as she had appeared, he had been tempted to simply reject the possibility that it had actually happened.

No Elumi had passed. He was stronger, faster, and cleverer than the average Elumi or he would not have gained the position he held, which was reserved for the elite warrior, the very best of the best.

It certainly could not have been a human.

And yet when he recalled the image to his mind, he had known it could be nothing else. There had been no wings. She had not worn the garb of any house of Pearthen, had born no weapon--and he had never seen hair in that shade on any Elumi in all his time.

It was, in point of fact, that bright flame of color that had drawn his gaze to begin with. Otherwise, he might not have seen her at all.

Death was a powerful incentive for vigilance, however. He could not afford the luxury of simply dismissing the incident as the product of imagination that he had suspected/feared it was.

It was his sacred duty to defend the gateway, and a matter of honor, but neither that duty nor the certainty that failure would be the forfeiture of his life had bothered him the most. In truth, the more he'd thought about it, the more certain he was that the human had taunted him and the angrier he'd become. Not only had a human, of all things, made a fool of him by penetrating his station when no Elumi had ever succeeded in doing so, she had thumbed her nose at him by zipping past him so quickly he could do nothing more than gape at her.

She would come again. He had known she would not be able to resist taunting him with her amazing ability.

And so he had waited, tensed for action, determined that if she breached the gateway again, he would not fail his duty. He would apprehend the enemy spy or die trying. As he had feared, she had, but he had been ready for her this time. This time she had not caught him by surprise with her stunning speed. This time, he had launched himself at her as she zipped past him and tackled her.

His success leavened his anger somewhat, but not entirely. He would have to report that his position had been breached. They would know even if he had been tempted to lie--and he was facing charges even though he had captured her. She had ruined his perfect military record.

He would be demoted and he would be banished to lower Earth, perhaps for a very long time.

Reaching the tower, Kirin landed before the entranceway and set the woman onto her feet. She couldn't be trusted not to bolt, however, so he held her tightly around the waist to prevent her escape as he opened the door. The door creaked from disuse, for it had been many, many years since the cell had held a prisoner. He shouldered the stiff door open, pushing the woman inside before he closed the door behind him, watching her suspiciously through the small observation window in the door. The moment he released her, she dashed away from him and backed up against the far wall, covering her breasts with one arm and the apex of her thighs with her other hand.

Until that moment, Kirin had been so preoccupied with his dilemma, so stunned to have his position breached, by a human of all things, he had not really looked at her as an individual. The demure pose immediately brought his focus upon her body, however, and the swath of naked flesh and soft curves sent a flash of heat through him. He'd never seen a human before, though he had studied their cultures in his bored youth--which was how he'd managed to pinpoint her language from the few words she'd spoken.

With an effort to detach himself from his surprising, and unnerving, state of arousal, he allowed himself to study her thoroughly.

She was similar to their women, though not as tall or muscled. The crown of her head just barely topped his shoulders. She looked soft all over, without any of the muscle definition to her body that he was accustomed to seeing. The Elumi women were strong, as fierce warriors as the men. Obviously, human women were not warriors at all or this one would not look so soft and rounded.

And tempting.

The flaming hair drew his eyes to her woman's place like a magnet despite her efforts to cover it and his efforts to ignore it.

He didn't know why only looking at her was enough to make his blood heat in his veins and pound in his temples, but there was no denying it did--as much as he would've liked to dismiss it.

She had surprised him--not just her speed, and her flight through his gateway, but when he'd caught her. The moment he'd landed on her, he had felt a strange sensation wash over him, for she was so slight it was not at all like tackling an opponent in battle. Her frailty had disarmed him.

He hadn't expected that much fight from one so puny and he was still more than a little bemused by it.

Dismissing his distraction with an effort, he forced himself to focus on the woman as his prisoner and enemy. He could not afford to think of her as a beautiful, desirable woman or his life would be forfeit--and she was not *that* beautiful. "Tell me how you found the gateway--how you breached it," he demanded harshly, realizing the moment he spoke that she was still affecting him, that he had not infused the words with the threat he had intended.

Danielle glared at him, struggling with indignation of her treatment and her 'fight if flight wasn't a possibility' instinct. She was beginning to get really scared now that she'd been imprisoned, and completely unable to convince herself that she was imagining what was happening.

She would almost have preferred to think her mind was gone.

Imprisonment meant she wasn't getting home anytime soon. She didn't even want to think about what else it might mean.

"Look, buddy! I already told you! I don't know anything about a damned gateway. I was testing my...." She broke off abruptly as a thought popped into her mind. What if her competitors had stumbled onto her finding? What if they'd somehow drugged her with--a hallucinogen or something like that just to try to get her to tell them about the pods?

"Who is buddy?" he roared. "Did he give you the key?"

Danielle jumped and then looked at him blankly. "I meant you."

"I am Archangel Kirin, guardian of the gateway!" he growled. "Who is buddy?"

Danielle began to think she wasn't the only one having a mental breakdown. "He looked a lot like you," she said hesitantly.

"He is Elumi?" he demanded, stunned.

"What's Elumi?"

She could hear him grinding his teeth all the way across the room. Abruptly, he snatched the door open and stalked across the cell toward her. Danielle felt her eyes get a little wider with each step he took in her direction until they felt as if they might simply pop from the sockets. He caught her upper arms in a bruising grip, lifting her feet free of the floor. "Talk!"

She needed no further prodding. "They're t-transporter p-p-pods. I--I invented them--to send p-p-people from one p-p-place to another. I don't know how I got here," she ended on a wail. "I don't know what Elumi is. I don't know anything about a key or a gateway. I don't even know where I am!"

He looked disconcerted when she burst into tears. He set her on her feet so abruptly her knees almost buckled. "I am Elumi."

Danielle's chin wobbled. "I thought you said you were Kirin."

He ground his teeth. His hands clenched and unclenched as it he was resisting the urge to grab her and shake her. "Do I not speak good English?"

Danielle blinked the tears from her eyes. "Yes."

He bent over, pushing his face so closely to hers that they were almost nose to nose. "I am Kirin, Archangel, whose duty it is to guard the gateway to Pearthen. I am an Elumi. *You* are a human. You should not be in high Earth. How have you learned to breach the gateway and gain entry into Pearthen?"

"I don't know," Danielle wailed like the child confronted by the parent with some misdeed. "I invented a machine. It wasn't supposed to take me anywhere except from one pod to the other."

The Elumi looked startled. He paled. "An invention? A machine?"

Sniffing, Danielle nodded. "I was the first to perfect it. There are others working on it, but I-I guess it isn't exactly perfect, though," she ended frowning. "I shouldn't be here. I'll have to check the data.... Can I go now?"

"NO!"

Danielle took a step back. Mopping the tears from her cheeks, she looked him over uneasily. "But--you said I wasn't supposed to be here. You can't keep me here! I'm an American citizen! I have rights!"

"Not here, you don't," he growled.

Turning on his heel abruptly, Kirin stalked from the cell and slammed the door behind him.

Once he had left the woman, he merely stood staring into the distance, however, trying to get his mind around what she had told him.

She had designed a machine that would allow her to breach the gateway.

She had designed it to allow humans to travel from one point to another.

Their borders would be overrun with humans! There were millions of them. There was not an army in Pearthen great enough--even altogether, with every kingdom united and every man, woman, and child fighting--to keep the humans from pouring through their lands like a plague.

He had to tell the king!

Uneasiness filled him immediately.

What if she was lying?

Could she be? Was there any other explanation for what she'd done?

He didn't think so. She had not flown, for she had no wings. She had been propelled in some manner, and that suggested the existence of the machine she had claimed to have built.

He was never to leave his post--under penalty of death-- but it would be nigh a month before his relief arrived. He did not think he could wait so long as that. She had said there were others. Even if he kept her locked up, others might perfect their machines in that time and pour over their borders.

He would have to risk it, he decided. He felt certain the king would consider the potential for disaster and forgive him for leaving his post under the circumstances. Either way he was almost certainly looking at expulsion. He would be banished for failing to prevent her from passing through his post. He might be facing death for leaving his post, but he would certainly be facing death if he remained where he was and did not report the danger immediately.

* * * *

Kirin had not considered the possibility that he might be seized the moment he showed his face, but such was the case. He had no sooner lit upon the ramparts of King Sorecet's fortress than an alarm went up.

"Traitor!" the captain of the guard snarled. "Seize that archangel! He has abandoned his post!"

"I have news for King Sorecet!" Kirin ground out, struggling against the hold of the two warriors that seized him. "It will mean your head, not mine, if you prevent me from carrying the news to him."

"What news?" Captain Daelin demanded, signaling to the two guards to hold.

Kirin narrowed his eyes at the captain. It was not that he distrusted the man, but he was not certain he trusted the man with his life. If he relayed his news to Daelin, there was no guarantee the man wouldn't simply report the news himself, as his own discovery, in order to gain favor with King Sorecet. "Human's have perfected a device that will allow them to breach our gateway."

Captain Daelin stared at him blankly for several moments and finally began to laugh, though there was little humor in it. "The solitude has turned your mind! They do not even know of the existence of the gateway. If they did, they are not the same as Elumi. Their fragile forms could not make the transition."

Kirin's jaw set. "I captured a human female. She breached the gateway twice. The first time, she moved so fast I could not catch her. I only caught her when she came again because I was prepared to intercept her. This is *not* my imagination. I questioned the prisoner. I tell you, she has invented a device that allows her to pass through our gateway. She told me there were others working to perfect the same device. If something is not done quickly, we will be overrun by the humans. I must speak with the king!"

Captain Daelin frowned, but he looked more thoughtful now, even slightly uneasy. "If what you say is true--and I do not believe it--then it would be something the king should know. I will not allow you to carry unverified information to King Sorecet, however. He is planning the siege of Nardu castle and he will not be pleased to be interrupted with any news at all."

He considered for several moments more and finally nodded. "I will see this human for myself and question her. If it is as you say, then you may keep your head and I will carry the news to King Sorecet while you bide a while in the prison to reflect on the inadvisability of abandoning your post--for any reason."

* * * *

Danielle felt weak all over when she saw the fierce birdman fly off. Her rubbery legs gave out abruptly, and she sat hard on the cold stone floor. He'd been so furious about her breaching his gate, she'd been terrified for several moments that he would torture the information he wanted out of her.

She was more than a little surprised that he hadn't, now that she thought about it, for he had been angry and tremendously agitated about the situation--which meant it must be something his people considered a serious infraction.

In fact, except for catching her to begin with, he had seemed very reluctant to touch her at all--almost like the thought of doing so unnerved him.

Relief not withstanding, she realized fairly quickly that she did not want to be in the cell when he returned. He hadn't tortured her ... yet. That didn't mean he wouldn't, and who was to say he'd be satisfied with the information she gave him? For all she knew, they considered breaching the gate enough of an excuse for execution. Considering his behavior, that didn't seem at all farfetched, for he did not strike her as the sort of soldier that would be easily unsettled. His face had been youthful--far more handsome that she'd noticed that first time--but there was knowledge and experience drawn upon it as well. His had not been the face of an untried, inexperienced boy but a hardened, seasoned soldier.

Picking herself up off of the floor, she looked around the cell. There was one window, high upon the wall and barred. Beyond that, there was no other way in or out of the cell but the door, which looked like it was made of the same material as the prison itself, and the door only had a tiny window--also barred.

The window was out of the question--both windows, for that matter, the one because she wouldn't be able to get her thigh through it, much less the rest of her body, the other because she didn't have frigging wings.

She was also buck naked, unfortunately, which meant she had nothing she could use to pick the lock. She moved to the door anyway to study it.

She almost felt ill when she saw how simple the locking mechanism was. If she only had a pin! A paperclip! A credit card might have done the trick.

Grasping the handle, she gave it a disgruntled tug.

It flew open at her sharp tug and she sprawled in the floor, too stunned for several moments to do more than gape at the wide open space beyond. He hadn't locked it? Boy, he must think she was a real moron!

Or maybe he'd thought she was too terrified even to consider trying to escape?

Or maybe he'd been so stunned by what she'd told him that he hadn't realized he hadn't locked it?

What did she care? The only thing that mattered was that he hadn't locked it.

Jumping to her feet, she ran outside before it occurred to her that the unlocked door might be some sort of trick. Fortunately, he was nowhere in sight.

Unfortunately, the prison had been built on a fairly high outcropping of rock.

She didn't waste time analyzing her fear of falling. That crazy birdman was liable to come back any time, and she had no desire to see just how pissed off he would be when he discovered he'd forgotten to lock the cage and his captive had flown the coop.

Slipping over the edge, she scraped the hide off every conceivable tender spot on her body as she slipped, slid, climbed, and fell from point to point until she landed on the mossy soil at the bottom.

Catching her breath, she listened for the tell-tale whine of electricity she remembered. She'd been really stunned right after he'd caught her, but she recalled the general direction they'd come--he'd landed right on the porch thingy outside the cell, not flown around to the front from a different angle.

The stream couldn't be too high off the ground. When he'd slammed into her she'd hit the dirt pretty quickly afterwards with only a little friction burn and bruising, no broken bones. It hadn't taken moments. The trip from air to ground had been more like a fly being spattered by a fly swatter.

The hair on her skin began to prickle when she'd been walking for maybe fifteen minutes. Knowing it meant she had to be close to the path, she stopped, sniffing the air for the faint trace of electrically heated air. Pinpointing the general vicinity, she raced toward it, zigzagging back and forth as the whine seemed to move away and then closer, leaping into the air.

Abruptly, so suddenly she thought for a moment that Kirin had hit her again, something powerful slammed into her back and everything went dark.

* * * *

Kirin saw his life pass before his eyes.

He and his escort of three were still some distance from the guard post when he saw the door of the cell standing open. He didn't dare look around for the woman. To do so would instantly alert his guards to the fact that there would be no prisoner waiting to be interrogated.

He hadn't bound her and he hadn't locked the door.

A cold sweat broke from his pores. He'd been so stunned by the news--so certain the pathetic creature he'd captured was too terrified to present any sort of problem---he hadn't considered she would even attempt to escape. Truthfully, once he'd realized that she had had to use a machine to travel, it hadn't occurred to him that there was any way she *could* escape.

He was a dead man. There wouldn't be any trial. He wouldn't get the opportunity to try to explain his mistake, let alone correct it.

He didn't have to worry about banishment. They would take his head.

He wasn't really aware of coming to a decision *not* to simply accept his disgrace and just punishment. Tensing, he waited until everyone began to slow to drop to the platform. The moment they began their descent, he shot for the gateway with every ounce of speed he could muster and went through.

Behind him, he heard shouts of fury. He didn't slow, however, until he found a defensible position.

Whipping his sword from its scabbard, he dropped to the roof of the high building and tensed for battle.

Two made it through the gateway directly behind him. The third either did not know the key to the gateway, or he had returned to report that Kirin had escaped.

He would worry about that later. At the moment, he needed to concentrate on keeping his head. And when he was done, he would find that twice damned human female and he would make her rue the day she had crossed him!

Chapter Three

Danielle literally fell out of the pod. Unlike her first trip through, however, she didn't allow herself the luxury of resting. The moment she hit the floor, she began to crawl frantically toward the console.

He might be right behind her. She had to shut the transport down--change the coordinates. Her fingers trembled as they flew over the keyboard, striking the wrong keys over and over. She stopped after a moment, dragging in a couple of deep, cleansing breaths to calm her frayed nerves. When she'd managed to calm the shakes a little bit, she began again, more slowly this time.

It seemed to take forever, but finally she had the entire system shut down.

Dead silence invaded the room. Her ears began to ring with the quiet. She'd been tinkering with the transporter so long she'd grown accustomed to the low background whine of the equipment.

She found herself shivering, her teeth clacking together like castanets. Finally, she pushed herself from her work chair and headed toward her bathroom. When she'd turned the shower on as hot as she could stand it, she slumped against the wall of the shower for some time and finally wilted to the floor, her mind curiously blank as she lay in the tub with the water trying to drill holes through her skin.

After a time, the heat began to seep past the surface and into her bones and the shaking slowed and finally stopped. Her brain began to spark and fire and finally random thoughts wandered through.

Pearthen, high Earth, birdmen--it sure as hell wasn't her idea of heaven!

That was the scariest man--whatever--she'd ever seen in her life!

Sitting up finally, she looked down at her hands. The green stuff from the plants he'd smeared her over still colored her skin. The scrapes and bruises she'd collected from her climb down the rocky outcropping were real. They stung.

She hadn't imagined that place.

She hadn't imagined that huge, muscle bound winged barbarian that had threatened her, imprisoned her--sort of.

What had she *done*?

Was her machine totally whacked? Or was it just some sort of fluke that had--what? Carried her into another dimension? It couldn't have carried her to another planet.

Ok, so maybe that wasn't any more farfetched than another dimension, but he'd spoken of humans like he was familiar with them. He spoke English remarkably well. He'd also referred to that place as Pearthen, high Earth. Unless he was a kook, and she really didn't think he was, then it had to be another dimension--unless there was something like the theoretical worm hole that was connecting his world to this one and they didn't know they were on another planet?

It made her head hurt just trying to untangle the gnarly thing. She wasn't going to get anywhere until she started analyzing the data the computer had collected. She might still not be able to figure it out without going back and she sure as hell wasn't going back to that place if she could avoid it.

She was seriously pruny by the time she finally shut the water off and climbed out. She might have been tempted to stay longer anyway, except that she'd run out of hot water.

While she towel dried her hair and combed the knots out of it, she considered if she felt up to turning the system back on. Deciding she didn't at the moment, she wrapped her towel around her and headed for her bedroom to look for something to put on. She was halfway between the bathroom and her chest of drawers when the voice of god spoke.

"Woman!"

Recognizing that voice instantly, Danielle let out a squawk like a dying chicken, sprang a foot clear of the floor, and touched down again with her legs already churning. Unfortunately, she had no idea from which direction the voice had come and her resemblance to a chicken with its head cut off didn't end there. She ran around in frantic little circles, searching for something she could use as a weapon, letting out another squawk of fright each time her foot touched down.

When she finally discovered that her nemesis was between her and the only exit from the room--except the windows--she let out another squawk and leapt flat footed onto the bed, still looking wildly around for something to throw at him or beat him unconscious with. Grabbing the lamp beside the bed finally, she whirled and flung it at him with all her might.

It was still plugged in. When it reached the length of the wire, it simply hit the floor.

The crash finally penetrated some of Danielle's panic. She stared down at the broken lamp for a moment before her gaze bounced to the winged barbarian.

He was staring at her in stunned amazement, as if he couldn't figure out what the hell she thought she was doing.

This wasn't really very surprising considering Danielle had no idea what the hell she was doing.

She saw, though, when she looked at him that he looked-- different. Gashes covered his arms, his thighs and his chest, some mere scratches, other oozing--something blue. The moment she froze, he made a flying leap for her, flattening her on the mattress with the weight of his body.

Stunned both by the attack and her sudden impact with the bed, Daniel hardly breathed. She didn't even try to move at first. As the edge of her shock wore off, however, it finally sank in that she wasn't crushed or mangled from the tackle. At about the same time she realized she wasn't incapacitated, she also realized that he hadn't so much as moved since he'd landed on top of her. Craning her neck, she looked down at the face planted in the middle of her breasts. All she could see was hair. When he still didn't move she reached shakily for the hair and picked up a lock to peer at his face.

He didn't twitch, but she couldn't see him all that well so she used the hank of hair she had in her fist to lift his head a little higher for a better look.

He was unconscious.

She might have thought he was dead except she could feel the warmth of his breath stirring against her bare skin.

A shiver went through as his breath skated over her damp, bare skin like the light caress of fingers.

Thoroughly confused, she eased his head down on her chest again, not because she was really concerned about hurting him, but because she didn't want his head slamming into her breasts. Placing a palm against his shoulder, she struggled to ease his weight from her enough to wiggle out from under him. She was damp with perspiration by the time she'd managed to free herself, and huffing from the effort.

Rolling off the bed, she stared down at him for several moments, wondering what had made him lose consciousness.

Shaking that off after a moment, she focused on what to do with him.

Call the police?

As tempted as she was, it took no more than a glance around her place to realize she didn't want cops crawling all over it, poking around her things. She hadn't let anyone in since she'd begun work on her project. She sure as hell wasn't going to call some of the world's nosiest people in to have a look around.

She also wasn't just going to stand around and wait for the giant, really pissed off, winged barbarian to wake up.

Remembering she had a roll of duct tape in the living room that she'd used to tack pieces of the pods together while she assembled it, she dashed into the other room and grabbed it up. He hadn't moved when she got back, thankfully, and she set to work with a will, taping his ankles together and then crawling up on the bed and grabbing first one arm and then the other.

His arms felt like tree limbs. She would never have thought anybody's arms could weigh so much! She was panting with exertion by the time she managed to get his wrists together behind his back and wind tape around them. It didn't help that she had to hold his wings up with her shoulders while she worked on him.

Weak with relief and the expenditure of energy, she collapsed on the side of the bed to catch her breath when she'd finished, waiting until she'd steadied her pulse and breathing before she finally rolled off the bed and searched for something to put on.

She didn't have much of a wardrobe. Every dime she could rake together had gone into the project and keeping body and soul together. She'd never been particularly interested in clothing anyway. As long as it didn't bind her and didn't cost much and served its purpose, she was satisfied.

Dragging a sloppy loose T-shirt from the drawer that bore the slogan 'I see dumb people', she pulled it over her head. She'd just stepped into a pair of panties when she heard a sound from the vicinity of the bed. Her head whipped around so fast a bone in her neck popped. Cold fear washed over her. He'd only shifted slightly, however, and she hurriedly grabbed a pair of pull-on knit pants, shoved her feet through the legs and jerked them up around her waist.

Moving back to her bed, she crossed her arms over her chest and studied the birdman frowningly, wondering what to do with him, but becoming less frightened and more worried about the fact that he was unconscious.

The only thing worse than having a live birdman in her bed was having a dead one. Visions of trying to dispose of the body danced through her head.

Anthropology wasn't her thing, but her scientific curiosity began to gain the upper hand.

She wouldn't have admitted it under torture, but her female inquisitiveness began to gain the upper hand over her scientific interest.

If she just ignored the fact that he was scary as shit when he was behaving aggressively and looked at him from a purely detached perspective--he was exceptionally beautiful.

Truth be told, she had pretty much had her nose in books her entire life and they hadn't been about anatomy--and she certainly hadn't had a lot of first hand experience so she didn't have much to compare him with--but she had never seen a more beautifully formed male body. He was pleasingly proportioned despite his fairly extreme size, arms, legs and torso in harmony--instead of stork legs and an ant body like the guy she'd last dated, who'd probably been almost as tall but not nearly as well built and certainly not as pleasingly proportioned. He was well muscled-- everywhere that she could see--which was most of him, far more than 'typical' in a naturally well built male, but not extreme like a body builder.

A long leather looking case was strapped to his back between his shoulders/wings. Pushing his hair out of the way, she grasped the ornate handle protruding from one end and pulled. A long, wicked looking blade slid into view.

It was heavy. It took two hands to remove it.

She cut her hand when she touched the blade to support the tip. Jumping in surprise, she lost her grip and the thing clattered to the floor beside the bed.

Staring in dismay at the blood that instantly began to ooze into her palm, she looked at him again after a moment. Sharp blade, obvious cuts, blue stuff smeared all over him.

Frowning at that, she leaned over him and touched the blue stuff smeared along his arms. It was still damp to the touch and she tested it with her fingertips and then sniffed it.

Metallic. Her heart clenched in her chest, her gaze flickering over the scrapes on his arms.

He was bleeding! She'd been standing here like a love sick teenager admiring his beautiful body while he lay bleeding to death!

Whirling around abruptly, she raced to the bathroom for a cloth and medical supplies, spilling half the contents from her medicine cabinet onto the vanity, in the sink and on the floor.

Band-Aids! That was all the hell she had in the cabinet? Band-Aids?

Grabbing a clean cloth, she wet it with cool water, wrung it out and hurried back to the bed. Pushing one wing out of the way, she dabbed at the blood carefully, examining each cut she revealed. She was only slightly relieved when she had cleaned both arms and saw that none of them looked deep. The wounds were already sealing themselves.

He'd had worse on his torso and thighs, though, she remembered.

And he was laying face down.

How the hell was she going to get him over to look at the wounds when she could barely lift his arms?

It was going to take a frigging crane.

Getting onto her knees, she placed one hand on his bicep and one on his hip and began straining to lift him high enough to roll him over, grunting with the effort. She'd only managed to lift him a matter of inches and was wondering if she could do any better with her feet and legs when he roused slightly and pulled away. Relieved when he rolled onto his side, she grunted and pushed until he rolled onto his back.

"*Marchete!*" he growled.

"Shut up!" Danielle snapped, mopping the sweat from her forehead and grabbing up the wet cloth again. "You're hurt. I need to see how bad it is."

Her hand was shaking so badly it was all she could do to manage the washcloth. Within moments it was so saturated with his blood that she had to run to the bathroom and rinse it. When she returned, she saw that he was struggling against the bindings. "Will you be still?" she snapped. "These cuts look they're closing but you're going to burst them open again if you keep that up."

Surprise flickered in his eyes. He went still as she clambered onto the bed and began carefully wiping away the blood on his belly. Seeing that the cuts were still bleeding sluggishly, but very little, she shoved his sarong out of the way and examined his thighs.

Puzzlement began to supersede her anxiety. When she'd finished wiping the majority of the blood off, she saw that none of the cuts were very deep. Frowning, she studied the gashes. Almost before her eyes, she saw them closing more tightly, becoming little more than red lines along his skin.

Her gaze flickered to his face. She saw that he was studying her. Pain still glazed his eyes, but there was something else in those deep blue depths, as well.

"How did this happen?"

Whatever had been in his eyes vanished at her question. Anger supplanted it. "It happened because my prisoner escaped and I had to fight for my life," he growled.

Danielle's jaw dropped. Guilt flooded her--unreasonably. She hadn't trespassed on purpose and she had no reason to feel guilty about running for her life. "None of it would have happened if you hadn't caught me to begin with," she said tightly.

"None of it would have happened if you had not breached the gateway."

Danielle studied him a moment and finally shrugged. "Ok. You're right, but it was an accident. Believe me, I don't want to go there again. I just need to study the machine and make some adjustments--I'm pretty sure."

"It must be destroyed," he growled.

Danielle's jaw dropped. "Are you out of your fucking mind? That thing will make me rich! Even if weren't for the money, I've invested every dime I have to my name and years of my life in this research! I told you it was an accident. Believe me, nothing could be further from my mind that going back. I can't imagine *any*body in their right mind wanting to go there."

"Then *I* will destroy it! I can not return to Pearthen until I have seen to it, until I can carry proof to my king that I was guarding the gateway as was my duty! Until then, there is a price on my head and I will not yield up my life for you, woman!"

Chapter Four

Danielle scooted off of the bed, plunking her hands on her hips. "I don't think so. You're assuming I'll let you, and I won't. It's mine! Your problem with your king is *your* problem!"

Growling furiously, he struggled for several moments and finally frowned in puzzlement. "What have you done to me? I can not feel my hands or my feet."

"I tied you up with duct tape."

His brows drew more tightly together. "You bound me?" he asked, his voice strangely neutral.

"You chased me."

"I did not. You ran."

Blood flooded Danielle's cheeks at the reminder. "What did you expect me to do when you'd terrorized me?"

He didn't seem to have an answer for that. "You fear me? Why did you bathe my wounds?"

Danielle looked away uncomfortably. "I thought you were hurt really bad. I had to see about the cuts, didn't I? I couldn't just let you bleed to death."

"But you bound me?"

"Because I didn't want *me* hurt, either!" She showed him her hand. "Look what that sword of yours did and I barely touched the thing!"

He stared at her palm for a long moment before his gaze returned to her face. "You have disarmed me," he said flatly. "If they come for me here, they will slay us both."

Danielle's eyes widened. A coldness washed over her. "They?" she said a little weakly.

"It is my duty to guard the gateway and see that none pass through who are not allowed. You breached the gateway, and because of you I left my post to report the machine. The penalty is death."

Danielle felt a little sick to her stomach. "But--you escaped and came here. They won't follow you. They can't, can they?" she asked doubtfully.

"Two already did. I slew them, but a third did not pass through. He will have reported my escape."

Despite her uneasiness about his claim, she frowned. "I don't understand this gateway thing. How did you follow me, anyway? I turned the machine off."

He thought it over and finally frowned. "I can not explain this in your tongue. There are no words."

Danielle pursed her lips skeptically, but she knew damned well it couldn't have been sheer blind luck. If he hadn't tracked her because of the machine, they would have to be able to track scents like a bloodhound, or heat signature, or maybe chemical signature.

That meant he was probably telling the truth about the others.

What the hell was she going to do? She couldn't just let the guy go. He'd probably throttle her and then destroy her work--not that the work was going to matter if she was too dead to enjoy it.

But if she didn't let him go, then the others like him were liable to show up and then they'd both be dead and she'd have the same problem.

She studied him uneasily. "If you'd give me your word you would go away, I might consider letting you go," she said hesitantly, knowing even as she said it that she'd have to be a complete moron to trust him.

"No."

Danielle's jaw dropped. She hadn't expected him to flatly refuse. After a moment, though, it occurred to her that he'd at least been honest about it--when she would've expected him to lie. Maybe she *could* trust him if she could get him to give his word?

He began struggling to free himself almost the moment the word was out of his mouth, distracting her. "If you keep that up, I'm going to bind you tighter."

"I can not feel my hands and feet," he said through gritted teeth.

In her enthusiasm, she'd bound him too tightly and cut off the circulation. She didn't have to be very familiar with biology to figure out what that meant. She was going to have to figure out some other way to tie him or he was going to lose the hands and feet from lack of circulation. "Well, I'm not going to let you go when you won't even give me your word about leaving," she said testily. "I'll see if I can figure out a better way to bind you, though."

Digging through the drawer in the bedside table, she found a pair of scissors and climbed onto the bed. "You're going to have to roll...."

She didn't manage to get the words out. Almost the moment she climbed onto the bed, he grabbed her, rolling on top of her. Danielle shrieked, ear splittingly.

Despite the siren racket, though, she heard him grunt, as if she'd kneed him in the stomach.

Gripping her shoulders, he lifted slightly away from her and Danielle followed his gaze as he looked down.

The scissors were buried in his stomach. Her own stomach clenched. "Oh god! Look what you made me do!" she gasped faintly, feeling blackness closing in on her at the sight.

Danielle surfaced from the blackness with the same sense of heaviness of climbing from a pool after being buoyed by the water for hours. She strained to lift her head, her arms. She couldn't move. Relapsing, she searched her mind instead, feeling nausea well inside of her again when she recalled what had happened.

Her eyes flew open at the memory and she looked around quickly for Kirin, more than half expecting to discover she couldn't move because she had a dead body on top of her.

He was lying beside her on the bed, studying her curiously, his hand supporting his head. She glanced down at his stomach. The scissors were gone. Blood had oozed from the wound but the wound itself was closed. Swallowing a little sickly, Danielle met his gaze again. "Puncture wounds can be really dangerous--and the scissors must have gone in two or three inches. You need to have that looked at by a doctor."

"I have had worse. It will heal."

"I'm serious! You need to have...." She broke off as she struggled to sit up and discovered she couldn't move. Glancing upwards, she saw why. Her wrists were bound with the tape to the bed. Lifting her head, she looked down and discovered her ankles were bound, as well.

She was also naked.

Her head jerked in Kirin's direction. "My clothes!"

He almost seemed to shrug. "I like you better without them."

Danielle blinked at him while that slowly sank into her mind.

Almost casually, he lifted his free hand and moved it over her belly. "Your skin is smooth, soft. Like your flesh."

Danielle's belly clenched so hard at his touch, the muscle cramped painfully. She winced, but he was watching his hand as he stroked it along her midriff and belly. "Exactly what do you think you're doing?" she asked with a touch of alarm. The 'demand' came out as a breathless sort of whisper, however.

"You touched me."

Danielle gaped at him. "I was trying to help you, you asshole!"

There was desire in his eyes when his gaze met hers. Anger subverted it. "Where is the machine? I must protect the gateway. It is my duty."

Danielle's eyes widened. She licked her lips, her mind scurrying around for any possibility of escape. This time, there didn't seem to be one. He'd underestimated her before. Obviously, he wasn't going to take any chances on her slipping through his fingers again.

But, what would he do if she didn't tell him? She was no masochist, but she'd endured a hell of a lot for that damned machine. As unnerved as she was, she couldn't bring herself to just tell him and let him destroy it.

Of course, it was in the living room in plain sight. All he had to do was look around the house and he was liable to decide to do just that at any moment.

He seemed interested in her, which probably would have flattered the hell out of her at any other time. All she could think about at the moment, though, was if there was any chance she could use his interest to her advantage.

It was unfortunate that she really had very little experience with men. She certainly had none in trying to seduce one, but she had a feeling she'd just passed up an opportunity. All she'd really had to do was to keep her mouth shut and let him 'explore.'

Thwarted of that possibility, she began struggling against the tape he'd used to bind her--the same tape she'd used on him. He'd broken it fairly easily, though, and she figured if she worked on it she should be able to also.

Wrong. The damned tape stretched but it only got tighter. When she glanced at Kirin again, though, she saw that his gaze was riveted to the contortions of her body as she bucked and tugged against the bindings.

He rolled away from her abruptly, presenting her with his back as he sat up on the edge of the bed.

"I don't see how it's going to do you any good to wreck my work," Danielle said crossly. "You already said they were going to execute you for leaving the gateway if you went back. Do you honestly think they'll wait and let you talk, when they already tried to hack you to pieces? And what kind of proof are you going to give them anyway? If you break the damned transporter, it's just going to be a pile of junk."

He stood up abruptly and stalked from the room.

Danielle could've bitten her tongue off. Now he was going to find the machine!

She tried to comfort herself with the thought that she could build another one, but it wasn't much consolation considering she was broke and would have to beg, borrow, or steal to come up with the money to buy components she needed to rebuild--assuming he didn't break her computer, in which case it could take her months to get everything figured out again. It wasn't like it was *all* inside her head.

* * * *

Kirin raked his hair back from his face with a hand that shook noticeably, struggling to shake off his arousal so that he could think. He could not think when he was anywhere near the woman.

It had been a mistake to give in to the impulse to study her body when she had fainted. He had not even tried to rationalize his actions. He had simply dragged the clothing from her body so that he could see her as he had not been able to when she had covered herself before.

Her skin was paler than his own, making the color of her hair contrast sharply. His curiosity had gotten the better of him and he had tested her hair with his fingers. The hair on her head was darker that the pelt on her mound, silky, and fine and straight. The brighter hair at the apex of her thighs was curly, nearly as silky--and far more fascinating.

It had taken an effort to drag his mind from it and bind her hands and feet, but he found the moment he had that she was far more of a distraction than before, for then he had glimpsed the delicate lips of her woman's place and he could not get that image out of his mind.

He frowned. She was a strange contradiction. She did not just seem soft and weak. She was. And easily frightened. And yet she fought him as if she thought she had some chance of besting him. Instinct, he supposed, but lacking any sort of logic for it was obvious she had no training whatsoever beyond the limitations of her physical body.

He could not give her credit for outwitting him before. That had taken little effort, he thought wryly, for between his disordered state of mind that she had breached the gate when she should not have been able to; his shock that she had escaped him the first time and very nearly done so the second trip through; his arousal toward her; and his horror at what she'd told him, he had certainly not had his wits about him. He could not think when, if ever, he had been so thoroughly rattled that he had lost the ability to think at all rationally.

What completely baffled him, though, was that, despite everything, his life had been important to her. She obviously did not know that he could heal far faster than she did. She had been concerned for him when he had passed out from the loss of blood and she had tried to help him.

He had treated her as his enemy, with very little regard for the fact that she was so fragile. Why had she not treated him as an enemy?

Clearly, he did not understand humans as well as he'd thought. He had believed they were very simple creatures, weak, not very intelligent--and repugnant because of their nearness to the lower animals of Earth.

She was not repulsive to him, far from it. He was fighting for his life and his freedom and he still could not discipline his mind to ignore the demands of his body each time he allowed himself to gaze at her.

He would have to put that from his mind. It was forbidden. He could not more surely condemn himself forever than to act upon his desires.

And yet he could not dismiss what she had said, either. Deep down, he knew that she was right. He had not been condemned to banishment. He would have been condemned to death if he had not fled--and if he returned, whatever he did, it seemed very unlikely that he would evade that fate.

His honor was at stake, though, not just his life. He had spent his entire adulthood as a warrior. His honor was everything. If he failed to protect the gateway--and his people, he would be dishonoring himself--not just his vow to his king.

In his heart, he felt that he knew what he must do, and yet was it reasonable to blindly follow all that he had believed in before when his whole world had tumbled around him?

He frowned. In one fell swoop, he had lost all--home, king, and country.

If would have been shameful enough if he had fallen from grace and been banished, but he had fallen so far from redemption, there seemed no way out.

He had been among the most honored of warriors. He had been promoted to archangel, a position much coveted since it was reserved only for the best of the best--the guardianship of the realm itself from intruders.

In truth, he had not appreciated it as another might have. The duty was tedious and mind numbingly boring. He would have far preferred to stay with his unit, to fight beside his comrades in the war for power that was being waged.

That hardly mattered now.

The woman was right, he realized. He could not return.

The hard truth was that no matter what decision he had made, his life would most likely have been forfeit. If he had not abandoned his post, if he had stayed and kept the woman captive while he awaited his relief, he would very likely have been condemned for dereliction of duty for not informing his superiors immediately.

The only path he could have taken that would not have meant his life was to have slain the woman immediately, and he had not even considered doing that. If she had been a warrior as he was, an enemy of his people, he would not have hesitated.

But the fragile, human woman had looked at him with great wounded eyes and he had turned soft--in the head!

He shook his head as if he could deny it, but he could not.

After a moment, he lifted his head and looked around the structure where she lived. Like the humans themselves, the abode was soft and weak, designed for comfort not for security.

A sense of both unreality and loss filled him. Could he grow accustomed to living among humans? Should he even attempt such a thing? His own world and people were lost to him, and yet it was forbidden for Elumi to live among humans, to interact with them and, regardless of his changed fortunes, he was not comfortable with the idea of simply discarding the laws of his own people.

Finally, he decided that this was not a decision that he could make until he had had time to accept what had happened. For now, he would focus on his duty to his people, the responsibility of protecting the borders of Pearthen.

The woman had said that she did not wish to go back, that she would change the machine so that it was not possible. He believed her. Perhaps it would be better to be her ally than her enemy?

Chapter Five

When Kirin returned to the bed chamber, he saw that the woman was still struggling with her bonds. For many moments, he stood at the foot of the bed, staring at the curling nest of bright hair that covered her woman's place, and at the soft pink petals between her thighs. Tension coiled inside of him again in a wave of heat.

His cock came to attention, pulling the blood from his head so quickly dizziness followed, disorientation.

How long since he had known a woman at all? He wondered, but he knew that was not the source of his dilemma. He assuaged the needs of his body when he was relieved of his post, and it had been little more than a week since he had returned to duty.

It was *this* woman--with her soft body and big blue eyes, with the fiery hair that was like none he had ever seen before. It was this woman's scent that drugged his mind and deprived him of wit or will.

Swallowing with an effort, he lifted his gaze to hers, trying to recall what it was that he had meant to say to her.

It eluded him.

"By what name are you called?" he asked finally.

She looked at him curiously. "Danielle. Dr. Danielle Logan."

Reaching down, he ripped the tape that bound her ankles to either side of the bed. He climbed over her then. Placing his legs on either side of her hips, he sat back, studying her, his buttocks resting lightly against her belly.

Her breath had caught in her chest. He saw a touch of fear in her eyes, but he saw more than that. He saw a reflection of his own desire.

It sent his own desire barreling out of control. For many moments he could think of nothing but sprawling atop her, feeling her soft body pressed tightly against his, sampling her lips, burying himself deeply inside of her and feeling her moist heat cupping his sex.

Leaning forward, he grasped the tape that bound her wrists one by one and freed her. When he looked down at her face, he saw confusion.

"You will fix this machine of yours, Danielle, so that none may use it to penetrate the gateway to my world."

She blinked several times and finally nodded, though he could see distrust in her eyes.

He lingered over her, not because he doubted his ability to subdue her if she tried to flee again, but because he still struggled with the need to taste the desire he had seen in her eyes.

He had seen fear there as well, however, and it was that
that at last tamped his clamoring needs, more even than the
fact that his laws forbade it.

When he sat back on his heels at last, she pushed herself
up on her elbows. "You're not just saying that?"

"On my honor, I will allow it--if you will give me your
word that you will do as you promise."

Her face brightened, broke into a smile of pure delight
that made Kirin's stomach tighten. "Oh you darling man--
uh Elumi! Yes, yes! I must fix that!"

When he moved away, she tumbled from the bed and
hurried from the room.

Bemused by the abrupt transformation, Kirin followed
her.

When he reached the large room, he saw her flitting about
from one thing to another like a brightly colored *flitterby*
seeking nectar.

She had not dressed, and he found himself distracted by
the bounce and sway of her breasts as she moved--and the
tight little pink tips of her breasts--and the curling thatch of
hair on her mound and her rounded buttocks. Propping one
shoulder against the wall, he immersed himself in studying
her to his heart's content.

* * * *

The moment the computer booted, Danielle flopped into
the chair in front of it and vacated it almost as quickly
when her warm ass came into contact with the cold plastic
seat. "Oh!"

Glancing around a little distractedly, she spied the T-shirt
she'd discarded earlier and grabbed it up, sniffed it to make
certain it wasn't rank and pulled it over her head. A pair of
pull on knit pants lay close by, but there was no sign of her
panties. Shrugging, she pulled the pants on and went back
to her computer, studying the data that scrolled across the
screen. Finally, she told the machine to print. Grabbing her
reading glasses, she shoved them on and snatched up the
paper as the printer spit it out.

"Do you have food?"

Startled by the male voice, Danielle glanced toward it in
surprise, wondering why he was still here. Didn't he have
someplace to go? Something to do? "What?"

"Food?"

She frowned, thinking. "Maybe. It would be that way." She pointed in the direction of the kitchen, then grabbed up the last of the printout, looking around hopefully for a more comfortable place to sit and study it.

There wasn't one. She'd moved all of her furniture out of the living room when she'd turned it into a lab. Grabbing a pen, she headed for the bedroom, peeled off the blue stained comforter, and crawled onto the bed to go over the data.

"There is only this."

When Danielle looked up distractedly, she saw that Kirin was holding a half of a pizza that was so dried out it was barely distinguishable from the cardboard box that contained it. "Oh," she said absently. "I guess not."

Kirin frowned at her. "Are you not hungry?"

Danielle thought it over and realized the pain in her stomach probably *was* hunger. "I don't have any money," she said apologetically.

"What is money?"

She stared at him blankly a moment, blinking, and then it dawned on her that he would have no reason to know what money was. "We use it to get goods and services."

He nodded, seemed to think it over for several moments and finally shrugged. "I will get food."

Surprised, Danielle merely stared at him, wondering how he was planning on getting food when he couldn't possibly have money. For that matter, she doubted he would even have any idea of where to get food. Before she could question him about it, however, he walked straight to the wall ... and went through it.

Danielle felt her jaw drop. Scrambling out of the bed, she dashed to the spot where he'd disappeared and touched the wall. Her palm tingled. Warmth suffused her skin.

He'd transmitted himself through the wall! He could *naturally* do what her machine did!

After several moments, she returned to the bed and sat down again, thinking that over. Wave length and speed! That was the key he'd been talking about before! It had to be the crux of her problem, as well. It wasn't just taking the machine longer to disassemble and reassemble when she transported larger, more complex objects. The complexity of doing so was altering the speed and wave length of the transmission.

She needed to figure out how to prevent that.

She was going over the schematics when Kirin returned as abruptly as he had departed. The smell of hot food wafted past her nostrils, immediately distracting Danielle.

"Food?" she said hopefully. "Oh! I am *so* starving! I can't remember the last time I had anything to eat."

Kirin's brows rose. "This is why you are like this." He held up his small finger.

Danielle gave him a drop dead look. "You didn't seem to mind the way I looked a while ago."

His eyes narrowed, but his lips curled faintly. "I do not mind, but I do not want to be stabbed by bones when I take you."

Danielle's jaw dropped. "When you ... what?"

After glancing around and discovering there was no table, he moved to the bed and settled on the mattress cross legged. Setting the bags he carried down, he began pulling boxes of food out. "When I take you for my woman," he said almost absently. "I have given it much thought and I have decided that there is no reason why I should deny myself of what I want. I will settle here and begin a new life."

Danielle decided she must not have heard him right. Or maybe he had meant something else? He seemed to have a very good grasp of English, but, because of the difference in their cultures, there were probably some things that just didn't translate well, or even at all.

Like when he'd tried to explain how he'd found her.

Danielle forced a half hearted chuckle. "I think that lost something in translation."

He studied her thoughtfully for several moments. "You wish to be wooed," he said finally. "I had not considered that."

Turning apple red, Danielle concentrated on examining the contents of the boxes. Why was it, she wondered, that she always seemed to end up with such analytical guys? Ordinarily, she didn't object to it. She was a scientist after all, but she couldn't think of anything that was more of a turn off than having I guy ask if he could kiss you--or whatever.

If he wasn't smart enough to catch the damned signals, or ballsy enough to handle a few rejections for taking the kisses, he needed to stay out of the frigging game.

He settled the box he'd chosen on the bed, stretched out on his side and propped on one arm. "I am a warrior, not a poet," he said.

Danielle slid a glance at him from under her lashes. "This is news," she retorted dryly.

He frowned as if considering her comment. "Business first," he said finally, nodding. "Protecting Pearthen must remain my first priority, even above my own desires."

Danielle reddened again. And desert later?

"You're not my type, actually," she said nastily.

"What is type?" he asked curiously.

She stared at him. Irritation surfaced that the insult seemed to have gone right over his head. She thought about being blunter, but she couldn't bring herself to be *that* rude. What could she say anyway? You're too pretty to suit me? I prefer spineless worms? All that testosterone makes me nervous?

His eyes narrowed speculatively. "You desire me," he said. "I have seen it in the way that you look at me."

"So--we're talking fucking here? Well, that's a relief. I thought you were talking about something else." She shrugged. "Why not? I haven't been laid in a while."

Anger glittered in his eyes. Before she could blink, he had settled one hand in the crook of her neck and shoved her flat, shifting over her so that his chest pinned her beneath him. Fried rice rained down over them as Danielle threw her hands up reflexively in an attempt to catch her balance. She let out a startled squeak just as his mouth covered hers.

Caught completely off guard, she had no defense. He blindsided her. The heat and hunger of his mouth flooded her instantly with a tidal wave of sensation. Her cleft moistened with arousal. Her belly clenched with a spasm of lust, and her breasts swelled, making her nipples engorge to near painful points against his hard chest.

She moaned into his mouth, almost animalistic, hungry, and needy.

The instinctive, defensive tensing of the muscles in her body vanished, melted away by the fierceness of his possession as he thrust his tongue into her mouth and explored the sensitive flesh, touching off waves of keen sensation that stole her breath. Blood pounded almost painfully in her body, depriving her mind of much needed oxygen and making it reel dizzily.

Her womb contracted, eager for fulfillment. Every muscle in her body seemed awakened by his kiss, honed to react to the slightest touch, the smallest movement.

She lay perfectly limp when he broke the kiss at last and lifted away to look down at her. Sensing his gaze, she struggled to lift the lead weight of her eyelids and gazed back at him, panting for breath.

His own breathing was ragged, his eyes glazed, almost fevered. "I frightened you," he said harshly, "and now I do not have your trust. I understand this, but you must understand that it was not something I wanted to do, or a lack of control, but my duty to my king. I am disciplined to control my anger. On my honor, I will never harm you. Or allow you to be harmed."

Danielle swallowed with an effort, struggled to assimilate what he was saying when all she really wanted at the moment was a little more out-of-control behavior.

It occurred to her, finally, when he moved away and helped her to struggle upright that he hadn't *been* out of control. He had kissed her to show her he knew damned well she was lying when she said she had no interest in him.

Damn his hide!

Still more than a little disoriented, Danielle looked around vaguely, trying to remember what she'd been doing before he'd kissed her. Food was liberally covering the bed around her, as if she'd thrown the box straight up in the air. Embarrassed, she felt color flood her cheeks as she concentrated on picking the food up and dumping it back into its container.

He handed her another box.

Danielle stared at it for several moments before she felt an insane urge to giggle. She bit her lip, wondering if it was hysteria, embarrassment, or true amusement.

The bed was a mess, however, and it occurred to her that Kirin hadn't missed the mark when he'd said he was just a soldier--plain, to the point, incredibly fast and aggressive but without much finesse. She chuckled.

He was studying the mess wryly when she peeked at him. His own mouth quirked upward on one side when she laughed. "Next time I will remember to take the box from you first." He shook his head. "You make me behave like an overeager, witless youth, Danielle."

She actually found that comment, and the sentiment, rather endearing.

Clearing her throat, she changed the subject. "I think I've figured out what happened with the transporter pods."

His brows rose questioningly.

She shrugged. "I won't bore you with a lot of jargon, but it's the wave length and speed--I think. It'll take me a few days to figure out how to adjust it and how much. Actually, I wouldn't have to adjust it at all if not for the little accident I had passing through your territory. I could patent it as is, since it's a working model. All I really needed to do was to prove that it worked, and I did that. Now I'm going to have to do some more experiments to see what will work and won't make the detour," she added slowly, realizing that that could actually take far longer than she'd originally considered. She would have to start the testing with larger objects of a similar size and weight to an adult human.... It might have to be adjusted any time there was a significant difference in the size, she realized suddenly--or would it? She would have to experiment with that, too.

"I can help you with this."

Chapter Six

Dragged abruptly back from her project plans, Danielle stared at Kirin blankly for several moments before a mixture of doubt and dismay filled her. "Exactly how do you think you can help me? You don't know anything about any of the equipment."

He studied her a long moment. "I will know when it is correct by the sound."

"You can't hear...." Danielle broke off, realizing she had no idea what he could hear.

He'd been waiting for her when she went through the second time, though, which might mean he actually *could* hear the transmission. But could he pick the signal out from others that were close?

He'd walked through her wall, which meant he possessed the natural ability to accelerate his atoms and transmit. He also knew the key to the gateway--the frequency she had her machine set to.

It occurred to her to wonder if it actually mattered or not. He would be satisfied, she felt sure, with an adjustment of the machine that he knew would not send humans through his gateway into Pearthen.

Which meant he would leave, right?

She was surprised to discover she had mixed feelings about that. She shouldn't have felt anything except relief at the thought.

Maybe it was Stockholm syndrome?

Get real! She hadn't been a prisoner much more than twenty minutes. That wasn't long enough to start empathizing with her captor.

But then it wasn't him, personally, that had scared the living hell out of her so much as it was terror at finding herself in an alien world when she had never expected to and had no idea what was going on.

It was being accused of a high crime and being imprisoned that had thoroughly rattled her.

He found her attractive--had from the first. She hadn't missed that despite everything that had happened. And it was hard to be indifferent about someone who found you appealing, especially when you were already fascinated with them on a physical level, because then chemical attraction also kicked in. He unnerved the hell out of her when he was in soldier mode, but physically, she thought he was hunk.

And, my god, he could kiss!

The suggestion that he wanted to have sex with her had had a certain amount of appeal. It had even more appeal now, when her body was still on slow sizzle from that kiss, more appeal that it should have all things considered.

She must have latent masochistic tendencies!

He was huge, scary, alien, and barbaric--way too manly for a wimp/nerd like her, and he was right, she didn't trust him. She knew what he'd said was true. If she'd crashed the gate of a government facility she might have been dead before they got around to questioning her. She would certainly have been scared just as badly, and ended up imprisoned and they would probably have beat the ever loving shit out of her before they'd thrown her in jail.

She wasn't at all certain she wanted to get to know him better. In fact, she was pretty sure she didn't.

She had to admit, though, that, purely on a scientific level, she was curious about him.

It was the testosterone thing, she decided, that primal instinct women still had that drew them to the strongest male, even when the logical side of her brain was screaming 'Run!', which hers was.

"Alrighty then. I guess we're all set. I'll concentrate on the data and work on adjusting the equipment and you can tell me when I hit a frequency that will safely transport."

He nodded. "We can not stay here long, however."

"Why not?" Danielle demanded, shifting gears with an effort.

"I was wounded in battle--near here. It will be far easier for them to track me to this place than it might have been otherwise."

Danielle's eyes widened. "Track you here? Oh! You can't stay here. I only have one bed."

"We will share."

She gave him a look. "Not if it means I'm liable to wake up with Elumi all around my bed, we can't."

He frowned. "You are right. It will be far better if we move everything elsewhere."

"What is it with this *we* shit? You go. It's you they're after."

His eyes narrowed. "I stay with the machine until it is changed."

"We can't move! My god. I've spent years accumulating all of this stuff! It would take a full sized moving van and weeks to pack and transport everything. Plus there's the little problem of where to move it to. This place is mine. I don't have money to get another place."

"Then *we* will stay here."

As an incentive, Danielle found that what Kirin had told her worked much better than being broke, better even than the prize--glory and wealth. It was amazing how nothing else seemed to matter when death was looming.

She didn't bother to ask him what would happen to her if the Elumi did come after him and found him with her. She had a feeling that was something she didn't really want to know.

But he'd said that it was forbidden for Elumi to consort with humans, and she thought that was probably because they didn't want humans knowing about them--which seemed to indicate to her that she would be 'erased.'

Unfortunately, although the fear of having a posse of Elumi catching up with them encouraged her to work until she was exhausted, a week passed and she only found several new ways to cook.

She didn't know whether it was more comforting to have Kirin around, knowing he was capable of defending her in case of need--or more unnerving because his being there increased the possibility that they would show up.

She couldn't help but feel guilty about such thoughts. It was her fault, after all, that he was in this mess. He had never accused her of ruining his life, but she knew she had, even though she hadn't done it intentionally.

She supposed that that explained, at least in part, why he had come directly to find her and why he stayed. Earth was an alien world to him. She was the only one that he had had any sort of contact with before--and a little familiarity under such circumstances was better than nothing at all, even though the incident that had thrown them together to start with had hardly been agreeable.

She suspected, if their roles had been reversed, she wouldn't have been nearly as forgiving about the whole thing as he appeared to be. She couldn't begin to imagine how completely unsettling it would be to suddenly find herself in a strange land, among strange people, who didn't even speak the same language she was used to and to know that it was forever--that she could never go home again. What she did grasp of it, however, made her feel really low.

When he began to disappear for longer and longer periods of time, she decided it had been inevitable from the start, regardless of what he'd said about deciding he wanted her for his woman. He was learning the new world he had to live in now. Once he understood it better, and he had carried out his final duty to his own people, he would probably find a dozen women far more appealing to him than her.

He was probably bored watching her putter around her lab.

And either he was as good at self-control as he claimed, or he had lied about being interested in her because he hadn't even tried to kiss her again, let alone anything else.

She was almost sorry he'd kissed her. As wonderful as it had felt, her body never really had settled since. Every time she felt him settle next to her on the bed, no matter how exhausted she was, she would tense, hoping that he would initiate something. Instead, he would merely curl around her almost protectively and drop into sleep, leaving her feeling anxious and weepy.

She suspected that was why she couldn't get the damned pods fixed. Try though she might, she could not recapture the same level of concentration that she had known before. No matter how deeply 'in' to studying the data she thought she was, she would hear his footsteps nearby and be instantly distracted. Or she would hear the sound of the shower, and she would think about what he looked like and wonder what he would do if she joined him.

Not that she had the nerve. She was a total wimp and not nearly as self-confident about her femininity as she was her brain and her abilities.

After a week of worrying that Kirin might try to 'prove' his appeal again, Danielle was so edgy that she began to think she'd be better off if he would just 'do' it so she could get it out of her system. She would never have thought that being promised she would "get her brains fucked out if only she did a thing" would be enough to make it impossible for her to get sex off of her mind.

It didn't help, at all, when she finally discovered that Kirin, after being mostly gone for over a week, had returned to watch every move she made broodingly, like a cat watching its prey and waiting for the perfect moment to pounce.

By the end of the second week, Danielle had decided enough was enough. It was bad enough to have a death threat hanging over her--which, thankfully, hadn't materialized--but to have the sexual tension added to it was driving her nuts.

The problem was, she didn't have a lot of experience, and she couldn't figure out how she could get it across to Kirin that she didn't want to wait.

He gave her the opportunity she'd been waiting for the day he returned wearing clothing like any human male--and minus his wings. Sitting in bed, Danielle had already finished eating before it dawned on her that something about Kirin was *really* different. She studied him frowningly when he got up and disposed of the food containers.

"Hey!" she said finally, surprise threading her voice. "You're wearing regular clothes! I mean human clothing."

He crossed his arms over his chest, leaning back against the door frame. "I have been for nigh two weeks."

Danielle reddened. "Really?" she said doubtfully, struggling to think back.

"Really." He dropped his arms and stood away from the wall. With calm deliberation, he pulled the clothes off and dropped them to the floor and then crossed the room, crawling back onto the bed.

Stunned, Danielle blinked at him in surprise when he started crawling purposefully toward her. After a moment, she cocked her head inquisitively. "You don't have wings. What did you do?" she asked, too aghast to appreciate his delicious nakedness.

Catching hold of her upper arms, he sat back and dragged her closer, peeling her shirt off over her head and tossing it to the floor. Goose bumps shimmied down her arms and back.

"I morphed. I do not need them if I am to walk among humans--and it is difficult to wear human clothing, which are not designed for winged beings."

"You can morph, too?" Danielle asked, pleased at the discovery and feeling warmed by his touch, his nearness.

He shook his head slowly. "You are not very observant, my love. I would be offended if it were not for the way that you look at me when you *do* notice that I am here. You are no longer afraid of me?"

Danielle blinked. Truthfully, she couldn't even remember when she had been afraid. She licked her lips, realizing that they were bone dry. "No, I'm not."

"Good," he murmured. Pushing her to the bed, he dragged her knit pants off and tossed them aside and then sprawled across her. "Because I have reached the limits of my endurance."

Chapter Seven

His bare chest against hers felt so deliciously wicked it took Danielle's breath away. She did not have the chance to catch it. He covered her mouth in a kiss of such searing heat and need that she felt as if she'd caught fire.

Her body rocketed into overdrive. Nerves sparked to life like a lit fuse. Her lower belly clenched and moisture suffused her cleft.

Memory had not served her well. His mouth felt far better than she remembered.

His lips were soft but firm. His taste was exquisitely male, provocative and intoxicating. He held her still, pressing her into the bed with his powerful body, imprinting the exotic, alien hardness of his muscles against her flesh.

"Mmm," she murmured when he broke the kiss at last and burrowed against her neck, nibbling at the tender flesh there and sending delightful shivers through her. "It's about time."

He pulled away to look down at her quizzically.

"I completed the project two hours ago," she murmured teasingly. "I think. And I have been waiting patiently for my reward ever since."

"Have you?" he asked, dipping his head to pluck at her engorged nipples with his lips.

Her breasts prickled pleasurably under the rasping scrape of his teeth. She bit her bottom lip, stifling a moan.

"Not ... very patiently," Danielle gasped, breathless.

Releasing her, he chuckled. "Finished, I meant?"

"Mmmhmm."

"I should check it."

"Now?"

He sucked the other nipple into his mouth, rolling it on his tongue. "Later?" he murmured when he released it.

Danielle speared her fingers through his hair and dragged him down for another kiss. "Tomorrow, maybe."

His mouth moved over hers with ravening need, infusing her with a craving that rapidly outstripped the desire she sensed in him. She kissed him back, stroking her tongue along his, dueling, following when he withdrew to explore his mouth as he had learned hers. He shuddered, sucking her tongue greedily. His callused, warrior's hands moved over her, rasping her flesh, touching off more heated currents, building a restlessness within her.

She gasped, breaking the kiss as his hand slipped between her thighs, delving the tender lips of her sex, arching her head back as his finger found her clit and teased it to a swollen, achy point. He sucked a hard kiss on her exposed throat and nibbled downward to suckle one pouting nipple again.

Her head swam with the sensation that flooded her. Her heart pounded in her chest, its pace quickening as her excitement accelerated beyond her control. He swirled a circle around her clit, pinching it gently, toying with the nub even as he nipped and sucked her nipples.

She moaned and clenched her thighs tightly on his wrist, rubbing her cleft against his stroking hand.

She wanted more. She didn't want to wait. She needed him inside of her. She felt as if she would die if he didn't possess her.

Blindly, she caressed his back and shoulders, his buttocks and then his belly, her fingers seeking his silken length. When her fingers closed around the breadth of his cock, he lifted his head on a hiss of a breath that sounded pained.

"I will explode," he said through gritted teeth.

"I will die if I can't feel you inside me. Now!" Danielle gasped, tugging his cock closer and forcing him to respond.

He groaned and ground against her hand, his muscles rigid with sensual tension.

Danielle gripped him, pumping him. He seemed to grow larger in her hand, harder--tense with near release.

She arched, writhing and moaning mindlessly, spreading her thighs wide apart.

Shaking with his own need, he opened his mouth over hers again, settling between her thighs and delving her cleft, seeking the moist heat of her opening. The swollen cock head parted her tender tissue, hot as a brand and incredibly thick.

She moaned into his mouth as he found her, as she felt him pushing inside, stretching her, filling her with the wonder of his possession. Her muscles seized, clutching him, hampering his progress until he drove powerfully inside, sank to the hilt and the mouth of her womb. He settled deep inside her core, so right ... so good.

Propped on rigidly straight arms, he looked down at her, his gaze dark and smoldering, searing her with his desire. He watched her a long moment, searing her with the thickness of his cock like a brand.

"You are my woman," he ground out hoarsely, his face tight with desire.

She felt the deepness of his intent in her soul. Her heart tightened with emotion, answering the primitive call with pure, unbridled instinct. She was his. She reveled in the moment, craved more.

"I belong to you," she murmured, drunk with lust.

He inched slowly out, making her channel tighten reflexively on his length to keep him inside. She whimpered, writhing, unable to control herself from clutching him hungrily.

He groaned, arching his head back as if in pain. Danielle caught the back of his neck, bringing him down and capturing his mouth in a desperate kiss.

His tongue speared hers, warring, tangling, retreating to suck hers into his mouth.

She whimpered, clutching his shoulders with ravenous need.

Pressing his shoulder into the bed beside her, he caught her hips in his hands, thrusting, working his heated length deeply inside of her until she tore her mouth from his, gasping for breath, groaning as if she was dying. She dug her nails into his shoulders, arching to meet him as he began to stroke her rhythmically, delirious with the surges of keen sensation and pleasure that wracked her as he stroked his engorged flesh along her channel.

She wanted it to go on forever, wanted to hold onto the wondrous feel of their bodies merging, but it felt too good to contain it. The tension coiled as she rose toward release, tighter and tighter until it abruptly reached the limit of containment and shattered convulsively. Fire rippled through her veins, making her melt beneath him. Her body quaked, clenching around his flesh, massaging him, milking him until he too uttered a groan as he reached his peak and fell over the edge into rapture.

He relaxed heavily against her when his body had finally ceased to convulse, gasping hoarsely, nuzzling his face against her neck.

Even as she lay there, her body continued to quake with orgasmic tremors, making her weak with satisfaction. She bit her lip, shivering with pleasure.

Danielle's arms tightened around him possessively. Drifting dreamily in the aftermath, she stroked her hands lovingly over his shoulders and back. Finally, dragging in a deep, shuddering breath, he rolled onto his side, carrying her with him and fitting her body snugly against his.

Tucking her head against his shoulder, he smoothed her hair and stroked her back caressingly. "I have found a place for us," he murmured after a time, when they had lain in blissful repletion until Danielle had begun to drift lazily.

"A place?" Danielle asked, surprised.

"Safe from the reach of the Elumi. It was once a fortress. The island is much like Pearthen--beautiful and temperate in climate. You will not need to worry that others will discover than I am not as you are. No one lives there now."

Danielle's brain was still sluggish from repletion and she could make no sense of what he was saying. "But--you found it? It belongs to someone."

"Us."

She pulled a little away from him. "You need money to buy something like that--a lot of money."

He seemed to shrug. "They seemed pleased to take the gold I offered them."

Danielle gaped at him. "Gold?"

"The yellow metal in the Earth."

"You found gold?"

"It is what we use in Pearthen for goods and services."

"And you found some."

He studied her a long moment. "Not exactly. It was mine. I thought it was worth the risk of returning for it."

"You went back!" Danielle gasped, horrified. "For that?"

He frowned. "I needed something to barter with to get the things that we would need. We can not stay here, my love. It is not safe and I gave you my word that I would keep you safe from harm. In time, they may cease to seek me, but for now it will be best if I find a place that I can more easily defend--perhaps will not need to defend at all."

"But--they would've come by now if they were going to," she said.

Kirin dragged her head back and placed a kiss on her lips. "They have been. Twice I have had to draw them away. Next time they will send more to take me and I am not certain that even I can triumph over four."

Danielle bolted upright. "You've been fighting? Those times you left, you were fighting for your life? Why didn't you *tell* me? My god! You could've been killed."

He studied her for several moments. "Would it matter to you?" he asked, intrigued.

"That's a horrible question to ask!" Danielle said angrily. "Of course it would matter to me."

"You will come with me then?"

It took a moment for Danielle to change gears. She was still in turmoil over the realization that Kirin could've been killed and she might never even have known it had happened. If he'd died, she might only have thought that he had decided to go elsewhere.

She shuddered in horror.

She didn't know what to think about the idea of moving to an island, but she supposed as long as she could get what she needed for her projects it didn't really matter where she lived. It wasn't like she was a social butterfly and would miss 'society.'

She certainly could not object when it could be a matter of life or death for Kirin.

"You still want me to?"

He studied her face. "That is not a question you should ask me. I told you that I wanted you for my woman. I think I knew the moment I first saw you that I wanted you for my woman and none other. You did not feel the same."

Danielle smiled tremulously. "You grew on me."

A smile lit his eyes. "In time perhaps you will come to love me as I love you," he murmured, stroking a finger caressingly along her cheek.

"Do you love me?" she prodded.

He chuckled. "I have said so."

"I like to hear it."

He cupped a hand over her cheek and kissed her deeply. "I love you," he murmured when he drew away again. "My poor little wingless alien woman."

Danielle smiled up at him. "I love you, too."

The End

BLOOD SIN

By
Kimberly Zant

Chapter One

I was on the most bizarre mission I had ever undertaken in my life. Adrenaline pumped through my blood as I cruised through the tiny southern town, searching for the sign that would point the way to me.

Part of what was pumping my drug of choice through my rapidly beating heart was fear. There was just no getting around that, because I wasn't stupid and I knew the risk I was taking. Part of the rush was pure excitement because I was just plain crazy that way and I couldn't help it, but part of it was also sexual.

I had a plan and if everything worked out just as I wanted it to, I was going to get the ride of my life tonight.

I braked when I at last spotted the sign: Holy Temple of the Warriors of God--15 miles.

My gut tightened. This was the place alright.

Flipping on my blinker, I made the turn and headed out of town, taking care to keep my lead foot from pressing the gas pedal to the floor. A lot of these little towns were notorious speed traps. It wasn't part of my plan to get caught by Goober and risk a night in jail because I had a serious problem with my mouth and authority.

The only thing that actually worried me about my plan was that I didn't have a clear mental picture of the layout of the Temple--hadn't even been able to find a decent exterior view for that matter, although the newspaper clipping had shown a good view of the garish red doors that fronted the 'Temple'.

It bothered me just a tiny bit that I hadn't actually used my training in years. I'd served in the military fresh out of high school. Not that I was a zealous patriot, or a glutton for punishment, or out for adventure, or even to escape my fruit cake of a mother. I'd gone in thinking I could earn my college money and party at the same time.

I'd come out four years later with the certainty that I was not cut out for submission. I was a natural dominatrix, but the military hadn't seemed to care for that particular talent since I was an enlisted stiff and supposed to follow orders, not give them.

Taking my college money, I'd headed off for my serving of education--no particular goal in mind. I just wanted the degree in whatever. It turned out there was a career just for me--management--and I'd enjoyed being the office bitch so well that I was damned near thirty before it finally dawned on me that I'd skipped something I didn't want to skip.

In all honesty, I didn't want to miss a damned thing. I knew it was unreasonable. Having your cake and eating it too just wasn't done, but I suppose I inherited some of my mother's unreasonableness. I'd decided early on that I was going to experience everything life had to offer, and taking half a slice wasn't acceptable.

I'd almost missed the kid and family thing--actually, I didn't particularly care whether I could rope a ring for my finger or not. I did want the kid, though.

Anybody that knew me well would have flatly vetoed the idea of me being a mom, but I figured dads didn't have to be pansies to be dads. Who was to say I couldn't be a hard ass and still be a good mom?

The trouble was, God--Fate--or Providence--was against me. I was outraged when I discovered I couldn't conceive and the worst of it was that the moment I found out I couldn't, I became obsessed with doing it.

Then I discovered that there were just some mountains that couldn't be moved and I'd hit one like a bug at ninety miles an hour.

Depression wasn't something I'd had much familiarity with before. I didn't deal with it all that well.

It got me to thinking about my mother--the fruit cake. As my uncle was fond of saying, she was a few cards shy of a full deck--a total religious freak. I still couldn't believe she hadn't been nominated as a saint after she died. Of course, she hadn't been Catholic, so I supposed that might have had something to do with it.

One of her weird religious experiences in particular popped into my head one day and since by that time I was really depressed and seriously obsessing over the 'problem' I began to wonder if there was anything to it. She'd always claimed she'd been visited by an angel and blessed with a child when she had been told she could never conceive.

Knowing my mother like I did, visited became raped and blessed--well, that was me and even I knew I wasn't a blessing. I didn't know who my father was, but I knew he wasn't any where around. Uncle Bill hadn't been too helpful. He'd just shrugged and said she'd gone off with some religious cult and came back knocked up.

I took an extended leave--maybe I'll be back, maybe I won't--from work. I'd been a workaholic for years and I didn't have expensive tastes. I figured I had plenty of money stockpiled if I needed it and I could always go back to making other people's lives miserable by making them work for their money if this didn't pan out. I'd been tracking 'sightings' of angels for months and I was just about ready to give up when I ran across an article about the cult I was even now bearing down on.

The claimed they'd captured a demon from hell and they were going to offer him up to God on the next full moon. They wouldn't let anyone see the demon--said it would get them and carry them to hell--but they were so excited about it I figured it was worth the drive down to Hicksville to check it out.

I didn't believe in angels, mind you. I believed in what I could see and hear, but something really freaky had happened to my mother. I'd tracked her medical records down and, sure enough, she *had* been diagnosed as 'unable to conceive' which was why her husband had dumped her and she'd joined the cult to start with.

I'm not sure exactly what I *did* think had happened, but I think somewhere in the back of my mind I was thinking aliens--which I had no problem believing in. I didn't particularly care if it was either as long as it could do the deed.

Hell, at this point, I'd have taken a demon. I was part whatever myself, according to my mother, which might explain why I was such a cream puff of a gal that I could wither a strong man's cock at twenty paces just by giving him the 'look' if he annoyed me.

I drove by the Temple, slowing so that I could get a look at it. Unfortunately, it was already starting to get dark and it wasn't easy to see since the building sat a good distance from the road. I drove a half a mile without seeing a road or driveway I could use to turn around and finally, after glancing at the road ahead and behind me, whipped the SUV I was driving around in a U turn and headed back.

It probably wasn't the best part of my plan to leave the vehicle so close to the Temple, but I wasn't a spring chicken anymore and I had no desire to try to outrun a pack of religious maniacs on foot when I could use a vehicle and make tracks faster. I'd had the foresight to rent a good all terrain vehicle, though, and I pulled off the road and into the brush. The brush was so thick I had a hell of a time getting out the driver's door. Making a mental note of 'will take time to reenter vehicle', I went to the back and opened it, dragging out a utility belt that I'd outfitted with every conceivable tool I might need to crash the party. Almost as an afterthought, I grabbed the nylon rope I'd brought and hooked it on the belt, hoping I wasn't going to need it.

When I'd fastened the belt around my waist, I debated whether I'd make more noise thrashing through the underbrush or skirting it. I opted for skirting it, mostly because I didn't relish the idea of stumbling along through the woods.

It was almost dark anyway, and I'd had the brilliant idea of buying myself a really cool black jumpsuit. I figured I needed to look hot to turn the guy/alien on and the best part was the thing had zippers from hell. I could slip out of it in no time at all. Getting back in wasn't as easy, but I figured if I didn't have time, I'd just leave it.

I studied the Temple as I skirted the edge of the woods, stopping now and then for reconnaissance. I knew there were bound to be cult members guarding place. The full moon wasn't due till the following night and, from what I'd been able to discover about the freaks, they were purifying themselves for the ritual, but I figured they'd still have guards. It didn't hurt to hope they were stupid and wouldn't, but I wasn't taking any chances.

I could hear the cult chanting from somewhere close by. It made the hair on the back of my neck prickle.

As I neared the Temple, however, I discovered there was another building behind it. The chanting was coming from the other building. Pausing in the shadows, I considered the situation. The building in the back must be like a dormitory, I finally decided. It seemed a little odd that they'd hold purification in the dorm instead of the Temple, but then they were pretty damned weird anyway.

The demon, I felt sure, was in the Temple.

There were two guards posted at the front and two more at the back. I'd have cussed a blue streak except that I was afraid they'd hear me. Sighing, I settled to think again. I was pretty sure I could handle one. I was also pretty convinced I couldn't handle two and certainly not if it meant taking them both down soundlessly to keep from alerting the two at the back of the building. There were windows all the way around the building, but from what I could see they were the kind that didn't open, just glass set into a window frame.

I looked up at the strange steeple that topped the building--strange because it wasn't actually a spire. Instead, it was more like a square tower. At the top was a real honest-to-God bell, which meant they would have a way of ringing it.

After a few moments, I realized why it was square.

There was a guard posted at the top. I hadn't noticed him at first because he had stopped, watching something at the rear of the building. I watched him for nearly fifteen minutes, realizing that he was bored stiff. He'd pace for a while, and then he'd stop and gaze off into dreamland for several minutes before he remembered he was supposed to be watching.

Did I want it that bad, I asked myself?

Irritated because I knew the answer--I'd come this far, I was damn well going to give it a good try--I began to work my way around the building, looking for some way to climb up.

Either the guy in the tower had had to climb up from the outside, or some dear soul had been working on the roof. I found a ladder just waiting for me. If was full dark by then. I checked to make certain I was out of the line of vision of the guards at the front and the rear, peered at the guy in the tower to make sure he was turned the other way, and then darted across the open lawn.

I was breathing like an asthmatic horse by the time I got to the top of the ladder. I couldn't wait to rest, however. I had to make it across the roof until I was under the tower and out of sight.

Pardonably pleased when I managed the short run without slipping and busting my ass, I settled at the bottom of the tower and waited until I didn't sound like an obscene caller before I moved to the rungs embedded in the tower itself.

Straight climb. That was going to be hellish, but at least the watch at the top couldn't see me unless he decided to look straight down. I climbed slowly to keep from overexerting my heart and lungs. When I was near the top, I paused to listen. Step, step, step, pause. Step, step, step, pause. At the second pause, I went over the top, landing cat like on the tower floor--which meant I sounded like a thundering herd of elephants and everything on the fucking belt rattled.

The guy whirled, but I already had my taser out. I hit him with a few thousand volts and released, leaping toward him as his knees wobbled and gave way. It was a near thing, but I managed to lower him to the floor without pitching either of us over the side.

When I'd settled him, I whipped my trusty roll of duct tape from the pocket of my utility belt and trussed him like a yearling calf. He came to just about the time I wrapped a strip of tape around his head and immediately began wiggling frantically. Glancing around, I saw there was nothing to tie him to. Finally, I hauled him to his feet and tied him to the corner of the tower figuring the other guards would at least see that he was still at his post if they looked, and he couldn't do anything I'd regret.

Tucking the tape in the belt again, I pulled out a small flashlight and examined the floor. Sure enough, there was a trap door. My heart was pounding with excitement when I pulled it open and looked down into the belly of the building.

Burning candles were all over the place. The smell of candle wax was almost enough to overwhelm me.

I was a lot more overwhelmed, though, when I discovered there was no ladder leading down from the tower.

What kind of morons built a tower that was only accessible from the outside?

Dropping to my belly, I hung over the drop for a better look. To my relief, I spied rungs running down the inside of the tower similar to those on the outside. The catch was that they ended at roughly the same place, and there was no ladder under the tower.

Shrugging, I reversed positions and put my legs through the opening, feeling around with one foot until I found a rung. I left nail prints in the wood when I finally came to the point of no return. My arm was just long enough I could brush the nearest frigging rung and not quite grasp it.

Taking a couple of deep breaths for courage, I lowered myself until I was hanging by both arms and made a dive for the rung I hadn't been able to reach. I caught it, but my palms were so sweaty with fear by that time I almost lost my grip. Slipping an arm through the rung to steady myself, I wiped my sweaty palms, blew on them until they were dryish and started down. When I reached the last rung, I turned to look down and gauge the distance.

There was a podium about ten feet below me. I didn't especially want to land on it and the idea of swinging to miss it didn't appeal to me a lot more. Sighing in irritation that nothing so far had been easy, I unhooked the rope from my belt. I'd brought it to tie up cult members if the need arose, not for climbing. I decided it ought to be long enough though.

It took me a good ten minutes to work knots into it to have something to hold onto and another five to tie it off to my satisfaction. By the time I had, I was sweating, partly from nerves and partly from the fucking candles.

Jeeze! Were they trying to roast the guy? Or just trying to make him feel at home?

My palms were wet again. I dried them and started down. It was hellish. I didn't remember having nearly this much trouble when I went through boot camp, but then again it had been a few years. The rope didn't quite reach. I dropped the last few feet before I'd had the chance to consider how I was going to get back up the frigging thing.

Not that it mattered. I doubted very seriously that I could climb up it. It had taken all I could do to climb down with gravity helping me.

I saw him/it as soon as I took my first look around. My stomach clenched in empathy. The bloodthirsty freaks had staked him to a cross and then hauled the cross up--to display him I supposed. Wings covered in feathers that were the inky, iridescent black of a raven's wings were spread on either side of him and staked or nailed in place.

Chapter Two

My heart failed me. I thought he/it was dead at first. I also thought it was fake, not the man part, but the wing thing. From what I could see, he looked like a man.

These people were crazier than I'd thought and I'd already given them credit for being some of the craziest fuckers not caged.

Something blue had been splashed onto him in several places. It dripped, forming small puddles beneath him.

Swallowing the bile in my throat, I moved closer.

Long black hair hung across his shoulders almost down to his pecs and pretty much obscured a look at his face, but the body--my ... my what a beautiful specimen of the male anatomy! I moved around him, studying the wings and discovered with a strange flutter in my belly that they were not only real wings, they were growing out of his shoulder blades.

The flutter of excitement became a tremor of revulsion. The blue hadn't been splashed on him. It was dripping from his veins where they'd wounded him. Bracing myself, I looked a little closer and saw that there was very little coagulation. It was blood, blue or not, and fresh. He hadn't been here long--like this. Otherwise he would definitely be dead as a door nail and I could see he was still breathing.

Obviously he'd fought like a demon--and made a good accounting for himself if they'd thought they had to stake him down and still bind him with wire.

He wasn't human, but he was an intelligent being.

Black hair, black wings, I mused. White, of course being the color of purity, it just naturally followed that black was sin. Crazy, stupid, backwards mother fuckers!

When I'd made a circuit and stood in front of him again, I discovered he'd lifted his head. His eyes were open. The irises were the color of ice, that next-thing-to-white sometimes but very rarely seen in humans, except his also had an iridescent shine to them like the eyes of a nocturnal animal. I shivered.

The face went with the body--masculine beauty personified.

So he had to be a demon because he was gorgeous and had black hair and wings?

Give me a break!

There was pain in his eyes--which I'd expected to see-- but it paled beside the absolute fury in them--which I hadn't actually expected and was surprised to discover made me more than a little uneasy even though he was trussed securely and couldn't get his hands on me.

Those, I saw, were balled into fists.

My stomach clenched again.

That explained the wire. He'd pulled free of the stakes.

"Speaky English?"

His eyes narrowed. "Not that version," he responded tightly.

I felt my face redden. It pissed me off.

"All right smart ass, so tell me--demon? Or angel?"

His gaze slid over me speculatively. "Elumi."

My brows popped upward in surprise. "Alien?"

"Elumi."

This was getting me no where fast. "I'm not with them."

That time his gaze moved past me. The hairs stood up on the back of my neck, but I discovered he was looking at the neon yellow rope I'd used to climb down. Apparently he'd been playing possum and had noticed my unorthodox arrival.

That realization pleased me. I figured it meant he was in a lot better shape than I'd thought, which meant alive enough to give me what I needed.

He was still breathing, after all. I figured he wasn't *that* much different from a human male.

Time wasn't on my side. I couldn't afford to finesse the deal. "I heard of this woman who did it with one of you guys and got pregnant, even though she couldn't conceive. Was that a fluke? Or can you do that?"

He gave me a speculative once over. I decided that meant yes. Otherwise, he would've looked at me like I was a fruit cake, right?

"Hell, I'm willing to try anything at this point or I wouldn't even be here--so here's the deal. You do me and get me knocked up. I'll let you go."

His lips curled back in a sneer that made my palms itch. "I will free myself, or I will die. I will not taint my line with the blood of a lesser being. It would be a blood sin."

Shock hit me first, but I recovered quickly. I gave him a drop dead look, which he actually weathered better than most men, but that only pissed me off even more. He talked like fucking me would be on a par with fucking a dog, and I damned sure wasn't a dog.

Alright, so I wasn't prime beef either. I was slightly aged beef, but I kept in good shape. I was no great beauty--like he was--but mirrors didn't crack when I looked in them either. Men, human men, usually gave me at least one look when I passed them.

I studied him speculatively for several moments, my hands on my hips.

Superior fucking asshole!

"You've done a dandy job of freeing yourself so far," I taunted, unable to resist the temptation to take a stab at him. The poison dart hit its mark. He gave me a look that sent a shiver down my spine.

He was better at 'the look' than I was.

Shrugging it off, I went back to considering my plan. Finally, I decided I might as well have a talk with his cock since I was here already. His cock might not be as fastidious as he was about mixing with the lower order.

The cross presented a problem, though.

After studying the ropes holding it up for several moments, I discovered with little surprise that the freaks had used a pulley system to lift it. Moving to the wench, I grasped the rope, found the release and braced myself. Fortunately, it didn't just disengage. After a bit of a struggle, I managed to lower the thing until it was against the floor.

Striding back to him, I stepped across the post he was bound to, placing a foot on either side of his hips, then squatted down for an inspection of the plumbing. Catching hold of the sarong around his waist, I flipped it up. I was a little surprised to see it looked pretty much like any other cock--slightly disappointed, actually. I was hoping for something a little different. All the same, it was pretty impressive equipment. It was adult sized, even flaccid.

At least it was going to be fun.

I stood up again, bent to grasp the zipper at the hem of my jumpsuit and unzipped the leg to the crotch, glancing at his face as I finished.

He was frowning, his eyes gleaming with suspicion and dawning outrage. Ignoring him, I squatted over his thighs again, grasped his cock and said hello big fellow. I heard his teeth grinding as I sucked on it experimentally.

I'd never figured out why they called it blowing when you had to suck the thing to inflate it.

It tasted pretty damned good--which was both a relief and a pleasure since necessity dictated blowing him and I wasn't keen on giving head--a little exotic, but meat just the same. In about two seconds flat, the monster awoke and it was fully twice the size erect as it had been flaccid--very impressive!

Unable to resist, I lifted my head. "He says yes."

He snarled at me, trying to jerk his cock from my grip. Shrugging, I returned my attention to what I'd been doing. Since time was of the essence and I figured I might have trouble moving fast enough to jack him off while I was astride him, I fell to work with a will. After a few minutes he stopped trying to get away and held himself perfectly still--as if that would avail him! Ha! I was a world class tongue flapper. *Nobody* talked more than I did, even when I was completely alone, which was most of the time. I had a tongue, and jaws, of steel. I could've sucked a blister on it if I'd wanted to.

He gave up trying to hold still, a clear signal that I'd gone way beyond his control. He began to make short, breathless sounds, trying to keep from groaning.

It turned me on big time. My own juices began to flow. I could feel my body burgeoning with desire.

Not that it mattered to the plan. I hadn't really considered getting off myself since it wasn't necessary, but I was turned on now. I got so carried away, I lost sight of the goal and almost screwed the pooch. When his cock abruptly jerked in my mouth, it snapped me out of it, though.

St. Helens was about to blow. Panting with my own arousal as well as exertion, I pulled his cock from my mouth, scooted up his thighs and lifted away from him, shoving his cock head into my opening. As wet as I was--as stiff as his cock was--it was still a hell of a tight fit. I was sweating by the time I'd managed to work him deeply inside, and panting so hard I felt more than a little light headed. I felt like I'd impaled myself on a fence post and had to concentrate to relax my muscles enough to allow a little movement.

Worried that I might have interrupted the process and he might still escape me, I began moving as soon as I felt my juices coating him, lifting up and bearing down again so that my channel stroked his member. I had to fight the urge to focus on my own pleasure instead of getting him off. Fortunately, I'd been right. He *was* about to blow. At just about the same instant my feverish ride took me to the top, I felt his cock jerk inside of me. Groaning, fighting the urge to simply hold still so that I could enjoy the sensations jolting through me, I kept moving, milking his body until his cock ceased to pump his seed into me.

Weak in the aftermath of the best climax I could remember having in a very long time, I wilted over him, struggling to catch my breath. His heart hammered in my ear, his own chest rising and falling in hard gusts.

I'd just begun to wonder it if was safe to linger a while longer and take another shot at collecting his seed when I heard a sound that made every muscle in my body tense for trouble. Jerking upright, I looked for the source.

A young female cult member stood just inside the chapel. As I looked at her, she dropped the jug of water she had in her hands.

Adrenaline flooded my blood stream instantly. I sprang off of my rape victim like he had catapulted me off with his cock. The girl was still trying to find her voice to scream when I reached her. Clamping a hand over her mouth just as she emitted a high pitched mouse squeak, I dug frantically for the taser. Finally, my hand curled around it and I jerked it from the belt, released her and gave her a good jolt.

She jerked all over, let out another squeak, this time of fear, and began to wilt toward the floor.

My ears pricked for trouble. I heard it bearing down on me. Grabbing a candle stand, I shoved it through the handles of the double doors, made a half hearted attempt to stamp out the burning candles I'd poured all over the floor and dashed back to my victim.

He looked furious enough to breathe fire. There was something in his eyes that told me he wasn't the least bit pleased with me.

"Hate to eat and run--but gotta go."

"You said you would free me," he growled.

I shrugged. "You didn't give to the cause," I pointed out--because there was no way in hell I was going to just turn the guy loose when he was looking at me with such promise in his eyes--promise of mayhem and bodily harm.

On the other hand, I couldn't bring myself to leave him at the mercy of those maniacs who obviously didn't have any. Digging frantically at my pocket while I listened to the two guards at the back pounding on the rear door, I finally managed to unearth a pair of wire cutters.

My hands shook as I clipped through the wires wrapped around his wrist. When I'd cut the wire, I had to rap him smartly on the knuckles to make him let go of my arm because he'd grabbed it the instant I freed him. Slapping the cutters into his open palm, I jumped back. "You wanted to free yourself. Do it."

Leaping over him, I dove for the front of the chapel and wedged another candle holder under those door handles before they got the idea to run around the building. They still didn't appear to have tumbled to the fact that there was an intruder inside. From what I could hear of their conversation, they were trying to figure out why the doors were stuck and apparently thought the girl was lying in front of them.

When I glanced around again, I saw I'd set fire to the chapel with the candles I'd dumped.

"Shit!" The whatever-he-was, had already gotten his other wrist free and was working on his feet.

That galvanized me more than the sounds from outside.

Nuts on the outside, fire on the inside and a totally pissed off whatever.

I looked up at the dangling rope, but I didn't figure I had enough adrenaline pumping through me to climb it again, even with fire--and brimstone--chasing me up. Glancing around a little frantically, I grabbed a hymnal and pitched it at the nearest window just as one of the candle holders bent and the doors burst inward.

They screamed. Grown men didn't usually scream when they saw fire. I knew instantly that the 'demon' was loose. Taking a running jump, I dove through the broken window, managing an awkward tuck and roll when I hit the ground on the outside--awkward because one of my arms gave. Pain shot through my arm, but I was too revved to pay it that much attention. Leaping to my feet, I sprinted toward the woods.

I could hear a good many shouts and a lot of screaming behind me. Some of it was screams to stop, the rest screams of terror.

Like I was going to stop! Get real! The yelling to stop only made me run faster. I was traveling at such velocity by the time I got to the edge of the road I had a hell of a time braking to make the turn, sliding halfway into the road like a baseball player sliding toward home base.

Rocks burned my palms as I clawed at the ground and finally regained my feet.

The adrenaline made it easier to snatch the driver's side door open in spite of the underbrush. Thankfully, I'd had the foresight to leave the keys in the ignition. I started the vehicle, yanked the gear into reverse and floored it.

There were a couple of screams behind me--first news I had that my pursuit was that close. I hoped the jouncing was just the SUV bouncing over the ruts, but I sure as hell wasn't getting out for a look. The smell of burning rubber and the scream of tires filled the cab as I slammed on the brakes when I hit pavement. Jerking the gear into drive, I floored it again.

The fire in the temple was already out of control by the time I zipped by. People were running in every direction. I got a glimpse of something really big leaping from the belfry.

A mixture of relief and nerves tightened in my belly.

He was free. I wasn't going to have to spend the rest of my life wondering--not that any of it was my fault. He'd gotten himself into the mess, after all. And the bloodthirsty kooks had caught him. It was their war. I was just a bystander.

My thighs were sticky with his seed, though.

Chapter Three

I decided, under the circumstances, to take the rental through the car wash before I returned it. When I'd washed it and vacuumed it several times, I returned it to the rental place, praying it had been too dark for anybody to catch the license plate.

I was pleased that I managed to behave perfectly calm and naturally.

I'd used a fake ID to rent the thing. I'd felt a little silly at the time, like someone playing spy, but it was a covert operation, after all, and I'd decided it was better to be safe than sorry.

I had reason to be pleased with my foresight.

When I left the car rental office, I spied a news stand. After studying it speculatively for a heartbeat, I dug a couple of coins out and bought one, then caught a cab and had him drop me off down town.

It was harder to act nonchalant when I got out of the cab. I hadn't taken the time to read the article on the front page, but the headlines had made me feel a little ill.

Satanists Burn Church

Like it was *my* fault the morons had frigging candles all over the place! In a wooden building, no less!

It took me an hour to reach the place where I'd left my car. I had to force myself to keep my legs to a brisk walk, but I wasn't rattled enough to draw attention to myself by running.

As tempted as I was to sit and read the article--just to see what lies they'd told--I started the car and left.

The drive back to the city where I lived took longer than I'd expected. I didn't get back to my apartment until the wee hours of the morning. I figured there were probably cops looking for me all over the place, so I'd kept to the speed limit like a good little girl instead of gunning the engine like I usually did whenever I was in a hurry to get somewhere--which was most of the time.

Exhausted, I dropped my gear on the floor by the door and headed for the bathroom.

A long, hot shower soothed my tension and the aches and pains from exerting muscles that hadn't been used in a number of years. When I got out, I grabbed a home pregnancy test and pissed on it.

The results were indecisive.

I was disappointed, but then I noticed the instructions said it took a few days for accuracy.

"Fuck!" Tossing the thing, I dried off, dropped the towel on the floor and headed for my bedroom.

I checked when I flipped on the light.

The what-ever-he-was was sprawled on my bed, his hands behind his head.

Without any rush, he threw his legs over the side of the bed and stood, dropping my wire cutters on the mattress.

I decided not to let him know I was intimidated. Crossing my arms over my breasts, I leaned against the door frame as casually as I could. "You didn't need to come to thank me."

His eyes narrowed. "I didn't."

"Or bring the wire cutters back."

He lifted his wings. It reminded me of those birds you see walking along the ground and shifting their wings threateningly to scare bugs out of the grass. I hated to admit it, but it made my belly clench painfully. I tensed all over.

The wings disappeared--just vanished. One moment they were there, the next he looked like an ordinary--well almost ordinary--man. I didn't ask him how he'd done it. I had a feeling he could do a lot of things and I probably didn't want to know about most of them.

His hands for instance. There wasn't a sign of the ugly holes that had been in his palms--or his feet. They hadn't just healed. The wounds might never have been there at all.

"You did not keep your bargain."

Outrage supplanted my nervousness. I dropped my arms and stood away from the door frame. "Because we didn't have one. You said no, remember?"

His eyes narrowed. "Yes. I thought perhaps you hadn't grasped 'no'."

I sighed irritably. The rape thing. "You'll live. You don't look too traumatized to me. And your friend gave it up willingly. What do you think--you're going to get your seed back? Sorry. Gone, gone."

He'd been stalking me from the moment he got out of my bed. It wasn't that I hadn't noticed. I just figured whirling to run would kick him into chase mode and I didn't really feel up to running at the moment. I wasn't dressed for it to start with and my knees felt all mushy, like they might not cooperate.

I didn't realize he'd gotten within reach until his hands shot out and his fingers curled around my upper arms. I was tensed and ready though. The moment he grabbed me, I grabbed his arms, jerked him toward me as I twisted and pushed one hip out and then gave him a shove.

Surprise flickered in his eyes when he felt himself falling backwards. He hit the floor hard enough to rattle the window glass and table lamp. I hadn't really thought past the hip throw. Instead of running like anybody with any sense would have, I leapt on top of him, straddling his torso and grabbing his arms just below the wrists.

He'd rattled me more than I'd realized to make me make such a stupid blunder.

For about two seconds, I had him. Two seconds later, he had me. Bucking, he pitched me off to one side and used his weight, which was a good deal more than mine, to pin me to the floor.

I looked up at him, trying to gather my wits. "So--I didn't catch your name the other day."

Something flickered in his pale eyes. Doubt? Surprise? "Gideon," he said through clenched teeth. "--Of Marceena."

I gave him a feral smile. "I'm Nicole. Do you think you could get the fuck off of me?"

To my great surprise and relief, he did, dragging me up by my arms as he got to his feet. Before I could order him out of my apartment, he caught me and tossed me toward the bed.

Now I was really stunned--and impressed. I was a lot heavier than I looked. I was trim and shy of average height, but I was almost as muscular as a gymnast from working out and muscle weighs more than fat.

Strong men had discovered I wasn't easy to lift and the guy had picked me up and tossed me like I was a Frisbee.

I hit the mattress and bounced, just grazing my tongue with my teeth. The pain distracted me. He landed on top of me before I figured out which way was up and rolled away.

The air left my lungs in an unlovely grunt.

I blinked up at him, trying to get my eyes to focus from the stinging that had brought tears to my eyes.

His expression almost made me sorry I'd made the effort. "You wanted to know what it was like to fuck an Elumi? I've decided to show you."

"Actually, I didn't. I just wanted the seed," I pointed out. I was always careful with the way I worded things. The English language was so open to interpretation people could twist just about anything you said into meaning whatever they wanted it to.

Obviously, I'd wounded his male ego. He didn't like the idea of being used and discarded.

"I wasn't as impressed with the experience as I'd hoped, to tell you the truth," I added confidentially, and not very wisely, I'm sure, but I was afraid if I looked too eager he might decide to punish me by *not* giving me any and the moment he'd offered my cunt had clapped 'oh boy'.

His lips tightened into a thin line.

He was beautiful when he was angry. There was just no getting around it.

My heart was palpitating so hard I began to worry if it would suffocate me.

Or worse, heart attack. I was no spring chicken, after all. I wasn't sure of just how much excitement the ticker could take.

And he was so rough and manly! And young, my God! And beautiful! How often did a gal like me get a chance at a young studly hunk! Not nearly often enough! Most of the men I ran into--young, old and in between, had no clue of what to do with a real woman. If a woman didn't look like they could break them in two with their fingers and whine and whimper, they practically peed their pants and ran like hell.

He shifted, pushing his knee between my thighs. I resisted, just enough to whet his appetite and keep from seeming too eager, and then spread them wide, drawing my knees up to give him better access. He curled his hips, thrusting forward. I felt the head of his cock and a wad of his damned sarong vying for entrance as his cock slipped along my cleft and connected.

I sighed irritably, because--really how different was it just to get poked? "No foreplay? I thought you were going to show me how much better you were at this than a human."

He planted his mouth over mine--to shut me up, I think.

I'd been hoping for it actually.

His mouth tasted divine. I had figured it would. I'd already had a taste of him and loved it. Heat curled in my belly. His chemical essence sent a rush through me like a drug. I sucked his tongue when he thrust it into my mouth and felt a hard shudder ripple through his body.

He was remembering what it had felt like when I'd sucked his cock, I knew. I was remembering it, too, and it played havoc with my senses. I caressed his tongue feverishly with my own, wishing I *was* sucking his cock.

Later, I was really stunned that that had run through my mind considering I wasn't *in* to giving head--I wasn't actually *in* to oral sex at all. I'd never had any trouble getting off and it pissed me off to come while my pussy was screaming to be filled. It was like half a fucking sneeze, too much and not enough at the same time.

Right at that moment, all I could think about was gnawing on his entire body.

The moment his grip on my wrists relaxed, I pulled free and ran my palms over his body, trying to feel everything at once. My mind was trying to tabulate the feel of hard muscle and silken skin at the same time it was recording the jolts of sensation feeding through every nerve ending in my body at a thousand miles an hour and threatening overload melt down when he hadn't done anything yet but kiss me.

I uttered a throaty complaint when he broke the kiss, but since he immediately began gnawing along my neck working his way downward, I forgot about complaining and arched my back, trying to hurry him toward my goal.

He knew what I wanted.

He teased me unmercifully, working circles around my engorged nipples with his mouth until I was nearly mindless with wanting.

I was going to kill him if he stopped.

When he lifted slightly away from me to look down at me I thought that was his intention. I saw, though, that he was torn--and confused--poor baby! I didn't know if it was because he'd expected me to fight and I hadn't, or if he was surprised that I seemed to have the same effect on him as he did me--truthfully I wasn't sure if I *did* have the same effect on him and I didn't especially care.

Don't stop now, I thought a little frantically. You haven't punished me nearly as much as I deserve!

I almost leapt out of my skin when he lowered his mouth to one desperately throbbing nipple and sucked it. My fingers acted entirely on their own, spearing through his hair and gripping his head frantically while fire poured through me in pounding waves. My mouth felt like it had been swabbed with cotton from all the panting and groaning I'd been doing by the time he decided to bestow the blessing of his mouth on the neglected nipple. I was still trying to gather enough moisture to swallow when he clamped down on it.

I came close to passing out with pure ecstasy as he suckled it. Holding on to my sanity with an effort, I began to wiggle a little frantically, trying to line up my hole with his pole, something I'd always found extremely frustrating with no hands, but I had to feel him inside of me, and I couldn't reach it without making him release my nipple, and I didn't think I could handle it if he stopped. My vaginal walls were cramping from the effort to clamp down on something hard that wasn't there, though, and I very quickly reached a state of extreme distress.

It took all I could do to save my life to refrain from screaming in tongues like the girl in the exorcist--Fuck me! Fuck me!

Actually, I might have. I wasn't certain afterwards and all I really cared about then or later was that he got the message. Shifting, he caught the beast and aimed it. I couldn't wait for him to feed me. I arched toward him the moment I felt his cock head butting the right spot, enveloping it. He grunted when my muscles grabbed him and tried to swallow him whole.

I flailed around a little wildly as he worked his way past almost painfully resistant flesh and finally impaled me to the hilt. I had to squeeze my eyes tightly shut and count to ten to keep from coming right that instant--but I was greedy. I wanted more of the good stuff before I let go of it.

Clamping my fingers into his buttocks, I dug in, wanting to pull him deeper still. He ignored my uncoordinated efforts and began to thrust smoothly in and out. I gasped in a lungful of air and held it, fighting the wall of pleasure that hit me each time he stroked my g-spot, trying to stave off the eruption I felt coming.

I quickly reached a point where I was too mindless even for that much thought, however. Almost the moment he kicked his thrusts into high gear and began pounding into me, my bubble of euphoria burst shatteringly. It wrenched a scream from my chest. Wrapping my legs around his waist tightly, I rode the crest until I was too weak to endure anymore.

I was only dimly aware of his own shattering release--the hoarse groan, the shudders that rippled through his muscles, the jerk of his cock inside me, the heat of his seed as it bathed my channel--but I clung to him tightly until the convulsions of pleasure tapered off to an occasional tremor.

Relieved, I let myself go limp. Every nerve ending in my body, it seemed, still sparked and throbbed in aftershocks from the ten plus magnitude eruption I'd just experienced.

I'd been drifting lazily on a current of supreme satisfaction for a while before I finally realized he'd lifted away from me and was staring at my face. I thought I was going to have to use a finger to get my eyelids unglued, but I finally managed to lift one eyebrow high enough to manage a slit of a view of his face.

It wasn't very helpful. I couldn't tell a damned thing about his expression.

Lifting a limp wrist, I patted his cheek. "Showed me, by damn, didn't you? Now that you've exerted your masculine supremacy, do you think you can take your plug out of the outlet? I'm really tired and this bed's only big enough for one," I murmured.

I sounded like somebody that had had about three drinks too many, but, really, it was a miracle I'd managed to wrap my tongue around that much. Only the desire to be left in peace to enjoy the fruits of my labors had spurred me to that much effort.

Obligingly, he rolled off. I rolled over onto my belly, stretching to get comfy. "Thanks!" I muttered into the pillow, because I was always polite and I never forgot the magic words, 'please' and 'thank you'. "Lock the door on your way out, ok?"

Chapter Four

Ordinarily, I couldn't exactly be described as little miss sunshine when I was rudely awakened, especially when I was really tired and thoroughly enjoying my sleep, but the finger examining my contented kitty had already reawakened my appetite. Just about the time I began to really enjoy it, though, two big hands grabbed my hips, lifting them clear of the bed until I had my knees under me.

"I don't do back door service," I snarled, "so watch where you put that thing if you want to keep it."

He probed my cleft, connecting with door number one.

As far gone as I was in zombie land, I'd have recognized that cock anywhere.

Sighing with a mixture of relief, pleasure, and a vague sense of martyrdom since he'd awakened me for round two instead of leaving like I'd asked, I tipped my hips up for him, bracing myself as he pushed. Despite every effort, I rooted the bed with my face. Vaguely irritated that he hadn't tried revving my engines a little more to get my juices flowing when he was hung like a frigging bull, I planted my palms on the bed and pushed upward, locking my elbows and bracing myself a little better before he could push again.

There still wasn't enough moisture to lubricate his path, and my muscles clenched, repelling the assault. All he actually managed to do was overbalance me so that I rooted the bed again, cracking my head against the headboard in the process. I didn't hit it hard enough to actually hurt--much--but it was enough to distract me and my body sucked up the little bit of juice it had managed to produce.

Grabbing my hips, he dragged me down the bed and tried again. I began to feel like an inch worm as we waltzed up the bed, but this time I at least had the presence of mind to duck when I saw the headboard looming. I crumpled against it like a bug hitting the wind shield of a car when he tried to pile drive me again.

He didn't give up easily. I had to say that much for him, but I sensed a hint of desperation in him as he dragged me down the bed again. I lifted my head. "In case you haven't figured it out yet, Einstein, you're either going to have to get a fucking shoe horn for that thing, or you're going to have to work on some lubrication."

He was breathing heavily when he grabbed my arm and flipped me over, partly from frustrated desire, partly from exertion and partly because he was really pissed off.

I gathered that he hadn't especially wanted me to enjoy it. He'd figured he would take what he wanted, like I had, and then leave.

I shrugged. Pay backs were always hell, but I figured I had it coming. If it would make him feel better I could try *not* to enjoy it. "Lu-bri-cation," I said slowly, in case he hadn't grasped it the first time. "Wait a minute," I added on a sudden thought. "I think I have something."

He caught my ankle as I crawled across the bed and grabbed hold of the drawer knob of the top drawer of my bedside chest. I flattened out, but dug blindly through the drawer anyway, discarding my assortment of dildos and vibrators until I found a tube like thing that actually was a tube. I held it up triumphantly as he dragged me across the bed again.

He snatched the tube from my hand, examining it suspiciously and finally took the top off and sniffed it.

"If it was something questionable, I wouldn't have given it to you to shove up me," I pointed out dryly, snatching it back and squirting some into my palm.

He grunted like I'd punched him in the belly when I grabbed his cock and rubbed it down.

When I had it thoroughly lubed from root to tip, I turned over, got on my hands and knees and waved my ass at him. He grabbed my hips, his fingers digging in tightly. This time when he thrust, his cock slipped inside of me instead of merely shoving me flat. I braced myself for the next thrust, trying to think bad thoughts.

I believed in fair play. I really did. I honestly tried not to enjoy it for his sake, because I could see he felt like I'd gotten one on him and he just wasn't going to be happy unless he had one up on me.

I didn't expect it to be any real problem. I'd gotten my cookie. I was satisfied. I'd actually gotten it twice in just a couple of days after a hell of a long dry spell--because I'd sworn off men when I discovered they couldn't give me what I wanted--either a kid or a good climax. If they enjoyed it, they wanted you to do things for them--like clean their nasty drawers, their apartments, cook for them-- and I didn't really have the time or inclination to tend to pets.

Besides, it was annoying to try to scrape them off without hurting their feelings.

I went over my laundry list in my head. I thought about getting my car waxed--which brought me to my legs and reminded me I was due for a leg and a bikini wax.

I totally lost the thread of my thoughts, though, when he sank to the hilt inside of me at last and I could feel all that rock hard flesh rubbing along my channel as he withdrew and thrust again.

It felt good and it reminded me of how good it had felt the time before, and the time before that.

Think bad thoughts, I told myself sternly, resisting the urge to moan as he began thrusting more quickly.

Dropping my upper body to the bed, I buried my face against the sheets in the hopes that I could muffle any sounds of pleasure I made as he began to thrust harder and faster. He had to be close. If I could just hang on a little longer.

My climax caught me completely off guard. Fortunately, I had my face buried against the bed. I felt confident he wouldn't notice, particularly since he came at almost the same moment.

I sprawled limply against the bed when he finally gathered himself and moved, dropping on the bed beside me. My mind was total mush. I struggled to gather my wits, trying to think how I'd behave if I felt abused and mistreated.

Slugging him probably wasn't a good idea. Besides, I didn't think I could manage it. I was feeling too weak.

If I was girly girl, what would I do, I asked myself?

Rage at him tearfully and throw things at him, my mind supplied, dredging that information up from some of the more obnoxious movies I'd seen.

I decided I couldn't pull that off either. It was me he had and me he was going to get.

Dragging myself off the bed, I headed for the bathroom. After adjusting the water, I climbed in. Tired as I was, I knew I wasn't going to get a wink of sleep with cum dribbling down my legs. I'd been too exhausted from my climax the first time to worry about it. This time I'd been working so hard *not* to enjoy it, I actually felt a little let down--like I'd almost got there but not quite.

So that was sort of a pay back, I decided.

He was gone when I made it back into the room.

Vaguely disappointed, I crawled into the bed, covered myself and dropped to sleep almost instantly.

I woke early, despite my nocturnal activities. It took more of an effort than usual to struggle out of the bed and stagger into the bathroom. I was only slightly more alert when I came out again and felt my way to the kitchen in search of my morning shot of caffeine.

Mixing my coffee, cream and sugar like a chemist until I was satisfied I had just the right number of grains of each in the cup, I took a test sip. It scalded my tongue and burned a path to my belly. Deciding to add a little milk, I stirred it again and trudged to my living room.

The newspaper I'd bought the day before was on the floor by the front door where I'd dropped everything when I came in. Ordinarily, I didn't like to mix bad news with my coffee, but I grabbed it up and read the article about my misadventures with the cult.

By the time I'd finished, I was wide awake.

Knowing journalists' tendencies to sensationalize everything, I tended to take reports with a grain of salt. I found it a lot harder to do that when the tale was about me and a pack of the most outrageous lies I'd ever seen in print.

No one had been killed, which I was grateful to hear, mostly because I didn't want to go to jail. I don't think my conscience would've been killing me with remorse if there'd been fatalities. I hadn't gone with any intention of actually hurting anyone and I certainly hadn't tried to do so while I was there. On the other hand, people like those sadistic cult members shouldn't be allowed to run free anyway.

If I hadn't gone, they would've been very gleefully preparing to murder Gideon by nightfall.

Thinking about Gideon reminded me that I'd forgotten to take my morning pee test--damn it!

Sighing, I tossed the paper down and finished my coffee, wondering what I was going to do with myself all day.

I wasn't used to doing nothing.

When I got up to grab the TV remote, I decided gym time might not be a bad idea. I was sore as hell all over.

Grabbing my bag, I stuffed what I needed in it and headed to the gym for a thorough workout. By the time I'd finished--workout, whirlpool, steam room--I felt pretty drained, but also much better.

Since I still had half a day to kill, I left the gym and headed for the office. Inside of fifteen minutes I discovered I'd been replaced.

I wasn't particularly disturbed. I didn't have to work--right away. My bank account was good and I hadn't even touched my savings.

I put job hunting on my mental 'things to do' list and decided to grab lunch and wander around the mall for a while. My sexy black jumpsuit hadn't weathered the mission that well. I bought another one and looked around the store a while before I left and headed down the mall.

I'd already passed the baby store--slowly--but decided to back track. It was reasonable, I assured myself. My test could come up positive, and then where would I be? Nothing for the kid and no idea what things cost.

The prices were pretty staggering. Besides that, I didn't know what the sex would be and I didn't really like the idea of taking the middle road and going yellow. I was an 'all the way' kind of gal. Once I knew for certain that I was, and knew what it was going to be, then I could knock myself out with frills or blue.

I kept looking anyway--because I just couldn't bring myself to walk out the door empty handed.

Finally, I decided on a baby book. It wasn't too expensive and I figured I could always use it for something else if my plan fell through. It was a nice book. Something like that was always useful.

When I'd made my purchase, I headed for the parking area, figuring the best way to avoid temptation was to leave the temptation behind me. I'd pretty much made a full day of it anyway.

Stopping by a newsstand on the way out, I grabbed a paper so I could study the classified ads when I got back to the apartment and see what sort of job openings there were.

There was another article about the church burning I discovered when I got home and sprawled on the couch. It was below the fold, though, so I figured they thought they'd gotten about all the mileage they were going to get on it. Arson hadn't been ruled out, but investigators weren't as certain as they had been before since they'd discovered the source of the fire was candles. They were saying now that it was *possible* that it was arson, but they couldn't rule out the possibility of accident or just plain carelessness since they'd found out there were lit candles all over the place.

The cultists were still screaming Satanists. One of the cult members claimed that she'd seen a Satanist fornicating with the demon the cult had captured. She was in the hospital undergoing psychiatric evaluation.

Dismissing it, I flipped through to the want ads, found a pen and started reading. I had a headache before I'd made it through the first column and decided to grab a bite to eat. My fridge looked like something from a refugee camp. Aside from a couple of twelve packs of canned colas, an over ripe tomato, a partial stalk of celery that was withered and more yellow than green, a quart container of milk that had about a half a cup of milk in it, and some boxes of take-out that contained some really funky, unrecognizable food type substances, the cupboard was bare.

The cabinets looked about the same. Discovering a can of tuna on one of the higher shelves toward the back--it was out of my line of sight which explained its presence--I opened it, squeezed the water out and looked around for something to go with it.

No bread. Dragging the boxes of take-out from the refrigerator, I dug around until I found a packet of mayo and squeezed it into the can, then looked for a bread type substance to go with the tuna salad. I finally managed to locate a partial bag of chips--stale--and tucked them under one arm. Grabbing the milk carton, I headed back into the living room.

The coffee table was where I did most of my eating at home. I'd never gotten around to buying a dining table, or stools to go with the built in breakfast bar. When I had everything situated, I settled on the floor with my pen, newspaper, and the food. I'd finished eating by the time I made it all the way down the second column of job listings.

Frowning thoughtfully, I went back over the possibilities I'd circled and scratched through the ones I decided didn't especially appeal to me. I had two left out of two columns.

That wasn't very promising.

Tired from sitting so long, I glanced at the clock and realized I'd missed my evening jog. Glad for an excuse to abandon something that was starting to depress me, I went to my room and changed into shorts and a tank top, then headed out for fresh air.

I wasn't much of a jogger, actually, not in the sense that I was always pushing myself to run a little faster and a little longer anyway. There was a playground area near the apartment complex and I limited myself to circling it a couple of times.

It was dark, but I didn't worry overmuch about that. It was a low crime area and besides I was pretty good at defending myself.

When I'd made my two circuits, I headed back to my apartment, feeling a little more clearheaded. I was almost at my door when I heard something land behind me with a soft thud and the distinctive flutter of wings.

I'd learned hand to hand combat when I'd been in the military. Part of that training had included martial arts. It wasn't any of the specific martial arts but rather a combination of several.

Whirling on the balls of my feet, I sprang into action, throwing three punches in rapid succession. He blocked all three, finally grabbing me and shoving me against the wall beside my door when I attempted a kick.

"It is I, Gideon."

Like I hadn't known that! "Oh. What are you doing back?"

He wasn't very pleased with the welcome. I could see that in the glitter in his eyes. Grabbing a handful of my hair, he dragged my head back and lowered his mouth to my neck. Barbarian! I thought fondly as a rush of pleasure exploded in a prickling wave across my body, moving outward from the point of contact.

Chapter Five

I could get used to this, I thought a little dizzily, feeling everything inside me go warm and mushy as he gnawed a path along my throat and finally covered my mouth as if he was starving and I was lunch, plunging his tongue into my mouth and ravishing the sensitive cavern with breathtaking boldness.

I had to suppose he hadn't figured out yet that it was impossible to rape a willing soul. He could be rough or gentle or anywhere in between. As long as he touched me I was a happy camper.

Actually, I thought a little dimly, he hadn't been gentle. I might not like that. I was rather fonder of the forceful conqueror than I should have been. If there was anything I knew about men it was that the very minute you started thinking about letting them become a habit, they were off to greener pastures.

That thought dampened my enthusiasm just a tad.

I broke the kiss. "The neighbors are bound to call the cops if they see me being assaulted by a big winged man outside my apartment. You think we could discuss this inside?"

While he was looking around to see who might have witnessed his arrival--which told me he hadn't actually considered that he might be seen before that--I unlocked the door and went in.

I'd barely cleared the door when he caught me, dragging me up against him and capturing my mouth again as he gave the door a push in the direction of closed. Everything in the room shook when the door slammed shut.

That was bound to attract a few rubber neckers--not that I cared.

By that time he had me on the floor. Carpet burn came to mind, but I was too interested in a different kind of friction to worry about that overmuch.

Grabbing my tank top, he shoved it up and over my head. I was prepared to balk when he grabbed my sports bra, but apparently he realized at once that it wasn't going to stretch over my head as the top had. He merely pushed it up above my breasts.

Capturing one with his hand, he covered the tip of the other with his mouth. I tensed all over as a jolt went through me like an electric current, gritting my teeth to keep from crying out and digging my hands into the carpet. He didn't linger overlong, just teased the nipple he'd sucked into his mouth for a few moments only, driving me wild with the need to gasp and thrash about feverishly, and then sought the mate to it to make me totally lose my mind. At about the same time he switched off, it finally occurred to me that he wouldn't have taken the time to warm me up if I wasn't supposed to be enjoying this. I stopped trying to dig a hole in the carpet and began stroking his back and anything else I could reach.

I loved the feel of his back. I suppose that made me a little weird, because most women seemed to go for the chest, but a strong, well muscled back was a definite turn on for me--and nice legs. Lucky for me he had nice everything.

Rapidly growing anxious for penetration, I ceased stroking his back and slipped a hand between us, trying to wrap my fingers around the erection that was rubbing bruisingly against my inner thighs. Instead of moving within reach, he pulled away. Rising to his knees, he grasped the waistband of my shorts and yanked downward.

I grabbed my panties and shoved them after the shorts. They tangled somewhere in the vicinity of my knees. I was still trying to wiggle out of them when he bent and scooped me up and headed for the bedroom. Somewhere between the living room and the bedroom I lost the panties and shorts that had been hooked on my foot and managed to disentangle my arms from the tank top, dropping that, too.

We crashed on the bed in a tangle of bodies that proved to be too much for the thin slats supporting the mattress and box springs. With a loud crack, the mattress fell through, tilting awkwardly. Grabbing me as we started to roll downhill, he corrected the imbalance by plopping me down on the high edge, which promptly fell through, leveling the bed once more.

Relieved of that worry, I groped between us again, searching. He lifted his hips, fumbled for a moment and then, after a brief struggle to free himself from it, tossed his sarong aside.

Surprised but pleased, I abandoned my pursuit of his cock, ditched the sports bra that was binding my arm pits and threatening to cut off circulation to my arms, and settled for an inspection of his ass. His buttocks were nicely rounded and firm with muscle like the rest of him.

He shifted upward along my body, settling his mouth over mine again. I grasped his hips, pushing up on him so that I could shove one leg under him. He responded to the demand. Settling between my spread thighs, he grasped his cock and guided it along my cleft--up and down. I couldn't decide whether he was looking for the right spot or trying to annoy the shit out of me. I maneuvered my hips up and down, trying to help him hit the bulls-eye.

By the time I felt his cock spreading my flesh I was just about ready scream with frustration. That mellowed considerably as I felt him pressing slowly but surely into me in short forays. I couldn't wait to take it all in. I lifted to meet him on his third thrust, pushing in counter until I felt his groin grinding into my flesh.

It was all uphill from that point. I curled my hips up until I could feel him stroking my g-spot with each thrust, pushing him to move faster and faster until rapture abruptly exploded around me. It was disappointingly short in duration, but almost the moment my body ceased to quake with release, it began climbing harder and faster toward a second climax. The second one hit me like an atomic blast. For several moments, I skated the verge of blacking out from the force of it. I was still quaking with the shocks when I felt him reach his peak and still shuddering in aftershocks when he finally collapsed, completely spent, on top of me.

Consciousness drifted in and out as I lay beneath him, trying to recover.

All I really wanted to do was grasp hold of the unconsciousness that kept teasing me and wrap myself up in it. Gideon was dead weight on top of me, however, and I was rapidly becoming too uncomfortable to drift off into lahlah land.

He roused enough to roll off when I started shoving at him--thankfully. It might have taken a crane to lift him otherwise. With an effort, I struggled out of the bed and headed for the bathroom to clean up. By the time I finished showering, I was wide awake, which was just as well since I discovered upon returning to the room that the ass was sprawled in the middle of my bed, dead to the world.

Sighing with a mixture or irritation and resignation, I dragged a nightie out of a drawer and pulled it on, then headed for the kitchen. No food had magically appeared, so I started cleaning out the refrigerator while I made a mental list of things to buy.

I nearly had heart failure when I turned around and discovered Gideon had followed me into the kitchen and was standing in the doorway--frowning as usual.

"I suppose you don't have your own place?" I groused.

Something flickered in his eyes. I wasn't sure what it was, but as much as I had enjoyed our latest round of fucking, it made me uneasy. I was starting to like it too much.

All right, so I'd liked it too much to start with, I amended mentally. I didn't want to get used to it. He'd move on sooner or later, and then I wouldn't have anything to play with but my vibrators--which did the job, but not terribly well.

"Not here," he said finally.

I waited to see if he would elaborate. He didn't. I wasn't surprised. I didn't think the man had even made a complete sentence in all the time I'd known him--all three or four days.

Granted, we were usually grunting and bumping uglies when he was around, but I'd still begun to wonder if he could actually put a whole sentence together. Beautiful but dumb? Or just not much for talking?

He struck me as an action kind of guy, actually.

He didn't strike me as stupid.

"And this is--where?"

"I told you, Marceena."

"Sorry. Forgot. Where's Marceena?"

"Beyond the gateway."

That was oh so helpful and informative!

I'd finished cleaning so I headed toward the living room to pick up where I'd left off in job hunting. He stepped out of the way when I pushed past him, following me into the living room.

I settled on the floor. He stood watching me for several moments and then disappeared down the hallway. I was wondering if he'd left when I heard the shower. Mildly irritated that he'd made himself at home, I finally dismissed it and went back to studying the paper.

The pickings were slim. By the time I'd read two more columns, I'd arrived at the conclusion that the paper wasn't going to be all that helpful. Even the few jobs I'd circled didn't especially appeal to me.

Maybe I was ready for a career change?

I was still trying to figure out what I might like doing when Gideon reappeared, dripping water since he'd only half dried himself, and sprawled out on the couch behind me. "Do you have food?"

"Nope."

He got up. "I will get food."

I was still staring at him in surprise when he simply walked through the wall and disappeared.

Actually, it wasn't simple at all, but it did explain how he'd come in and out of my apartment without any trouble at all. While I watched, wings sprouted from his back around his shoulder blades. The wall sort of wavered and rippled and then he walked through.

Jumping to my feet, I strode to the wall and touched the spot. It felt perfectly solid--oddly hot to the touch, though.

Particle manipulation?

I was no scientist, but it seemed to me that he'd somehow scrambled the atoms--or something like that anyway. Feeling really odd, I returned to my spot and stared at the floor for several moments, trying to gather my thoughts.

Abruptly, it occurred to me that I ought to log that incident. I'd never known a damn thing about my own father. I hadn't really suffered over it, but I'd been a little curious. Supposing I actually did conceive? The kid might want to know.

Moving to the door, I dug through the packages I'd left there and unearthed the baby book, feeling pleased with myself now that I'd justified spending the money. When I'd settled at the table again, I started flipping through it, searching for a place to record the little bit of information I had about Gideon.

There wasn't really a place for it, I discovered, but there were several lined pages in the back for notes. While I was trying to compose my thoughts, it occurred to me that a description was in order. A photo would've been better, but a narrative sketch was better than nothing at all. It started out objectively enough, but by the time I'd made notations about his approximate height, weight, age and build, I was really getting into it and getting downright poetic about the color of his eyes, the faint cleft in his chin, the shape of his lips and so forth.

The lights dimmed, distracting me. I looked up, thinking there must have been a power dip, and discovered Gideon standing over me, staring curiously at the book.

The smell of hot food wafted from the bags in his hands.

I recognized the logo on the bags. "The cops aren't on your tail, are they?" I asked a little uneasily, studying the bags.

"No," he responded, without concern, leaning down to deposit the bags and then snatching the book from my hands while I was distracted by the food.

I frowned at him, mildly irritated until it suddenly flashed through my mind what I'd been writing. Three shades of color washed over my face before I could get to my feet. He held the book out of my reach. I punched him in the gut. When he bent over, I snatched the book back.

He chuckled. Despite my irritation, I liked the sound. Deciding he couldn't have had enough time to actually read what I'd written, assuming he could read English at all and my chicken scratch in particular, I closed the book, tucked it beneath one thigh and explored the contents of the bag.

It was filled with greasy fries and sandwiches. Grabbing a sandwich and a handful of fries, I used the newspaper for a place mat. He hadn't brought drinks. I had to suppose he couldn't wait around to fill cups.

I was starving. I hadn't had anything but a salad at lunch and the tuna a little earlier and I'd been working out half the day--besides the workout I'd just finished in the bedroom, but I couldn't eat without something to wash it down. When I got back from the kitchen with two cans of soda, Gideon was sprawled on the couch, reading the fucking book.

For once, my temper got the better of me. Stalking to the coffee table, I plunked the cans down and made a grab for the book. I wasn't certain if I overbalanced and fell on top of him when he held it out of my reach or if he jerked me down, but I sprawled heavily. Grunting, he dropped the book over the arm of the couch and wrapped his arms around me before I could roll off.

He was grinning up at me when I pulled far enough away to glare at him. "You think I have beautiful blue eyes?"

My eyes narrowed. I could feel blood pulsing in my cheeks, though. "I think you're an asshole."

Without looking the least bit outdone by the comment or repentant for pissing me off, he released me. After a brief struggle, I managed to get my feet under me and get up. When I leaned down to grab my book, he planted his face in my ass, nipping one ass cheek with his teeth. I came upright like I was spring loaded and rapped him soundly on the top of his head with the book.

He let go, rubbing his head and chuckling at the glare I sent him as I stalked around to the other side of the coffee table and sat down. Sliding from the couch, he crossed his legs and settled across from me, digging through the bag. "What sort of book is this?" he asked when he had finished downing the first sandwich in about four bites.

A sent him a resentful glance. "Just--a book," I muttered. I really didn't want to talk about it at all. I most particularly didn't want to explain it, not after he'd been so nasty about giving up his damned seed to start with. *If* I'd conceived, it wasn't going to be anybody's frigging blood sin.

I didn't know why he was so damned possessive about his seed anyway. Sure he could do things I couldn't, but I wasn't inferior, no matter what he thought about it.

"Why did you describe me?" he asked curiously.

"I've got a piss poor memory, that's why," I snapped.

I discovered when I glanced at him that he was studying me speculatively. I didn't especially care for the look. It seemed a little too knowing to suit me. I cast around in my mind trying to think of something to distract him and finally just decided to see if I could pry any real information out of him since he seemed inclined to talk.

"What are you doing here anyway?" I asked.

"I enjoy fucking you."

Chapter Six

"Thanks for clearing that up," I said dryly. I decided not to point out that it had taken some enthusiastic persuasion on my part to convince him to part with his precious seed to begin with. He seemed to have dismissed our less than amiable 'first date' and I suppose he had decided he might as well enjoy himself since the dirty deed was done without his consent and couldn't be undone.

It rankled that he was so offhand about the situation, but I decided I thought it was refreshingly honest even if the dart did break the skin. "I mean here, on Earth, not here in my apartment."

"I am banished."

That sounded promising, and intriguing. It pricked my interest enough that I dismissed the sting of his last remark. "Oh? Kill somebody? I know it wasn't your winning personality."

He gave me a look, but I could tell I'd managed at least a tiny prick in return. Finally, he shrugged. "I failed. King Edric was not pleased over the outcome of the battle. All were slain save me, our General, and a handful of others, for we were taken by surprise. General Titiane was beheaded. The rest of us were banished to lower Earth."

I felt my brows rise almost to my hair line and my jaw go slack. Partly it was because that was the longest dialogue I'd heard out of the man--uh--Elumi. Partly it was because it sounded more like something out of a novel than fact. Mostly, though, it was because I was stunned at the barbarism he described. Here I'd been thinking he must be from a really advanced race of people and he talked like he'd stepped out of the middle ages.

"I need my sword," he added after a moment, confirming my suspicions. "I have found a warrior of Garyn. If I take his head, I can return through the gateway."

I discovered I was having a hard time wrapping my mind around most of what he'd said. The last comments punctured my absorption with untangling the puzzle, though. "Why the head?" I asked curiously. "And why do you need to use a sword? Why not just shoot the poor stiff?"

He looked more than a little indignant. "There is no sport in using the weapons humans use, no bravery in killing from a distance, no skill to speak of."

Those snide comments got my temper up. "I'll have you to know I was in a war--uh--in the military myself! It *does* take skill to shoot, because I can't hit the side of a fucking barn at twenty paces. And you try lying on your belly in a ditch while bullets whiz over your head and let me know how much guts it takes to stick your head up and shoot back! We sure as hell don't do it for sport!"

He looked me over keenly. "This is why you seem different," he said finally, as if he'd figured out something that had been puzzling him about me--like why I was weird?

Obviously, we had a whole lot less in common than I'd previously considered. Not that I'd spent a lot of time thinking about it, because, really, what was the point? The one thing that had been crystal clear to me from the beginning was that he didn't belong in my world. It hardly mattered that now I knew I didn't belong in his either since I wasn't likely to be invited over anyway.

Not that I would've been interested in being invited. I figured we had enough violence in 'lower Earth'.

I didn't much care for the fact that that connotation made it sound like hell, though. *His* world sounded pretty hellish to me.

I had to wonder if he was talking about another dimension. I'd never thought that theory of other dimensions existing at the same time and in the same space made much sense, but he'd mentioned the gateway before. And he didn't talk about it like it was another planet-- unless the gateway was like a transporter?

After brooding over it for several minutes, I realized I should probably write some of this down. I hadn't been lying. I really did have a terrible memory--that was the main reason I was so careful to keep everything around me in order. It wasn't because I was a neat freak, but because I had to have a place for everything or I'd never find it again. Before I'd disciplined myself to put things in a specific place, I'd had a bad habit of wandering around with things in my hands and setting them down at random--with no memory of where or when. Now I just deposited everything beside the door when I came in until I had the time and felt the inclination to sort it and put it in its proper place.

I was a little reluctant to dig the book out again after he'd teased me about it, but I figured I ought to pump him for information while I could. There was no telling when he might disappear for good and I could miss my chance.

"You still didn't explain the head thing," I pointed out, dragging the book out and flipping through it.

"Remove the head and there can be no doubt the enemy is slain--and it is easier to carry. Another wound would mend."

Practical, I decided. It didn't sound quite as barbaric that way. "Could mend, you mean."

"Would," he corrected me.

"An arm or a leg...."

"Would grow back."

My jaw dropped. "You're not serious."

"In time, yes. A warrior could be very weakened that way, and could be slain before he had time to regenerate, but he might also escape."

I don't know why that stunned me so much. I'd just seen him walk through a wall. I'd already seen the way he could pop those wings out and use them whenever the mood struck and then make them disappear again.

My fingers began to cramp with all the scribbling. It occurred to me, though, that this might not be the sort of thing a kid should be reading. After a little thought, I flipped through the book to the family tree.

"Father's name?"

He was frowning when I looked up at him. "Ulrich," he said slowly, obviously a little puzzled at the change of subject.

I spelled it phonetically. "Mother?"

"Yes."

I rolled my eyes. "Her name?"

He thought that over for a while. "I don't remember."

I decided not to pursue that. It sounded a little too personal. "Date of birth?"

He had his head tilted curiously when I glanced at him again. "I do not remember that either."

"Come on!" I snapped, irritated that he was being so difficult about coughing up the information I wanted. "How old are you then?"

Something flickered in his eyes. I knew before he opened his mouth that he was going to lie about his age. "Fifteen hundred, ninety three."

"You remembered the year, huh? I wonder how that would equate to our date?"

"Not the date. Age."

I dropped the pen and slammed the book closed. "Fine! Don't tell me!" I said, surging to my feet. Stalking into my bedroom, I slammed the door behind me and climbed into bed, punching the pillow.

He followed me. The man--Elumi--was a glutton for punishment.

I didn't know whether to punch him or kick him when he climbed into bed beside me as if he'd been invited and rolled over, throwing an arm and leg over me. "Nineteen hundred thirty," he muttered with the air of somebody confessing a dark secret. "But I am still in my prime."

Uttering a snarl, I crawled out from under him, snatched the pillow out from under his head and the blanket off, then stalked back into the living room and settled on the couch.

"Twenty three hundred, you ill tempered wench!" he yelled at me from the bedroom.

I ignored that remark.

"All right, damn it!" he growled from the door of the living room. "Twenty five hundred. I swear it on my dead mother!"

I rolled over and glared at him. "You don't even remember her name!"

He stared at me for a long moment as if I'd slapped him, then abruptly stalked across the living room and disappeared through the wall.

"Good!" I yelled at the ceiling, figuring he was somewhere in that vicinity by that time. Getting up, I gathered my bedding and headed for my bed again.

I woke up some time later with a head between my legs and a tongue in my kitty. I was thoroughly aroused by the time I roused, however. I might still have been tempted to swat him except that the moment I'd run him off I'd begun to feel guilty about my comment about his mother.

Besides, it felt too damned good to make him stop. His mouth was hot. His tongue was talented and waves of exquisite sensation were pouring through me.

I was really torn. I could feel the tension inside of me building rapidly toward release. I wanted it. At the same time, I was enjoying the feel of his tongue and mouth too much to rush things.

Then there was the fact that I never had nearly as good a climax if it was just clitoral.

I decided to compromise and enjoy it until I was really close.

When I felt the first rush, I grabbed two handfuls of hair and tried to dislodge him. He grabbed my hands and held them and kept right on teasing me. I groaned when the first convulsions of pleasure began to wrack my body. By the time he decided he was done, I was screaming and trying to escape. He shifted, crawling up my quaking body slowly, teasing my still sensitive flesh until I thought I couldn't stand it. I groaned in complaint when he began teasing my nipples.

My vaginal muscles clenched so hard when he tried to push inside of me my belly cramped. I wasn't sure I wanted him there at the moment, but I was too far gone to utter a verbal complaint beyond the moans and groans, and besides, he hadn't gotten his. I was surprised and not altogether pleased when I felt the tension building in me again when he finally filled me completely and began to move rhythmically along my channel. It wasn't displeasure so much as the anxiety that I was going to get halfway there before he came and then crash and burn.

He stayed with me, lifting my legs to his shoulders so that he was hitting my g-spot in just the right way. The second coming almost blew my mind. I was still shuddering with the aftershocks when he found his own release.

He did the strangest thing when he'd stopped shuddering. Instead of rolling off of me and giving both of us a chance to catch our breaths and cool down, he slipped his arms around me, dragging me over as he rolled until I was lying half on top of him and then he nuzzled my neck and kissed me for several minutes--long enough I'd just decided he meant to start over when he stopped and went to sleep.

That was so disconcerting it almost woke me up completely. As it was I lay for a long time wondering if he was losing interest before I finally got too tired to worry about it anymore.

Dawn, my least favorite time of day, made its presence known by finding every chink in my fucking curtains and pouring blinding daylight against my eyelids remorselessly. I tried to move but discovered I was pinned down by something heavy, and hot--that was breathing against my neck. It took me five minutes to wiggle out from under him. I felt a peculiar pang when I glanced over at his sleeping face.

Deciding finally that it was just sensation returning to my numbed body after a prolonged period of poor circulation due to the lead weight Gideon became when he was asleep,

I got off the bed and staggered toward the bathroom to take care my morning ritual.

Lucky for me the effort to get out from under him had heightened my mental capacity a good bit over my general condition first thing in the morning. I'd already flopped on the pot before I remembered the test--but I probably wouldn't have remembered it until I was done if I hadn't been semi-alert. Grabbing one from the cabinet, I wrestled with the packaging, trying to clench until I could get the test strip out. After moving it back and forth in front of me for several moments, I managed to get it in focus and figure out which end to hold and which to pee on.

When I was done, I set it on the lavatory counter and crawled into the shower for a quick clean up. The shower woke me a little more and I was able to actually get my eyelids open by the time I got out and headed for the lavatory to brush my teeth.

Halfway through that chore, I glanced down at the test.

Positive. Pregnant.

I swallowed my toothpaste. My stomach, always delicate first thing in the morning, instantly rebelled and I nearly threw up. The heaves were bad enough, but I finally managed to calm my stomach and rinse my mouth. Picking up the test strip, I studied it in disbelief, trying to figure out how I could've fucked it up, or if I was misreading it.

It was pretty straightforward and simple, though. Pee and wait. And then it says pregnant or not pregnant.

Yes! I mouthed in silent jubilation and then did a little victory dance around the bathroom. When I'd made the circuit, I met up with Gideon in the doorway. A jolt of surprise and dawning embarrassment for my juvenile behavior went through me. Right behind that, guilt kicked in and I shoved the test strip behind my back.

His brows rose questioningly.

"I was working out," I lied, pushing past him and heading for the kitchen. Adrenaline was pumping through my blood so rapidly I hardly needed coffee to wake me up. I made it anyway, partly because I needed something routine to do to calm me down and partly because there wasn't anything else in the house to put in my empty stomach--except the leftovers from the night before. I didn't think I could face cold burgers and fries this early in the day, though.

I kept catching myself smiling. It was dampening not to be able to give vent to my excitement and sense of victory, but sour puss would probably not be pleased about it and I didn't want my enjoyment ruined by a party pooper.

Oddly enough, when I took my coffee and headed back into my room to dress and discovered Gideon was gone, I felt deflated.

Dismissing it after a moment, I moved to the mirror to study my stomach, wondering how many days along I was and when I could expect to start looking pregnant. I tried to leaven my excitement with a reality check--I was only a few days along. It might not stay put.

I couldn't convince myself that it wouldn't, however. I hadn't even managed to conceive before. This had to be IT!

It was really distressing to think I was going to have to wait months and months before I had it. It dawned on me, though, that I should be making plans. Nine months didn't seem nearly that long when I looked at it that way.

Dragging a notebook out, I went into the living room, checked the time and started making phone calls. I couldn't get more than two doctors even to give me a ballpark price for prenatal care and an approximate hospital cost. When they found out my age, they started adding other possible expenses.

It irritated me. I wasn't that damned old!

After making an appointment with one, I settled down to tabulate expenses and then checked those against my assets. I was relieved to see that I was still OK as far as finances went. I had enough to get me through, even if I couldn't find a job, but what then?

Chapter Seven

The urge to light out for the baby shop and start collecting everything I could conceivably need for baby was nearly overwhelming. When I finally realized that I just couldn't sit still any longer and behave like a rational human being, I grabbed my purse and headed for the grocery store.

I hadn't brought the list I'd made.

It didn't matter. The cupboards were bare. I needed pretty much everything.

I'd already made one pass through the store tossing things into the buggy at random when I realized I was a pregnant woman. I had to eat the right things. Once I'd breezed back through putting everything back on the shelf I'd decided wasn't nutritious enough, my buggy was almost empty. I went through slower the next time around, reading the labels on everything until I had a blinding headache and was tired besides.

When I'd gotten home and put everything up, I fixed myself a light lunch and sat down to eat it while I worried over my plans.

I didn't like the idea of daycare. I knew it was what working women everywhere had to do to make a living and I still didn't like it.

Unfortunately, I wasn't independently wealthy.

Tired from worry and nearly a week of spending half of every night fucking, I finally crept into my bed and took a nap. I didn't feel a lot better when I woke up, primarily I decided because I just wasn't used to taking a nap during the day.

The fact that Gideon hadn't appeared was merely coincidental.

I finally decided he had gone off to search for his missing sword.

His behavior the night before made me a little uneasy about it, though, which in turn annoyed me as soon as I realized I was worrying about it. I figured I ought to be old enough and wise enough in the ways of the world by now not to get too wound up about something like that.

It was bound to happen sooner or later and with most men, human men anyway, it was usually sooner. I realized after a while that I was actually surprised and a little flattered that it had taken him most of a week to start looking for greener pastures.

There was no getting around the fact that it put a crimp in my enjoyment, but after a while I was able to focus on the problem again.

Along about bedtime, when he still hadn't shown up-- which was purely incidental to my thought processes--it occurred to me that I never had actually particularly liked living in the city. My early childhood had been spent at the old family farm. My mother had decided to move us up to the city to be closer to her brother and his family, but I still owned the old farm.

The kid would probably like the farm better, too. Of course it wasn't really a farm per se. We'd just called it that because it was outside the city limits in the country. It hadn't been a working farm since my grandfather's time and I was certainly no farmer. The old house was pretty much falling down, too.

I decided, though, that before I spent a lot of time job hunting in the city, I'd just take a ride down and check the old place out. It was situated almost ten miles out from the nearest town to it, and that town wasn't big enough to be called a city or even much of a town. I should see if there were any job prospects and just how bad the house looked now.

The following morning I rose and packed a small suitcase, figuring I might want to hang around a few days if the house wasn't in too bad a shape. It seemed probable that it could take me at least a few days to check out the job market alone.

The farm was a surprise, not altogether pleasant. It wasn't in as bad a shape as I'd feared, but it was pretty grown up and the house was definitely in need of repairs. The main surprise was that it looked a lot smaller than I remembered from my childhood. That wasn't the bad part, though. The bad part was that it resurrected memories. My mother had actually been fairly rational during that stage in my life. She'd already been heading toward fruit cake, but there were good memories tied to the farm and those made me miss her--or at least the her she'd been when we lived on the farm.

I spent several days just rambling around the farm and house making notes on what needed to be fixed and whether it was something I could do myself or would need to hire someone to do.

I was in town getting estimates on doing those jobs I couldn't when I happened upon a job opportunity. It wasn't management, but I hadn't expected to land anything in that area anyway, not in such a small town. It *was* a job running a small office which was still within my range of expertise.

The girl that worked there was getting married and planned to be a housewife.

Quaint! I didn't know women even did that anymore.

It seemed like fate, though, so I jumped on the opportunity.

Once I'd made arrangements for the repairs I needed done, I packed up and headed back to my apartment in the city. I only had a few weeks to figure out a way to get out of the last few months of my lease and make arrangements to move.

All in all I was pleased with the way things were coming together. I wouldn't be making nearly as much money as I'd made before, but it wasn't going to cost me nearly as much to live either. The country air would be better for the kid--unless it had allergies--and I was ready to get out of the rat race and slow down.

Plus, I hadn't thought about Gideon more than a few times a day in the entire time I'd been at the farm and then only fleetingly.

It still bothered me that I'd thought about him at all, but I took it with a grain of salt. I had pretty thick skin, but I was also a creature of habit and Gideon had hung around long enough I'd started getting used to him. Then, too, there was the great sex thing. It was so rare to find somebody who had that effect on you a woman could be pardoned for getting addicted to the good stuff.

I was not happy when I got back to my apartment and found Gideon laying in wait for me. I was so fully occupied with my own thoughts and trying to get my key in the door that the soft thud behind me barely registered. When he grabbed me from behind I nearly shit a squealing worm.

I elbowed him in the rib cage just for scaring me.

He grunted, his arms going slack enough I managed to pull free. "You total ass hole!" I growled, whirling on him furiously. "You scared the living hell out of me! What are you doing here?"

He looked surprised and then almost as angry as I was. "Why did you leave?"

I stared at him for several moments, caught completely off guard. Nobody had kept track of me in so long I felt totally disoriented at being questioned. "I had things to do," I said shortly, angry that he'd had the gall to question me at all, particularly when he came and went without a 'by your leave'. Opening the door of the apartment, I entered, dropping the suitcase by the door.

It was too much to hope he wouldn't follow me.

I wrestled with my anger for several minutes after he'd followed me inside and slammed the door hard enough to rattle the room. Finally, reason began to thread its way through the anger and I realized that, aside from being startled, I was being no more reasonable than he was. I dragged in a deep, cleansing breath and let it out slowly. "Sorry," I said as apologetically as I could manage. "You scared me. It made me mad."

That seemed to leaven his anger somewhat, but I could tell he was still struggling with it.

"Why were you looking for me anyway?" I asked, flopping on the couch because my knees still felt as weak as water.

Several emotions flitted across his face in quick succession, too fast for me to catch. Finally, he turned to pacing the room, thinking. "I have not found my sword," he said finally.

"Ah!" I nodded. That explained a lot. "I figured you would've already gotten your man and lit out for the gateway."

He frowned, but whatever he'd started to say, he seemed to reconsider. "He knows I am here and I have nothing to fight him with. Until I can find the sword, I must keep on the move or it is my head that will be carried through the gateway."

I felt so ill at that comment that I thought for several moments I might actually throw up. Not once since I had been gone had it occurred to me that Gideon was in danger. I suppose I just hadn't completely grasped his situation. Maybe I hadn't believed it at all. Regardless, I had spent more time mentally berating him for heading off for greener pastures than anything else.

Finally mastering the unsettling emotions roiling through me, I managed to focus on the problem. I didn't want Gideon to get killed. I much preferred to think of him leaving and going home to that possibility.

It would make my life easier anyway. He'd said he enjoyed fucking me. Until he'd had his fill, he would come back whenever the mood struck him and I'd be a sucker and let him because of my own needs. I couldn't allow that. I was just as 'in' to self deception as the next person, but I was no fool. I was already too attached to Gideon for comfort. There was always the possibility that familiarity would breed contempt, but it wasn't something I was willing to gamble on when there was just as much chance that familiarity would breed addiction.

"I don't suppose a different sword would do?" I asked, wondering even as I said it where the hell I'd find one. There were plenty of places around that made reproductions, but I had a feeling that wouldn't be close enough.

His look told me no. I sighed. "Why don't you tell me how and where you lost it to start with? Maybe if we backtrack, we can figure out what happened to it?"

He glared at me. "I have done that."

"You haven't done it with me. And I happen to be more familiar with this world than you are."

He was silent for several moments, pacing, either trying to decide whether it was worth the effort, or trying to decide where to start. "I had run upon an enemy soldier-- the Garyn I spoke of--and engaged him in battle. We fought for many hours, for we are very evenly matched in skill and strength. We were moving all the time that we fought, sometimes in the air, sometimes on the ground. As it grew dark, I managed to wound him, but I was also at a disadvantage, for we Elumi can not see as well in the dark as in the light."

I rolled my eyes at that since I was fairly certain humans were a lot more disadvantaged in the dark than the Elumi were.

He frowned. "We are not invincible," he growled. "We heal quickly, even great wounds, but there is still pain and weakness from loss of blood."

"Sorry," I muttered, wishing he wouldn't talk about that since it made me hurt just remembering what he had looked like when I'd found him. "Tell me everything."

It took him a moment to pick up where he'd left off. "He wounded me, as well. Still, we fought on. I thought I had wounded him worse, for he began to slow and I could see that he wanted to break off and retreat until he had healed to fight again. My own wound began to pull my strength from me, though, and although I managed to wound him several more times, he caught me, as well, and I think we both began to realize that neither could find victory at that point.

"We withdrew finally by mutual agreement. I had to find a safe place to allow my body time to heal since I could not know if he would grow strong faster--or if there were other enemies around who could take my head while I was too weak to fight.

"By the time I had found a place where I believed I would be safe, I was not very clear in my mind--and it was not as safe as I had thought. The humans came when I was barely conscious. I fought them, but I was weak and easy for the four of them to overwhelm. When I woke again, I was as you found me."

I was more than a little unsettled by the time he'd finished. I was deeply distressed. Guilt crept into the mixture for my part in his mistreatment, but I was far more furious at what those cultists had done to him. I had to fight the urge to rage over what they had done, which made it that much more difficult for me to think objectively about his problem.

"You were in an abandoned building when they found you?"

He shrugged. "So I had thought."

"Maybe an abandoned building," I amended. "You don't recall having the sword when you were taken from the building?"

He gave me a look. "I was not conscious."

I felt like crying, but stifled the unfamiliar urge. "Not very helpful. So you wouldn't remember anything about the trip to the temple either?"

He shook his head.

I thought over what he'd said. "It must be around there somewhere," I muttered finally. "Even unconscious, I doubt they would have considered going far with you. Believe me, those cowards were a lot more afraid of you than you were of them."

He looked surprised. "I was not afraid. I was angry. If I had had only a little time to rest and heal, they could not have taken me. I was angry that I was so weak that I had been taken so easily."

Now that he mentioned it, I recalled pretty vividly that he had been very, very angry. I'd thought at the time that it was because of me. Now I wondered if he had been so furious simply because I was another human who'd come to torment him.

I sighed. Water under the bridge now, but it was certainly something to make a mental note of for future reference-- don't get so wrapped up in what you want that you forget to consider someone else's feelings.

There were a lot of ways 'what goes around comes around' could manifest itself. Gideon had gotten his revenge for what I'd done in a way I doubted he'd even considered.

"We'll have to go back there," I said decisively. "You'll have to go with me because I can't fly. And we'll need to disguise you. I don't want to take a chance that any of the cultists will recognize you and try something else."

"I am strong now. I would welcome the opportunity to fight them again."

"I'm sure you would, and I can't say I blame you. Thing is, though, humans take a dim view of wholesale slaughter. If you waded in and whacked off a lot of heads, every cop for miles around and half the federal government would be looking for you--which might not bother you since you can always head back across the border. But it could make my life hellish and I'm just not going to go if you won't give me your word that you won't do anything that'll land me in jail. I've got other plans for my life."

Chapter Eight

He gave in easier than I'd expected, which made me more than a little suspicious. From what I could see, the world he hailed from was all about vengeance--taking it and dishing it out. Considering the circumstances, I would have wanted revenge myself if they'd done to me what they'd done, and tried to do, to him so I could relate to the desire for it. I just hoped he could contain himself until I was out of the picture.

He seemed to take it as a matter of fact that as long as he was there anyway he might just as well take care of his needs. On an emotional level, I wasn't nearly as enthusiastic as I had been before because I found I couldn't be as objective and detached about it. On the other hand, I couldn't think of any way to object that wouldn't give my feelings away. Besides, I did enjoy it. I figured I might as well make hay while the sun was shining.

Having done without for almost a week--half a week anyway--I discovered I couldn't contain my enthusiasm anyway once he got the juices flowing. Since the route of indifference wasn't possible, I decided to go the other way and tease him to the point of rough, quick sex to minimize the temptation to go all mushy and stupid about it. It worked like a charm, because, I suppose, he'd done without, too--maybe not--but I didn't want to think about that. He was hungry enough to convince me he'd gone without and that was all that really mattered.

Since I figured the sooner done the better, I took some measurements and headed out to the mall the following morning to find clothes that would help him blend in. The price tags were a real shock, enough that my practical side kicked in.

New clothes were going to be a lot more noticeable than older clothes. I didn't want to make him look like a homeless man either, but Gideon was drop dead gorgeous. Women were going to notice even if the men didn't. As much as I wanted to dress him 'pretty', I decided that wasn't such a great idea and began searching for stores that recycled clothing.

It was exhausting, but I finally found a couple of shirts and pairs of pants I thought would fit him reasonably well. I didn't bother with undies. He went around swinging in the breeze now. I figured the pants were going to be more restrictive than he liked. Topping the stack off with a pair of tennis shoes and cap with a visor to hide as much of his beautiful face as possible, I paid for it and headed home again.

Gideon was pacing my living room when I got back, not surprising since I'd told him I wouldn't be gone long.

I was happy to see the clothes fit him--not happy with the way he looked in them. There was just no making the guy look bad.

He hated the shoes worse that he hated the clothes, and he was pretty unhappy about those.

That long, beautiful black hair had to go. I knew it, and yet I just couldn't bring myself to cut it off. Finally, I brushed it back from his face, secured it with a pony tail stretch band and tucked it under his cap.

He liked the cap.

Probably because he looked like hell in it. One could always count on a man becoming instantly attached to anything that looked like shit on them.

The first part of the trip didn't go well. Gideon twitched, complaining about the restriction of the clothes and the fact that he couldn't get out of them very quickly if he needed to. The shoes pinched and the trousers were strangling his cock and balls.

I told him to do like every other man I'd ever seen, play with them until he was comfortable. I also pointed out that he wasn't supposed to get out of the clothes quickly because he'd promised me he wasn't going to do anything violent.

I had to slap his hand when we stopped for lunch, because he was still trying to adjust himself. He glared at me, but subsided, merely shifting and wincing like he had a stake up his ass from time to time.

Patience, Nicole! I told myself. The man had never been trussed up in clothes before. I was sure it wasn't something he was going to get used to either, because he would be ditching them as quickly as he could.

I whiled away the second half of the trip talking--mostly to myself--about the farm and what I would do with it. Despite everything, I was really looking forward to a change in my life, maybe *because* of everything.

I didn't get so wrapped up that I talked about my plans for the kid. I figured we'd pretty much made our peace on that subject. There was no sense in starting the war all over again by reminding him of what I'd done. Besides, I thought I'd feel better if we could end this affair on a high note. Fighting was no way to end it.

Toward the last, as we came closer to the town, uneasiness loosened my tongue even more. I really didn't relish returning to the scene of the crime so soon *after* the crime. It was risky. I was fairly sure no one had seen me well enough to recognize me except the girl I'd hit with the taser and as far as I knew she was still in the loony bin. I wasn't one hundred percent certain, though--of anything.

Since I figured two strangers asking anything at all about the cult or the fire would be enough to arouse suspicions, I merely drove around town until I found a real-estate company. I was nervous about taking Gideon in, but more nervous about leaving him outside in the car--which I knew he wouldn't stay in.

The receptionist glanced up when we came in, did a double take when she caught a glimpse of Gideon and was instantly transformed into borderline retarded. "Can I help you?" she stammered, falling all over her tongue.

It thrust me immediately into territorial bitch mode. I'd realized I would have to introduce Gideon. He didn't look a thing like me, so I didn't think it would be very believable to claim him as a relative. On the other hand, I thought he looked a little too young to be my husband--young enough it might attract attention to us that I didn't want.

Under the circumstances, though, it took all I could do and then some to keep from digging my claws into him and screaming 'mine!'

I managed a tight smile. "My--uh--brother and I are looking for a place around this area."

The girl looked at me blankly.

I forced a chuckle, ignoring the look Gideon gave me. "He's my half brother actually."

She was having trouble gathering her wits. I could see that, and also the speculative gleam that had come into her eyes when I hadn't staked my territory. "Of course we want something that would be big enough for his wife and kids, too," I added sweetly.

Her face fell, almost comically, except that I didn't feel much like laughing. She asked us to take a seat, but before we had, the agent came out of his office and invited us in.

For a man who must spend a lot of time at his desk, he looked pretty good. He wasn't hard on the eyes either.

Of course I knew all the charm he was pouring on was aimed at my pocket book, not me, but it soothed my wounded ego that he at least appeared to find me attractive.

"What're you folks looking for?"

I frowned. "Actually, we've only just begun and we're not entirely sure. What I was hoping for was to get a map of the area and a listing of the properties that were available."

He frowned, obviously not pleased at the idea that he wouldn't be able to follow me around and press for a sale.

"That way I could eliminate the ones that were totally unsuitable and once I've taken note of the one's that interest me I could get you to show them."

"Something in town? Or in the country?"

I glanced at Gideon. His eyes were stormy. I had a feeling he was going to give me hell when we left. "The countryside," I answered, giving the guy my best smile.

He began searching his desk drawers for files, giving us his spiel about the county and town while he was at it. Producing a map, he began sorting through his listings and marking spots of interest.

It took almost an hour. My face was starting to cramp from smiling. "Goodness," I drawled sweetly when he finally ran out of breath and listings. "This could take a while. We'll look these over and get back to you in a couple of days. Thank you so much for all your help."

"I'd be delighted if you'd let me take to dinner this evening. We could talk about the properties you've looked at over dinner and drinks." He glanced at Gideon. "Both of you," he added belatedly, looking more than a little uncomfortable.

I pretended to think it over. "Actually, we're really tired from the drive and I'd like to look at a few of these today. Maybe tomorrow?"

"What was that all about?" Gideon growled when we'd gotten back into the car.

I kept my smile with an effort, waving to the realtor, who'd followed us out. "Getting information without arousing suspicions," I retorted.

"He did not take his gaze from your breasts," Gideon said harshly.

"That was the idea," I said dryly. "It's why I wore this blouse. If a man's mind is on his cock, it isn't on other things."

"You were trying to--entice the man to fuck you?" he demanded, outraged.

I rolled my eyes. "Of course not! I didn't even know it would be a man before I got there. I just figured if it was a man I would want to distract him, that's all. I didn't want him asking a lot of questions about us or why we were thinking about buying a place anywhere near this hick town. He wasn't bad looking, though," I added, mostly because I was still ticked off about the way that *girl* had practically drooled all over Gideon. I hadn't noticed whether Gideon was encouraging her or not, mostly because I refused to look and see, but he certainly hadn't *dis*couraged her and neither had my lie that he was married with kids for more than a few minutes and she was not only young, she was pretty. Not that she actually had to be pretty as long as she was young.

I pulled off and parked as soon as I saw a likely looking spot, opening the map to study it. Gideon, still boiling mad, had apparently decided to give me the disapproving silent treatment.

Ignoring his bad humor, I studied the map until I'd located the temple and then checked to see how many places near it were up for sale.

Of course, I was depending on the possibility that it was fairly close, and also that the cultists hadn't just taken the sword when they'd taken him, but I figured Gideon had already thought of the cult himself.

"You checked the temple and the other buildings?" I asked, just in case.

"Yes."

Sighing, I put the map away. Three of the places were right on the same damned road as the temple. There was no way to avoid going by it.

The first place I stopped turned out to be a house for sale. I couldn't see any sign of a barn or other structure on the property, so I kept driving. I couldn't resist glancing toward the temple as we passed. Raw new lumber met my gaze. Cult members were running around the burned hull like ants.

They were rebuilding.

At least half of them paused to watch the car pass. Obviously not too many cars came this way.

My belly clenched as uneasiness flooded me. It was unnerving to have so many psychos looking at me. Very casually, I propped my arm on the armrest and propped my face in my hand because I didn't want to be recognized but I also didn't want to make it obvious that I was trying *not* to be recognized.

A little further down the road, I spotted an old barn in the distance. It looked like it was about to collapse in on itself. It wasn't one of the properties the realtor had marked, but I figured we might as well look.

"I have looked here," Gideon said when I turned off the road and headed toward it.

"It won't hurt to look again."

There was no sign of the sword, of course. I hadn't expected it to be easy to find. If it had, Gideon would already have found it, but I was still disappointed and I became more disheartened and more uneasy as the day wore on. Darkness fell and we'd still had no luck. I didn't like the idea of staying in town overnight, but there wasn't another town of any size for miles.

Once we'd gotten a room for the night we went out to eat. There were no fast food joints which left us no choice except to go to one of the local diners or do without. Everyone stared, hard. I tried to tell myself it was just typical small town nosiness. I knew that was probably all it was, and it still made me uneasy.

Gideon had spent most of the day scowling at me. I was surprised he stayed angry. Ordinarily, he didn't nurse his temper. It was rather like quicksilver, erupting fairly easily, but dissipating just as quickly.

Mad or not, he saw no reason to let the bed go to waste only for rest. In fact, he hardly let me get any rest at all. I wasn't sure what he was trying to prove, or if he was trying to prove anything at all, but my legs were so wobbly and sore the next morning I couldn't walk without wincing.

We got off to an early start. We'd checked every place close to the temple the day before. We widened the search, driving down every back road we came to and stopping at every run down barn and storage building. By noon, I'd begun to seriously consider the possibility that it would never be found. Maybe the cops had found it and it was sitting in their evidence room? Maybe some kid had found it and took it off to play with it? Maybe the cultists had taken the sword after all and had hidden it somewhere?

Day two was as much of a bust as day one had been.

I considered fobbing the realtor off when he called to ask me to dinner. Instead, I accepted, deciding I'd tried everything else. Maybe I could pump him for information and discover something.

Gideon did *not* like it. He was even less happy about it when I insisted on going out alone with the guy, but after I'd pointed out that I wasn't likely to get anything out of the man if Gideon was going to be glaring at him over the table the whole time, he got pissed off and left.

I had a headache by the time I met the realtor at the local country club. I was vaguely amazed that they even had one, but I supposed there were rich white men all over the south and whither they were, there was going to be a club.

By the time our dinner was served, I already knew the man was going to be no help at all. He bounced back and forth between flirting outrageously with me and flirting with my pocket book.

He tried plying me with drinks even though I'd already told him I didn't drink--which wasn't strictly true. I did drink occasionally, but I was pregnant now. Alcohol would not pass my lips.

I was ready to go as soon as we'd finished eating-- actually before we finished, but I figured I had to be polite and not behave as if I couldn't get loose from him fast enough. On my way to the ladies room to calm down and regroup, I just happened to glance at the paraphernalia that had been mounted on the walls as decoration.

I came close to passing out when my gaze landed on a long sword. I had to make myself walk past it. I was shaking by the time I got into the lady's room.

"It was just a replica," I told myself. I didn't believe it, though. I was no expert at such things, but I'd seen enough war memorabilia to know that sword didn't look like any I'd ever seen from any period of world history. The hand guard and hilt were gold, encrusted with gems like I'd never seen, and even the blade was different, wide like a medieval broad sword, but shorter and serrated at the tip almost like a hunting knife.

The G was the biggest giveaway, though.

Chapter Nine

By the time I'd calmed down a little, I realized that it wouldn't necessarily look suspicious just to gaze casually at the wall. There were a lot of things on it--old pictures, old tools and weapons--all antiques I supposed. When I left the ladies' room, I strolled by, stopping several times to examine things I had no interest in, just so it wouldn't look suspicious when I got to the sword and lingered long enough for a thorough look.

I hadn't imagined the initial. There was a design that reminded me of a medieval coat of arms, not exactly like those I was familiar with but similar enough I thought that was probably what it was.

I don't know why I did so unless I sensed that I was being watched, but I glanced toward the tall window as I started to move on. Gideon stood framed in the glass. His gaze wasn't on me at that moment, however, but on the sword.

For a handful of heartbeats our gazes met. I saw triumph in his eyes. The next moment, that strange phenomenon I'd seen before began, except this time I was looking at Gideon, not behind him. The glass, the wall, the air seemed to ripple. Gideon's form vanished. A coolness brushed along my arm. When I glanced down at the prickle of sensation I saw the sword was gone.

He'd taken it and no one save me had even noticed.

An odd assortment of emotions washed through me--gladness was uppermost, though, because I knew Gideon had his sword now and he was going to be alright.

I moved on after only a moment and stopped to study a few other items for good measure. The realtor got up and pulled my chair out as I reached the table again. I sat, heavily. My knees felt unaccountably weak. My thoughts were still chaotic, but I didn't want to sort them at the moment. I needed to be alone. "I've really enjoyed this."

"You'll like the dessert even better. I took the liberty of ordering while you were gone."

The polite smile I'd pasted on collapsed. "That is so sweet! But I'm watching my weight."

"Just a taste."

I should have insisted on leaving then. I didn't want to be present when someone noticed the sword was missing. Not that I could be blamed. I didn't have it. And I refused to feel guilty about the guy ordering desert. It wasn't my problem that he'd ordered something I didn't want. I didn't really like being rude, though, and it couldn't take long to eat a bite or two. "I suppose. I really do need to get back, though. I'm just exhausted from driving around and looking at places."

To my relief, the dessert arrived fairly quickly. I didn't see anything particularly special about it. It was cake, and not especially good cake--bone dry, in fact. I took a bite and washed it down.

"Did you notice the sword?"

I looked at him blankly, trying to pretend I had no idea what he was talking about. I couldn't keep my damned color from fluctuating, however. "Sword? Oh, that strange one."

He chuckled. "The only one on the wall. I found it a while back. No idea where it came from or what it was doing in that old barn, but I figured it would look good on the wall and make me look good if I donated it."

"Oh," I said, stalling while I wracked my mind to think of something to cover my slip. Obviously, he'd noticed me looking at it. I didn't especially want him to notice it wasn't there anymore so I resisted the temptation to say 'what sword?', knowing he'd instantly look. "I wasn't paying much attention," I added lamely. "I suppose it's a replica?"

He smiled.

A wave of dizziness washed over me.

"You think it's a replica?"

"I'm not really up on antiques, to tell you the truth," I managed, beginning to feel really odd. "You know--I don't like to be rude, but I think my fatigue is starting to catch up to me. I think I'm going to head back to the hotel."

He frowned. "Sorry to hear that. Let me walk you to your car."

I didn't really want him to walk me to my damned car. I just wanted to get out of that place. Gideon had his sword.

I hadn't gotten the chance to say goodbye. I didn't want to think about that, though, because I had a bad feeling that if I let myself think about it I was going to end up squalling.

A harder wave of dizziness hit me when I stood up. I had to put my hand on the table to find my balance.

"A little too much to drink, huh?" the realtor said, smiling.

I blinked. "I haven't drank anything but tea."

He chuckled, nodding at the couple at the next table. "Why don't you let me give you a hand?"

By the time we'd made it to the wide front porch of the club, he was practically carrying me and I knew I was in serious trouble. He'd put something in my drink while I was in the bathroom.

Stupid! Stupid! That was how the guys always slipped the date rape drug to their victims and I should've known better than to drink anything I'd hadn't been keeping an eye on. But how was I to guess the guys in Hicksville were doing it, too?

"I think I should drive you."

"No! No! I'll be fine," I said, but the words were slurring together as if I really was drunk.

"You know, I owe you one for that trick with the damned taser," he said almost matter-of-factly as he marched me down the stairs and into the parking lot.

As far gone as I was, that comment didn't take more than a couple of seconds to compute. "The guy in the tower? That was you?"

"I recognized you almost immediately. I might not have if you weren't still with the demon, you Satanist bitch, but you're in league...."

He didn't get the rest of the sentence out. Something huge and black slammed into him, hitting him so hard he flew backwards several yards and into the side of a parked car. I sprawled out without his support. When I finally managed to struggle upright, I saw an avenging angel standing over him--my angel. I could tell just by his stance that he was disgusted the guy was out cold and unable to present any kind of challenge. "Gideon," I said in pleased surprise. "You here?"

He turned at the sound of his name and moved toward me. Kneeling, he scooped a hand under my shoulders, running his free hand over me as if to check me for injury. His palm lingered on my belly for several moments, making me wonder what was going through his mind. Apparently satisfied, he slipped his other arm beneath my knees and stood up again. I wrapped my arms around his neck and dropped my head on his shoulder because my head was spinning and felt too heavy to hold up.

"I didn't get to say goodbye," I muttered.

"What did he do to you?" he asked sharply.

"Date rape drug, I think," I slurred. "Something in my tea, anyways. But you rescued me."

"I need to take you home."

"Can't. Need my car. And my suitcase," I pointed out, holding onto consciousness with a supreme effort.

He kissed me, to shut me up, I think. "I'll get them for you later," he said when he lifted his head to look down at me again. "Right now I just want to be sure you and the babe are safe."

My stomach went weightless. I had a feeling I was no longer on the ground, but I wasn't entirely certain. I struggled to remain conscious just a few minutes longer. There was something I wanted say, but I was having a hard time thinking of it. "Take care of yourself, Gideon," I murmured finally.

Light was shining in my eyes when I woke up. I felt like I'd been on a drinking binge. Everything on me hurt, but my head most of all. Groaning, I rolled over in the bed, dragging the pillow over my head to block out the light.

Sleep eluded me. Finally, I threw the pillow off and struggled upright, thoroughly confused when I looked around at my room. I frowned, but to save my life I couldn't remember getting there. A few snatches of memory flitted through my mind, but it was like a dream one couldn't quite remember, just random, blurred images.

I had gone back to Hicksville, though. I remembered that. I'd gone with Gideon to find his sword because he needed it to get home.

The sudden urge to blubber like a baby rolled over me without warning like a tidal wave.

I couldn't remember anything about last night--not after seeing the sword. Gideon had it now, though. I knew that. Had he brought me home? Or had I, horror of horrors, driven myself and lost all memory of it?

I supposed it didn't really matter. I was home. I'd done what I'd set out to do. I'd helped Gideon. I didn't want to think about the enemy he'd gone after, but I knew he had. I comforted myself with the knowledge that at least he had a weapon now to defend himself with.

A few painkillers and a shower later, I still felt like shit. I spent most of the day lying around the house and sleeping. I spent the following day almost the same way.

On the third morning, I got up and kicked myself in the ass. I was going to be a mom. I was supposed to be planning, celebrating--looking forward to the rest of my life.

After I'd showered and dressed, I went out for boxes and to rent a moving trailer. I wasn't carrying that much with me--the house was furnished. By the time I'd packed up what I wanted to take with me I discovered I didn't even really need the trailer. I threw the boxes into it anyway.

I still had a month left on my lease. After wrangling with the manager a while I finally paid the thieving bastard for the month I wasn't going to be in the apartment and left. As soon as I'd made all the calls I needed to to have the utilities turned off, I got in my car and drove away without looking back.

I wasn't going to look back at all, I told myself. I was just going to look forward from now on.

I entertained myself on the drive to the farm with deciding on a decorating theme for the kid's room.

I remembered as I drove up in front of the house that I'd forgotten to cancel my appointment with the obstetrician. I dismissed it. I needed a local doctor now and I might not even have to wait three or four months just to get an appointment.

The work I'd paid for had been done since I'd been here last, most of it anyway.

I hadn't had the lights turned on and the well wouldn't work without electricity.

Unhitching the trailer without emptying it, I rushed back into town to take care of that and beg them to send someone out so I wouldn't have to sit in the dark. The woman promised to try, but she didn't look very hopeful of actually managing it. Since I didn't think she'd manage it either, I stopped by *the* supermarket and bought bottled water and candles.

I was sitting at the kitchen table like someone about to perform a séance when the lights abruptly came on. I leapt up from the table with an Indian war whoop and did a little dance around the kitchen table.

When I'd made the circuit, I came face to face with a grinning face at the kitchen door. My heart nearly stopped.

"Everything working now?"

I turned red as a beet. Moving to the door I snatched it open and stared at the utility man, trying not to think about the hopeful jerk my heart had given when I saw a male face in the glass. "I was afraid I'd have to spend my first night here in the dark."

"Mildred told me you were going to be out here alone in the dark if I didn't come. I couldn't have that. You want to check the tap and make sure the pump's on?"

"Oh. Good idea!" I moved to the sink and checked. "Yahoo! That's working too! I don't know how to thank you enough for coming out so late."

He grinned at me. "You can let me take you out sometime."

I stared at him blankly, abruptly uncomfortable. Get back up on that horse, girl! I chided myself, the sooner the better. He's cute. He's got charm. "Maybe when I'm settled in?"

When he'd left, my shoulders slumped with relief, and then I kicked myself. A hair of the dog, Nicole!

But I didn't want a hair of the damned dog. I wanted Gideon.

I wasn't going to think about that, though. I'd promised myself I wasn't going to look back.

Settling in took so much work that time flew for me. I didn't have much to move in, but there was a hell of a lot of stuff to wade through and move out. My mother, apparently, had never thrown anything away--so much for thinking she wasn't already dotty before she left the farm. I found boxes filled with nothing but used wrapping paper and bows, stacks of newspapers, magazines dating back to forever.

I'd hired workers to take care of the repairs I didn't feel competent to handle, but there were a lot of 'small' things I had to take care of myself. Before I knew it a week had passed.

Half way through my second week in my new home I heard a knock at the front door. Startled, I backed down the ladder I was working on and stepped in the tray of paint I'd left at the bottom. "Shit! Damn it to hell! I'm coming! Give me a minute." I yelled the last in the direction of the front door. "Or maybe a half hour," I muttered to myself.

Slipping my shoe off, I hopped on one foot to the bathroom and shoved my foot into the tub. The shower came on instead of the tub spout, thoroughly drenching me. Fuming, I finished rinsing the paint off my leg and grabbed a towel, drying off as I hobbled through the house with one shoe on and one off.

When I'd snatched the door open, I simply stared blankly at the man standing there, trying to get my mind around the strangeness of seeing him dressed like an ordinary human being.

He stared back at me, his gaze traveling slowly down my paint and water spattered form before it returned to my face.

"I thought you'd gone home," I managed finally.

Something flickered in his eyes. "I couldn't. I missed you."

My chin wobbled. "I don't think I can do this anymore, Gideon. I was just starting to get used to not having you around. I really do love fucking you, but...."

"I love everything about you. I don't want you to get used to not having me around."

I blinked in surprise. "What did you say?"

He hooked a hand behind my head and jerked me tightly up against him, smiling down at me. "I could not go back. I've no heart for the war anymore, and I could not survive long anyway when I can think of nothing but being with you. I will stay with you and our child."

"Here?" I didn't realize until much later that he'd spoken of my pregnancy as if it was something he'd known all along--but then, perhaps he had. The Elumi were bound to be aware that they were potent breeders, on human females, anyway.

He looked around the house. "Yes. Here. Wherever you are."

I didn't know whether to laugh or cry. I did a little of both. "You sure you're cut out for this world? You're not going to change your mind? I love you, too, but I don't think I could stand...."

He kissed me. I think it was just to shut me up, but it still felt absolutely wonderful!

The End

DARK THRALL

By

Celeste Anwar

Chapter One

Once upon a time, Raphael had been the greatest seducer in all the land of Pearthen. His sexual prowess was renowned, and his skills in the bedroom highly sought by the voracious and timid alike.

Raphael loved women. He loved their skin and smell, tasting their curves and breasts, listening to their lilting voices. He enjoyed wooing them almost as much as he enjoyed making love to them. He'd had the pleasure of many courtships--far more than he cared to admit, especially in light of the fact that it was because of a woman that he'd been permanently banished to Earth. He had no hope of regaining entry into Pearthen, and since he'd become one of the fallen, he'd been unable to settle down into the comfort of his old ways.

Even before he had been banished, Raphael had always preferred to make love, not war, as the Earth saying went. There was certainly no incentive for him to hunt down his enemies after he had been expelled from Pearthen, when doing so would not regain the favor he had lost or free him from his banishment, and yet he had been forced into fight and/or flight too many times to count.

Raphael was tired. He was miserable, and he was lonelier than he had ever believed possible.

He had endured the misery of having no company but his own for quite some time before it dawned upon him that, just as he had no reason to fight his enemies, he also had no reason or incentive to abide by the laws of Pearthen which forbade him to interact with humans.

He lived on Earth now--forever. He was an Earth person, if not a human. There was no reason at all why he should not settle among them and look about for a companion and produce a child.

All he needed to do was to find the right woman, but to do so he realized he must first learn to blend in with the native population. As little as he cared what the laws of his former land were, he had learned a lesson from his banishment. He could not flaunt his conduct. If the humans realized that he walked among them it might create a disturbance that the Elumi would notice and then banishment would not be his punishment. He would be beheaded instead.

After observing the mating habits of humans for quite a while, he finally decided that he had mastered the technique and decided that it was time to test his knowledge. Since the majority of the mating appeared to take place in specific buildings in the city that he'd chosen to live in, he shifted into his purely human form and procured himself clothing that he thought would be suitable for the ritual.

When he was satisfied that he was dressed properly to pass, and enticingly enough to attract the female of the species, he made his way to the gathering place he had chosen and hit his first road block. The man at the door demanded ID and ten bucks. As far as he knew, bucks were deer, a species of cattle known to roam the forests of Earth. And not only was he not certain how he would catch these animals, but he also wasn't sure how he was to get them to the man.

Deciding, finally, that perhaps he hadn't observed closely enough, he moved aside and waited for a human man to go through. He was distracted by the fact that there were far more females going in than there were men. And not only did the guard at the door not ask for ID, he also didn't ask for ten bucks. Thoroughly confused by now, and far more interested in following the women in than waiting to see more, Raphael was just wondering if perhaps he should draw the man off into the alley and challenge him to a fight, when a male human arrived. The male human was asked to produce an ID and ten bucks, just as he had been, which at least relieved him of the suspicion that he'd been singled out.

Curiously enough, the man pulled out a small container and handed the guard a thin rectangle and a green piece of paper. The guard looked the stiff rectangle over, looked at the man, and handed it back. He put the piece of green paper in a drawer, hit the back of the man's hand with something, and the man went inside.

Raphael retreated a short distance to think that over. Obviously, what he needed was one of those square things, because that had the ID and the ten bucks in it. He decided he would have to relieve one of the human males of one of those objects.

Retreating to the corner of the building, he propped one shoulder against it and settled to wait. He'd been waiting for a few minutes when a likely looking prey appeared. Sizing him up, Raphael decided this one would be easier to take than most, not that he was particularly worried about it. He knew he was a good bit stronger than the strongest of human males, but he thought that it wouldn't work the best in the world if he found it necessary to struggle with the man. It might draw unwanted attention.

This one was a full head shorter than him and as thin as a willow switch. Rafael was fairly certain there'd be no problem at all. As the man walked by him, he grabbed him by the scruff of his neck and hauled him into the alley.

"I have need of your ... thing," Raphael said, slamming his victim into the wall.

The male's mouth worked, but no sound emerged. His eyes looked like they would pop from his head.

"I need your thing," Raphael said more emphatically.

"Oh fuck," the man finally said.

Raphael frowned. He knew that word. *That* word definitely lay in the range of his vocabulary, but there was no way in hell that he was going to fuck a male to get what he needed. "No fuck. Just give it to me."

"What do you want?" the man whined.

"It's sort of ... square. And it has ID and ten bucks."

The guy looked almost relieved. "God damned foreigners can't even speak English and they're robbing people...." He dragged something from his pocket and held it out.

Raphael released him and took it. "Thank you," he said politely. "You can go now."

He waited until he'd seen the man run away. When he was certain the man was gone, he went back up to the guard at the door.

The guard looked him over. "I told you you had to have an ID and ten bucks. What's the matter? You deaf?"

Forcing a feral smile, Raphael handed him the object he had procured. The guard looked at him strangely. After a moment, he opened it up. Sure enough, it contained one of the square things. He took that out, looked it over, and then looked at Raphael.

"This says your name is Chris Smith. You're twenty one years old, blonde haired, blue eyed, and you weigh one hundred and twenty five pounds ... and you're female."

Raphael frowned. The man had spoken much faster than he could grasp the strange words. He could see, though, that the man was waiting for some sort of response. "Yes."

The man stared at him for several moments and finally took a piece of paper out of the wallet and handed it back to him. "Next time, try rolling a man. Just a suggestion."

Raphael was still thinking that over as he made his way into the building. It worried him to think he might have difficulty telling the male human from the female. He had been certain that the human he had captured had been a man. He'd never had that problem before, and he began to wonder if he really did want a female human if it was so difficult to tell them apart from the males.

He was distracted from his disturbing thoughts by the deafening rumble of thunder inside the building. It was also far darker inside than it was outside. Flickering lights added to the confusion. He stopped when he reached the main room, still debating with himself as he surveyed the sea of humans as to whether to proceed or to retreat until he had had time to study the humans a little more closely. There was hardly even room to move. He realized, however, as he glanced towards one particular spot in the room, that this was definitely the place.

There, men and women bumped and gyrated in some strangely erotic mating dance. Lust immediately surged through his blood, seeming almost to pound in time to the beat he could hear in the noise. He would find the woman here.

Threading his way between tables and chairs and people of all shapes, sizes, and colors, he stopped when he reached the mating floor, surveying the possibilities. Almost at once, his gaze was drawn to one particular female and a sensation like he'd been punched in the belly struck him. Her coloring and build reminded him painfully of the women he had known in his own world, but the similarity ended there. She was tall for a human female but she was not as tall as an Elumi women, and she was not muscular as the warrior women of Pearthen were. She looked as if she would be soft to the touch. Her hips curved outward, her waist deeply inward. When she turned, he saw the soft globes of her breasts bounced gently and swayed mesmerizingly with her movement. The way she moved set blood to pounding in his temples and his groin. He knew the moment his gaze met hers that fate had smiled upon him. This was the woman he wanted. This was the woman who would bear his child.

* * * *

"Oh. My. God. Look! He's beautiful! I can't remember the last time I saw something that looked that good," Diana gushed. "Jesus, I could lick him like a tootsie pop. MmmMMMMMM."

"Chocolate or vanilla?" Isabel asked with a laugh.

"Little bit a both. Long black hair, dark eyes, muscles everywhere. I think he might be Indian. Da-yum. Whatever he is, I don't care. I'll take one."

Izzy couldn't help herself. The way Diana was drooling, she had to see. As casually as she could, she turned to look. Almost as if her movement had drawn his attention, he seemed to zero in on her. They're gazes collided across the room. The man was fuckin' tall! Her heart was hammering like a war drum when she whirled back around. "Dammit! I made eye contact. You know you can't make eye contact in these places. Diana, why the hell didn't you warn me he was looking this way?"

She chuckled. "Didn't figure it mattered."

"Is he gone?"

Diana's eyes widened. "Uh...."

"No. He is here," a man said behind her.

Oh shit.... Izzy turned around and met ... chest. Very nice, mus-cly chest. The black jersey top he wore left little to the imagination and exposed his belly and a happy trail that disappeared into his tight black jeans. He was also sporting a damned impressive erection.

"I would like to perform the mating dance with you," he said above her.

Izzy tore her gaze from his crotch and tilted her head up. He was at *least* half a head taller than her, and she was six foot tall. That put him at like ... what? Six foot five? She'd never been around a guy that tall. She was pretty sure she didn't like it. "Uh. What?"

He frowned and looked confused. "I would like to perform the mating dance with you," he said a little louder. The music stopped about halfway through the sentence. Into a virtually dead silence echoed the words "mating dance with you."

Izzy felt her face turn bright red. Diana cackled. "Another time," Izzy said politely. "This dance is over."

Another song started about that time, but Izzy made good her escape, trying to batter her way between gyrating dancers and the exodus of those leaving the dance floor. Someone snagged her arm, jerking her to a halt.

She knew exactly who it was, but she stopped and threw him a glance that was a mixture of indignation and surprise. "Excuse you."

Looking uncomfortable, he released her arm. After glancing around for several moments, as if he was trying to figure out where he was at, he looked down at her again. "I did this wrong?" he asked.

Izzy was intrigued, in spite of herself. She was a sucker for a sexy accent, and he had one she'd never encountered before. Besides, as intimidating as his size was, Diana was right, he was gorgeous. "You're not from around here, are you?"

He looked downright uneasy when she asked that. "I am human."

Izzy felt her jaw drop. That was probably the most peculiar statement she'd ever heard, even from a foreigner.

I am American, she could understand, but I am human? What was with that? Obviously, he didn't speak English nearly as well as she'd thought at first. She sighed. She'd always been a sucker for stray cats--especially when they were cute. "Come on, I'll buy you a drink."

He didn't argue. He followed her as docilely as a puppy. When she glanced back at him, she saw that his gaze was riveted to her ass. He didn't look the least bit disconcerted when he met her gaze. There wasn't much subterfuge about the guy. She decided she liked that though.

"I like that," he said, pointing at her butt.

Izzy stared at him a moment. "Thank you."

"You're welcome," he said politely, and then smiled as if he realized he'd said something clever.

He had a very sexy smile ... and dimples. She'd always been a sucker for dimples.

They settled at the table that Diana was already occupying. Diana looked him over like he was a choice piece of beef. "Do you have any brothers?" she asked.

He frowned. "I don't know this word."

Diana exchanged a glance with Izzy. "Guess that's a no," Diana said glumly. "You know any others that look like you do?"

"Not here," he said.

"What would you like to drink?" Izzy cut in.

He stared at her a moment and finally looked around. "One of those," he said, pointing.

Diana gave him a look. "The girl or the drink?"

Izzy kicked her under the table. The guy glared at her. "I have chosen this woman," he said, pointing at Izzy.

Izzy and Diana exchanged another glance. Izzy turned to look in the direction he'd pointed. The woman at the table next to them had one of those fruity, tropical mixed drinks with a little pink umbrella sticking out of it. "One of those?" she asked a little doubtfully.

"Yes," he said. "Thank you."

Izzy and Diana exchanged another look. Shrugging, Izzy signaled for the waitress. "What is it called?" she asked him.

"What?" he asked curiously.

"The drink? What's the name of the drink?"

"I will ask."

She grabbed his hand when he moved to stand up. "Never mind, I'll just tell the waitress you want one that looks like that. What's your name, anyway?"

"Raphael."

"Ooooh," Diana purred. "I like that."

Izzy kicked her under the table. "Go find your own, dammit."

Sighing, Diana got up and left. As she passed by the back of Izzy's chair, she leaned down. "Find out where his friends hang out, dammit. I want one of those."

Izzy nodded.

"What did she ask?" he asked curiously.

"She said she wanted one just like you. She wants me to ask you where to find them."

He looked surprised. "She cannot go there. *I* cannot even go there anymore."

That sounded intriguing, but since Izzy was in the process of ordering drinks, she had time to consider whether she really wanted to know that much about him or not. She finally decided, since this was most likely going to be a one night thing, there wasn't much point in pursuing that interesting little tidbit.

She couldn't help but notice he hadn't asked what her name was. "My name's Isabel. Izzy for short," she volunteered. "Are you Italian by any chance?"

He seemed to think it over. "No," he said finally.

That accent was driving her crazy. Tall, dark, and named Raphael. Where would he be from? "Spanish?" she said.

"No."

"South American?"

An expression of comprehension crossed his features. "I am from the Kingdom Marceena on Pearthen, high Earth."

Izzy frowned. "I never was worth a shit at geography, but that don't sound at all familiar to me. Is that someplace in Europe?"

"No." He hesitated for several moments. "You are a beautiful woman. Your eyes remind me of the sea of Benatar."

Since her eyes were mud brown, Izzy had a little difficulty with that compliment. "Thank you. I think."

The drinks arrived. Izzy was never more grateful for a distraction. Digging into her purse, she produced her wallet and paid for the drinks. When the waitress had left, she noticed Raphael watched her place her wallet in her pocketbook. She felt a little uneasy about that.

"What are those green things?" he asked curiously.

It took her a moment to figure out what he was asking. "You mean the money?" Izzy asked blankly. "How are you getting around if you don't know what money is?"

"I haven't been here that long. This is a thing of value, that you trade for other things of value?"

"What planet are you from?"

He looked a little surprised, doubtful, uneasy--maybe even a little pleased, as if he couldn't help but be pleased that she'd noticed he was different but at the same time it worried him that she had. "Pearthen."

Izzy was beginning to think that they had a little more than a language barrier going on here. The man had a body to die for, a gorgeous face, an accent that made her warm and wet, and he didn't really *seem* stupid, but he seemed *very* strange. She might've thought he was a mental patient, but he didn't seem crazy, just sort of ... alien.

She took a few swigs of her drink. When she looked at him again, she discovered he'd downed the entire contents of the glass and was munching on fruit. He pulled a wallet out of his jeans pocket and opened it up. Pulling the bills out, he laid them on the table and asked her to explain how much they would buy.

The guy was needy in more ways than one, couldn't count his money and didn't have a lot to count when it came to that. Izzy decided that Plan A was really the best one to go for. A one nighter, definitely.

She was a little unnerved by the mothering instinct he provoked in her. He seemed--was so lost, so out of his element that she had to fight the protective urge that rose inside her, but she didn't want anyone else's problems. She had enough problems of her own. "What do you say we just go to my place? Cut the bullshit and get down to it?"

He looked surprised but pleased. "We fuck now?"

Izzy chuckled. "Not 'til we get to my place."

Grabbing his hand, she led him from the club. As they threaded there way through the crowd toward the exit, she caught Diana's eye as she passed and threw her friend a wave and a wink. Diana glared at her and shot her a bird.

Izzy was still chuckling as they left the club. When she glanced at Raphael, she saw that he was shooting her a bird.

"What is this?" he asked.

"It's a hand signal."

He winked at her. "What is this?"

"You don't miss much, do you?"

"No. What is it for?"

Izzy chuckled. "Diana's my best girlfriend. I told her I was taking you to my place. She signaled back that she understood." She felt a little uneasy about his ready acceptance of her explanation. She supposed she really ought to have gone into more detail--explained that such gestures could have a wealth of meaning--but she figured that was close enough to what had transpired between her and Diana.

Chapter Two

They took a cab to her apartment. She figured it was best since there was no telling where Raphael lived, whether he'd even *have* a bed, or any kind of protection. Unlocking the door when they reached her apartment, she entered, flipping the lights on as she went. He followed behind her, leaving the front door open.

"Shut that," she said. "Do you want anything to drink?"

"I've had enough," he said.

All righty then. Cut to the chase. Smiling, she strolled back to him, taking his hand in hers and leading him to her bedroom. She released his hand when they reached the bedroom and moved to the bedside lamp, flipping the switch twice to keep it dim, but with enough light to get down to business. "I hope you still have that play purty ready for me," she said in a purring voice, turning to look at him where he stood near the door.

Moving to the bed, she sat on the edge and crooked her finger at him in a "come hither" gesture. He didn't need much provocation. He sauntered across the room, peeling his shirt off as he approached her, and then unbuttoning his pants.

Izzy resisted the urge to fan herself at the private strip show. He might be strange, but his body was damn fine. She couldn't wait to touch him, could feel her body revving already when she hadn't even touched him yet. She'd never been with a man so fit before. Most didn't give a shit about how they looked.

She just hoped he was good in bed.

He stopped in front of her, his chest rising and falling with deep, excited breaths.

Her pulse quickened. She hooked her fingers in his waistband, tugging him closer to unzip his fly. The zipper sounded loud in the room, heightening her anticipation. She parted his fly and pushed his pants down his hips.

He wasn't wearing underwear.

Izzy felt her eyes widen as she revealed his erection. His cock stood out from his narrow hips, thick and engorged to a deep, fleshy red.

It seemed a shame to cover it up, but mama didn't raise no fool. She leaned over and took a condom out of her bedside table, tearing it open with her teeth.

"What is that?" he asked.

Izzy rolled it onto his length and looked up. "Protection? Tell me you've used condoms before."

"What is it for?"

Great. One of those. She shouldn't have been surprised. Most men would rather play dumb, and this guy was obviously not American--he had to be from some backwater country that didn't believe in giving women the option of *not* being pregnant. "It's to keep your little tadpoles from swimming up my channel and getting me pregnant."

He frowned but said nothing.

Izzy peeled off her top and threw it on the floor, cutting off further conversation. His frown turned as he clenched his jaw and looked at her hungrily.

Heat bloomed at her breasts and spread up her neck and down her belly.

He knelt on the floor and cupped her breasts. A sound that was half groan, half sigh escaped his mouth.

He buried his face at her neck, sucking the hollow behind her ear as he massaged her breasts.

Fire shot through her blood, warming her, making her wet with desire. She moaned and clutched his forearms, easing her legs open to allow him closer access.

He nibbled her neck, up and around her jaw until he found her lips and covered her mouth with his own. His tongue plunged inside, tangled with hers.

Izzy sucked his tongue, reveling in his moan of pleasure into her mouth. He tasted wild, exotic and tangy from the drink and fruit he'd consumed. She ran her hands down his back, cupping his tight ass. Mmmmm. He felt good. She'd never be able to go back to scrawny men now. Just feeling his muscles flex had her sex watering in anticipation.

He groaned into her mouth and pushed her back on the bed. Breaking this kiss, breathing raggedly, he crawled on top of her and covered her with his body.

He ran his lips down her chin and throat, kissing her collarbone, her chest. Ragged, hot breath wafted her skin, his tongue cooling and heating her all at once.

He reached her bra and nibbled her nipple through the satiny fabric.

Tendrils of muffled sensation crawled along her nerves.

Izzy groaned in frustration.

He pulled at the fabric with his teeth and fingers, then lifted his head to study her chest with a frown. Impatient, he snapped the bra in front, jouncing her breasts free.

A satisfied sound rumbled in his chest. He descended, ravishing her breasts, nipping, nibbling, sucking. He seemed everywhere at once, his hands, his mouth, his tongue. She felt devoured, like a delicacy he couldn't seem to get enough of.

He was just rough enough to leave her wanting more.

Izzy touched his massive shoulders, excited by the muscles working there, his arms bulging. She could feel the strained power in his body, his excitement invoked by her body and exploratory touches.

Her breasts felt heavy, swollen. Her nipples excruciatingly erect and painfully ignored when he moved down her ribcage in a nibbling path to her belly. He met the waistband of her skirt.

She gasped when he ripped it, too, tugging it off her hips with impatient roughness that turned her on more than she thought possible.

His callused palms touched her hips, eased off her panties until she was completely naked beneath him.

She'd had enough foreplay, and yet, she couldn't seem to encourage him enough to go ahead and take her. He seemed determined to take his time, to stoke her arousal as high as he could before going further.

She enjoyed it, but she hated it.

He nibbled her lower belly, her hips. His fingers teased the thin runway of hair leading to her pussy. Her stomach clenched on a spasm of arousal. Her cleft tightened, and she could feel her arousal saturating her folds.

He nipped her mound with his teeth, surprising a gasp out of her. Her thighs tensed as he pushed them apart. She bit her bottom lip, clutching the covers in a death grip as he nuzzled her slit.

She could feel his breath cooling her wet folds, heightening sensation, deepening arousal. When his tongue swiped her slit, her body reacted with a violent spasm of pleasure. She bucked, sucking in a hard, loud breath as he plunged his tongue into her vagina.

Muffled groans and slurps reached her ears, breaking through the pleasure hazing her mind. Her clit throbbed, pulsing with the rapid beat of her heart.

"You taste different than I expected," he murmured when he pulled free, breathing heavily on her sex. "But very good. I enjoy tasting you." He nibbled her clit, sucking it into his mouth like a sugary treat. "Mmmmm. The more I have, the more I want," he said, finishing on a growl as he buried his face in her cunt.

Izzy clamped her thighs around his head, surely smothering him, but she couldn't help herself. She arched, bringing her hips closer to him, grinding herself against his mouth, reaching for the ultimate bliss.

He pried her legs off and moved over her, settling his hips between her legs. His chest brushed her achy nipples, squeezing her breasts as he lowered to her.

The thick head of his cock nudged her entrance, moving into position to part the tender lips of her vagina.

He nuzzled her temple, holding himself above her enough to avoid crushing the breath out of her lungs. He moved his hips, rocking, teasing her with the slide of his length against her, slipping in her juices, moving maddeningly against her clit.

She jerked involuntarily, coming up hard against him. Izzy groaned in frustration, moving beneath him, her vaginal muscles clenching with carnal hunger.

He pushed forward suddenly, the thick head stretching her opening, moving inside with the sensation of a cork exploding from a bottle. Her body's lubrication increased, making her wetter with the edge of pain, the forceful invasion.

"Isabel," he groaned, kissing her ear as plunged to the hilt and sent every nerve ending in her cunt screaming with undeniable pleasure.

* * * *

Raphael panted above her, holding perfectly still as her woman's channel clamped down on him in a rippling movement that had sweat popping out along his skin. His cock felt on fire, liquid heat engulfing his length. His muscles burned with restraint.

She moaned beneath him, trying to move on his cock, urging him to action. Her thighs slid against his legs, so soft and satiny that he ached to touch them, explore her with his tongue. He'd been too eager to begin--he realized his mistake now, his impatience. Her fingertips danced across his back and shoulders, creating a firestorm of pleasure he hadn't experienced in years.

He gritted his teeth, trying to control himself.

She was so damnably tight, almost milking him. He'd never experienced anything like it before in his life.

Even the sleeve she'd put on him couldn't muffle the sensations rioting from the shocking clutch of her muscles. Her body wanted the seed he would put into her. The condom was no barrier to him, should he wish it otherwise, and he did. He would put a babe in her belly tonight.

Sweet mercy. He shuddered. His body shook with a lust he couldn't explain.

He groaned and pulled from her. As he drew slowly back, she tightened on him, her muscles trembling.

He propped on an elbow, moving a hand between their bodies to stroke her clitoris. It was warm and swollen and wet, plumping to a rigid pinpoint of need the moment he touched it. She cried out his name, arching her back as he tweaked the point and flexed his cock deep within her.

Raphael had never known a time when his control had been so weak, his sexual appetite so great. How could this human arouse such hidden desires from him?

The knowledge that she would now be his increased his appetite, seared his brain. His woman.

He slid his lips over her ear, bending deeply to reach her jaw. He sucked the sweet skin at the corner of her lips, pinching her clit with his fingers and rolling it until she whimpered and her back arched.

She was intoxicating, her smell, her taste. Had Elumi women been so sweet? So seductive? Was he just so desperate that any woman would feel so good?

His blood thundered through his veins, making his cock throb with the violent beat of his heart.

"Raphael," she cried out desperately, digging her short nails into his shoulders.

The gripping tunnel of flesh encasing his length was too much to resist, maddening him with desire. A savage growl ripped from his throat, and he plunged inside her once more. Propping his arms on either side of her head, he thrust into her, groaning as her body loved him, coaxed him to the pinnacle of pleasure.

Her body arched. She cried out, going rigid beneath him, and he knew she'd reached her climax. Her cries echoed around him until he wanted to explode.

He closed his eyes, driving into her again and again. The milking pull of her muscles was hypnotic, drugging.

He gave in to the violent need taking root, so savage it threatened to tear him apart. Pleasure erupted inside him, making his cock grow harder, stiff as an oak shaft. He pushed, melding through the thin sleeve to spew his seed deep inside her as it erupted from his cock head. He orgasmed, releasing just enough within her depths to secure the creation of his child ... and the binding of his beautiful Isabel to him.

Chapter Three

Euphoria such as he had never known warmed Raphael as he gazed down at his prize, stroking her soft flesh, which pleased him so much that he could not resist touching her, even though she slept now. He could not recall ever having experienced a union more completely satisfying. He wondered if it was entirely due to the fact that she was his perfect mate or if it was because he had placed his son in her belly.

He thought, perhaps, that it was some of both.

She would breed a fine son for him. He supposed that he should be appalled that it would not be Elumi, but a combination of human and Elumi, but he found that it pleased him to think of their seeds combining as he had mated with her, that he would have a child that was a part of him and a part of her.

Perhaps he would have felt much the same if he had chosen an Elumi woman, but he had never had any interest in doing so when he had had the opportunity and he no longer had that option.

The wonder of this, and a good part of his euphoria, was that he no longer cared.

He frowned thoughtfully after several moments.

He had been completely focused for some time on finding a companion. He had not thought beyond that and he realized that he had erred. He would be a father. He must consider how best to protect his child. It would be fragile. There was much that it would need to learn and grow into the strong son that he had envisioned. Plans needed to be made and executed before he welcomed it into this world.

With that thought, he skated his hand downward over Isabel's body, settling his palm on her flat belly. Had he sparked life, he wondered with a flicker of doubt? He could sense nothing, but he realized after a moment that he was simply far too anxious. Days would pass before he could be certain, perhaps many days.

And in that time, his child and his woman would be most vulnerable.

Frowning, he sat up abruptly.

It was not safe for him to linger near his woman--not now. He should have thought about that, instead of indulging himself. Their mingled scents might draw his enemies.

Standing abruptly, he moved into her bathroom and bathed himself, carefully removing as much of her scent from himself as he could. When he was reasonably satisfied, he shut the water off and left her abode. Morphing, he took to the air and returned to the abandoned building that he had claimed as shelter for many months.

He began to pace and think when he had alit, trying to decide if it would be best to stay as far away from Isabel as he could, or if it would be better to stay near her to guard her and his child.

Finally, he decided that, for a few days at least, it would be best to keep his distance. He could use that time to find a safe place for his family. The centers of population drew the fallen. There, they knew they were most likely to find the enemies they sought, hiding themselves among the humans.

He must find a place of remoteness, and when he had, he would need to fill it with the things that would bring pleasure and comfort to his companion, for he knew humans were creatures of comfort.

* * * *

Izzy stretched and yawned, her back muscles tightening with the movement. "Mmmmmm," she hummed, leisurely opening her eyes to an empty bed and room.

That was a surprise. She had thought Raphael was the needy type, the sort to want to hang on for a while--the kind of man that inevitably wore out his welcome before he left and usually had to be run off.

It was a little disconcerting to discover he wasn't quite what she'd expected. Maybe he'd been playing her?

Dismay hit her like a brick. Rolling out of bed abruptly, she looked around a little frantically for her pocketbook. Relief filled her when she discovered it was untouched, all of her credit cards and money accounted for, but then she was almost more puzzled than before. He'd seemed lost, but wasn't? It hadn't been scam--which she should have thought about before. She was just damned lucky it hadn't been!

Shrugging, she dropped the purse and headed for the bathroom to perform her morning ablutions and get ready for work.

The rat race sucked, but someone had to do it.

When she got to work, Diana met her before she'd even gotten settled at her desk.

"Dish, girl. I want every nasty, raunchy detail. Did you cum more than once? What did his dick look like? Is he a good kisser?"

"Jesus, Diana!" Izzy looked around to make sure no one was near enough to hear Diana's excited chatter. When she saw the coast was clear, she looked at her friend a long moment, trying to decide how much to divulge. She didn't know why she wasn't comfortable talking about her night with Raphael, but she found that she *was* reluctant. "He was ... good."

Disbelief was patent in Diana's expression. She rolled her eyes. "Come off it. Is that all you're gonna tell?"

"All right. He was very good." Isabel grinned. "That's all I'm sayin'. Ladies don't talk."

Diana gave her a look. "I ain't never heard that one before. Give it up. It had to be better than what I got saddled with last night. He pumped on top of me--I kid you not--three times, came, then got up to leave. I was glad to see his sorry ass go. Not only did I not get my cookie, I didn't even have fun *almost* getting my cookie! That guy was so lame! I can't believe I saw Rafe first and *you* got him! I am so jealous!"

Izzy patted her shoulder sympathetically. "I asked Raphael like you asked me. He said he knew others like him, but you couldn't go there. He said he couldn't even go there anymore. Isn't that strange?"

Diana had perked up immediately at the first part of Izzy's speech, but by the time Izzy finished she was looking morose. "Guess they're not handing out visas, huh?"

Izzy frowned. "I don't know. I have to wonder ... Whoops. There's the boss. Scram."

Diana scrambled back to her work station, and Izzy turned on her computer to answer customer complaints. She loved Diana and normally told her everything, but this time was different. She might have thought it was because Diana was acting all weird and jealous, but she didn't really believe, deep down that Diana was that serious. She probably was envious--she would've been if the shoe had been on the other foot--but Diana knew the score. A guy picked whoever he picked. A gal said yes or no.

It wasn't about Diana. She couldn't quite figure out her hesitation in talking about Raphael, but it wasn't because she was afraid it would hurt her feelings. She just hadn't wanted to share. It puzzled her--*he* puzzled her. She was being silly, she knew, but damn, the boy knew how to work *it*.

There was just something about him....

She couldn't recall ever coming so hard in all her life, and she was a little embarrassed about how vocal she'd been the night before. Even after he'd rolled off her and pulled his dick out, tremors of pleasure still rippled through her for almost an hour afterward.

There was no explaining that, and she wondered now just how alert she'd been. She'd had a good bit to drink. No doubt her memory was fuzzy on all the particulars.

It was just as well. She doubted very much that she'd ever see him again.

A man like that was too sexy to be with one woman.

* * * *

Diana thought the best cure for the no man blues was to go out clubbing. Since it was the weekend, again--she wasn't about to let Izzy sit at home and be miserable by her lonesome, which was why she was now sitting at the bar, letting the bone shattering beat of dance music vibrate her organs to liquid form.

Diana went off dancing, but Izzy didn't feel up to it, so she moved to a table in the back, as far from the noise as she could get while still maintaining a good scoping position.

The club was packed with pumping, grinding, sweaty bodies. Izzy sipped a coke, surveying the room. She'd pretty much been satisfied with her last encounter, and she wasn't really looking to score--which was one of the reasons she was sticking with plain coke--no alcoholic beverages tonight. She wasn't taking any chances she would fall for the next guy's line.

All the men looked basically the same to her: average, nothing special but nothing bad--just ... boring. As she watched them, she kept thinking about the way Raphael had stood apart from the crowd in every way--just plain magnificent even before she'd taken a roll with him.

And that had been mind boggling.

It was a damned shame he'd turned out to be like so many others, she thought with disgust--eat and run.

She was dwelling a little too much on Raphael, she realized.

Damn, I've got it bad, she thought and then determinedly turned her attention back to the room.

As she looked out over the crowded dance floor, her gaze locked with a man's, as if magnetized.

He stopped and looked at her. The room seemed to disappear. The color of his eyes seemed almost electrical, like a glow jumping out at her across the room. Long blonde hair cascaded over his shoulders, and he was tall--as tall as Raphael. Despite the fact that he was as fair as Raphael had been dark, she couldn't help but wonder if he was of some relation to Raphael. Something in the bone structure of his face seemed familiar, and it couldn't be a coincidence that two extremely tall, well built men would frequent the same club within a week of each other.

Izzy swallowed a sudden lump in her throat when he moved, walking towards her. He stopped when he reached her table and pulled a chair out, sitting down.

She gave him a look, arching a brow. He damn sure hadn't been invited to sit down. What balls!

Tilting his head, he sniffed. "You smell very good."

Goose bumps flitted along her spine--not the happy kind. There was something wrong with this guy. She could practically see aggression oozing from his pores. She was probably just overreacting. She chuckled nervously. "I hope you couldn't smell me across the room."

His lids lowered. He caught her hand where it rested on the table and brought her fingers to his lips. "What if I told you I could?"

Izzy raised her eyebrows and pulled her hand free. His accent perfectly matched Raphael's. Where the hell were these guys coming from? And why were they so fuckin' weird? "Uh. Then I'd have to worry my deodorant's not working like it's supposed to."

He sighed. "You humans can be so crude."

Humans?

Her uneasiness deepened. She'd thought it was kinda cute when Raphael had informed her that he was human. This guy worried her--everything about him, but especially the reference to humans. "I think you better leave. My boyfriend will be back soon."

Her belly clenched as a slow smile curled his lips.

"I count on that." He stood then, bowed, and left.

Izzy was feeling seriously creeped out by the whole episode by the time Diana came back to the table.

"Hey, what's wrong?" she asked, looking Izzy over worriedly.

"Nothing," Izzy said. "I'm just ready to go home. Think you'll be okay here?"

"Yeah. No biggie. Call me tomorrow, okay?"

"Sure."

Grabbing up her purse, Izzy pushed her way through the crowd. She was about halfway through the hallway that led out when she was suddenly grabbed. She reacted violently, expecting that creep had gotten hold of her. Whirling, she slapped at the hand gripping her arm, pulling up short when she saw it was Raphael.

"Christ! You need to learn not to grab people like that," she said, clutching a fist to her racing heart. "You just about gave me a heart attack."

He frowned, his gaze flickering over her assessingly. Catching her hand, he sniffed the backs of her fingers then lifted his head and cast his gaze around the room. There was anger in his eyes when he met her gaze again. "You were with a--man."

Izzy gaped at him and finally snatched her hand back. "I most certainly was not! Not that it's any of your business. I haven't even seen you in a week."

If anything, his frowned deepened. "You are not safe here."

"No shit, Sherlock." At his puzzled look, she dragged in a calming breath and softened her tone. It really wasn't his fault she was upset. Well, it was sort of, because she was really pissed that he'd banged her and disappeared, but he hadn't scared the shit out of her--which had on her edge and was why she was so snappy. "I'm sorry, but I'm having a really bad night."

After studying him a moment, she moved toward him. Looping her arms around his shoulders, she leaned close as she looked up at him. "Want to come to my place?"

His face remained impassive, but she saw his eyes still gleamed with anger. "You are my woman. I protect what is mine."

She could argue with that--odd thing was, she didn't find it nearly as annoying as she would've thought she would-- but right now, as much as she hated to admit needing anyone, she wanted some protection. Or at least the *illusion* of feeling protected.

Instead of arguing, she slipped an arm through his and led him outside. She'd parked her car in the back, and they walked around the building. The streets were devoid of people or cars--most everyone had settled into whatever club they'd chosen for the night, and there'd be no great exodus until after last call.

A streetlight flickered above them. Sounds of bugs tinkling against the glass drifted down.

Raphael stopped abruptly, pulling her up short. Puzzled, uneasy for some reason she couldn't entirely fathom, she tugged his arm. "My car's right there," she said, pointing to the red Dodge.

A rush of wind ruffled her hair. Pulling free from her grasp, Raphael suddenly pushed her away, leaping back even as he sent her flying backwards with the force of his blow. Izzy gasped in stunned surprise and fell on her backside, instantly bruising her tail bone and scraping her palms.

Too stunned to feel anything at all, she looked up to find a man confronting Raphael, the same one that had bothered her in the club.

Oh fuck!

"I knew I'd find you here when I smelled you on your human whore, Raphael," the man growled.

Raphael bared his teeth, circling the stranger in a fighter's stance, slightly hunched over, his arms held out on either side of him.

Abruptly, the man whipped a sword from beneath his overcoat. The blade gleamed wickedly in the light and Izzy felt downright faint looking at it.

Gasping, Izzy scrambled to her feet and looked around quickly for her purse. She found it, dug out the pepper spray buried at the bottom, then fought the urge to giggle hysterically as she thought about how ridiculous it was to use spray against a man wielding a five foot long sword.

Dismissing her misgivings, she shrieked, drawing the man's attention. When his head whipped around in her direction, she screamed again and sprayed him in the face.

"Run!" she yelled at Raphael.

It was right about that time that Izzy discovered that the pepper spray didn't seem to have any effect on him. He roared and charged her, raising his sword.

She couldn't move. Her brain and every muscle in her body seemed to shut down as she stared at the face of death.

Raphael tackled him from the side, knocking him from his path of doom and jump starting her brain into action once more.

Her heart pounded in her throat so hard she felt like throwing up. Gasping, she whirled and headed for her car, frantically trying to find her keys. She found them after a frantic search, jammed the key in the lock and looked around for Raphael.

The two men were locked in a deadly embrace, each one wrestling for dominance, but there was no doubt in Izzy's mind that this was no mere bar fight, but one each man seemed determined to take to the death.

Jumping into her car, Izzy started it, jerking the gear into reverse and flooring it as she backed out of the parking space. She felt the bump and crunch as she connected with another car, but she ignored it, training the headlights on the fighting men. They'd stripped to the waist, both of them--or torn each other's shirts off and they pounded on each other and slung each other around. The blond guy had lost his sword somewhere in the rounds. If she had to, she'd run that bastard down.

Gritting her teeth, she leaned down on the horn. A pathetic, tiny beep whined forth. She grimaced, revving her engine threateningly, turning on her brights.

They released each other at the same instant. Wings sprouted from the man's back and then Raphael's.

Izzy's jaw dropped.

For several moments, Izzy wasn't certain she even breathed. Stunned, she watched as they disappeared into the night sky.

Oh my fucking god!

Still too stunned to behave on any level other than instinct, she punched the car into gear and hit the gas. The tires spun, squealing on pavement several seconds before the car finally lurched forward.

Izzy sped all the way to her apartment. Parking out front, she switched the car off and nearly broke the key trying to get out and climb out of the car at the same time. When she'd managed to scramble out of the car, she ran inside, firmly locking the door behind her before she ventured any further. Still shaking, she grabbed the nearest thing she could find that looked like a weapon--a candle holder--and checked her meager apartment, making sure she was alone before she finally collapsed on the couch.

Her mind seemed to be set on pause. No actual thoughts ran through it--tumultuous emotions but nothing she could grasp. After a few minutes, her mind shifted gears, replaying the scene outside the club over and over again. Wings--both of them. A sword. Strange accents.

They weren't human.

They were angels.

Chapter Four

Isabel shuddered and rubbed her arms to warm herself. The movement produced pain. Her palms hurt. She looked down at them in surprise, soaking in the scrapes and bruises. She'd forgotten that Raphael had pushed her out of the way just as the man leapt toward them and she'd fallen. She was filthy from the pavement and sore. She needed a shower.

It took several tries to get up because her knees were so weak they kept buckling and dropping her back onto the couch. Finally, she managed to lock the watery joints and peeled her clothes off, heading toward the bathroom. She turned the water on until steam filled the cubicle.

Stepping in, she let the water course over her skin, washing away the dirt and ache in her muscles. Her skin turned a bright pink under the onslaught, but she didn't care. It felt good, and she didn't leave until she'd used up all the hot water and her muscles felt like jelly.

Exhausted but at the same time rejuvenated, she dried herself off and slipped into a camisole and panties before leaving the bedroom.

Raphael lay on the couch.

Shock made her take a step back and lean weakly on the door jam. Her heart skipped a beat--stopped dead still in her chest, actually, for several moments.

Battered, bruised, and dirty, he was perfectly still on the couch, lying with his arm draped over his eyes. Something blue trickled down a slash on his arm.

Blood. *Blue* blood.

"How ... how did you get in here," she asked, more than a little weakly.

He moved his arm, lifting up his head to look at her. "There is no lock on Earth that can keep me out--any Elumi for that matter."

Oh god. What the hell did he mean about locks anyway? Was he that good at picking them? "So you *are* an alien?" It was more of a statement than a question.

He frowned. "I am Elumi, from Pearthen. High Earth. It is...." He paused, as if considering how best to explain it. "...another dimension of your planet, but a part of it."

"Like heaven? Y'all looked like angels out there. Except, not any angels I ever heard of." Izzy stayed by the door. She wasn't sure what to expect out of him now, but she felt better having the distance between them at the least.

He waved her words away. "You humans and your preoccupation with the heavens and deities." Pushing himself to his feet, he strode across the room toward her.

Izzy squeaked and backed into the bathroom, locking the door and backing up until her legs hit the toilet.

Raphael moved *through* the door into the bathroom with her.

Her legs gave out as blackness swam across her vision.

The next thing she knew, she was on the couch. Raphael was looking down at her, a half smile curling his lips. "The babe has taken root. I suspected but wasn't certain I had succeeded."

Izzy's eyes rolled around in her head. "Wh ... wha ... what?" She sat up as his meaning hit her. "What baby? What the hell are you talking about?"

He took a seat on the couch beside her drawn up legs. Leaning toward her, he rested a hand on her knee. She slapped it until he pulled it away.

He frowned. "I gave you a baby."

"No hell you didn't."

He looked perplexed. "Why do you yell?"

"No reason. I just like yelling when I hear news like that. How the fuck could you get me pregnant? I put a condom on you myself. If it comes to that, how could you even tell?"

"If I choose to go through a barrier, I can. It matters not where that barrier lies."

Izzy swallowed and touched her stomach. The image of Raphael passing through the door without any trouble flashed in her mind. She felt queasy.

"And the pregnancy thing? How'd you know that?"

"My enemy found you. The change has already begun. My seed has taken root in your belly. He could smell my child within you, as can I."

Changes? Baby? Smells? Izzy's head pounded. She massaged her temples. "What about this guy?" she asked abruptly, her heart clenching in sudden fear. "Is he going to come hunt me down?"

"No. I killed him."

"You what?" she screamed, leaping up from the couch.

He looked at her in surprise. "I could not let him live. He would only have returned, again and again until he killed me. I did not particularly want to die so I killed him."

"Jesus Fucking Christ! What'd you do with the body? Did you leave it there? Are the police going to be hunting you? Or coming here to my apartment?"

He gave her a look--as if she should know better than that. "That is forbidden. Humans are not allowed to know of our existence and they would certainly know if we left bodies lying around. I placed it and the head inside your conveyance until I could heal myself and dispose of it."

"It--and his head?" Izzy asked weakly, feeling faint *and* nauseated. "You're saying--you didn't even have a weapon."

"I used his sword to cut off his head. That is the only way to kill an Elumi."

She stared at him in dismay. Slowly, something he'd said a few moments earlier turned in her mind and produced a fresh shock. "My conveyance? My *car*?" Izzy wilted onto the couch again, fanning her face to keep from blacking out. "Please tell me you're not serious. Am I on Scare Tactics? Candid Camera from hell?"

He held his side. She could see blood seeping through his fingers and her stomach clenched in sympathetic pain despite the insulation of her shock. He grimaced. "I could not leave it lying there. The laws aside, the others would assuredly find me. As a matter of fact, I do not believe you should venture out until a suitable period of time has passed. When the babe has consciousness it will be able to protect itself from detection."

"Others? There's more of you?"

He nodded. "Many Fallen."

A surreal horror engulfed her, mingling with sympathy. She could see he was badly hurt, but damn his hide. She didn't need this shit.

"Okay, the first thing we need to do is get rid of the body while it's still dark ... and before it starts stinking up my car. Then I'll take care of your wounds. You stay here and keep some pressure on them. I won't be gone long."

He looked surprised and then disapproving. "I should go with you. You are too small to lift him and I do not want you to be alone--now."

She didn't know whether to laugh or cry that he was so worried about her when he was so weak he could hardly stand. Getting up decisively, she pushed him back, ignoring the smear of blue fluid on her brown leather couch. "No. I mean it, Raphael. You stay here. Where I'm going, you'll just be in the way. Think you'll live until I get back?"

He regarded her a long moment. "Yes."

She nodded and went out to her car. There was nothing in the backseat. For a minute, she wondered if maybe he'd just been joking around, then she thought about the trunk. She popped it open.

Sure enough, there was the body.

Izzy gagged and slammed it shut, then ran back inside. Raphael sat up and gave her a quizzical look.

"You're coming with me. No way am I touching that thing."

* * * *

By the time they got back from the swamp, it was nearing dawn. Raphael had pitched the head into the bog like a quarterback throwing a football. He'd also easily disposed of the body. The dumping was comical in a grotesque kind of way. Almost as soon as he had launched the body into the bayou, a gator had bellowed and dragged the carcass deep into the water--which was good, because she hadn't thought about bringing something along to weigh it down. She wasn't really in a state of mind to think about forensic evidence and the practicalities of weighing someone down so they wouldn't float to the top of the water.

Normally, she thought she would've been sick over the whole episode. She supposed it was the fact that the body wasn't human that allowed her to cope with it. The blue blood looked more like paint than actual blood. Or maybe it was because it simply hadn't seemed real at all? She'd always been a horror buff, so seeing a dead body seemed more like a bad gore movie than something real. Surreal, actually.

Or maybe it was because she'd just had so many shocks already that she couldn't take in any more?

She was a nervous wreck by the time they got back to her apartment and exhausted, both physically and emotionally. Unfortunately, she still had to tend to Raphael's wounds.

The first thing she got him to do was bathe in tepid water. He hissed initially at the coolness of the water as it struck his wounds, but fell silent and grim faced after a few seconds. She closed the door then cleaned up the couch and laid out a sheet and pillow for him, then gathered what medicinal supplies she could find--mostly band-aids and rubbing alcohol.

She was digging under the sink to see if she'd stuck some peroxide under it when something touched her ass.

She jumped, grazed her head on the lip of the cabinet, and knocked over three half empty bottles of cleaner. "Ow." She gave him a look. "You've got to stop ... uh ... where's the big towel I put out for you?"

Izzy looked up his gleaming wet body, standing above her like the Colossus of Rhodes. Water trickled down his thighs and calves and streamed in rivulets down the ripples of his belly, accentuating every lovely, muscled inch. His long black hair hung in thick, saturated locks around his shoulders, with tiny tendrils clinging to his forehead and cheeks. He had a small towel draped around his hips like a short Roman skirt, barely covering his groin area from her view.

"Is something wrong?" he asked, clutching his wounded side.

Izzy snapped out of her stupor. "No. Nothing. Everything's fine. Let's get you ... uh ... wrapped up."

She went back to the bathroom, grabbed the big towel, then draped it around his shoulders and pushed him down into a seat at the kitchen table. Now that he was clean--and naked--she could see his wounds weren't nearly as bad as she'd thought. What she'd thought were bruises must have been dirt, because there was no discoloration on his skin anywhere other than around the half dozen cuts, and those looked more like scratches. They were already healing. The gash in his side was the worst, and it had stopped bleeding. It probably needed stitches, but even if she'd thought she could stomach doing something like stitching him up she didn't keep a needle and thread. She dabbed alcohol on his wounds, surprised that he didn't flinch since it had always burned the crap out of her. When she was satisfied she'd disinfected everything, she folded up some paper towels and taped them to his side with half a box of band-aids.

Izzy rubbed her tired eyes and straightened from her crouch at his legs. "Okay. You get to sleep on the couch. I'm headed for bed." She walked to her bedroom door and stopped to look at him. "Do not disturb. Got it?"

She didn't wait for an answer. She shut her door, locked it and then crawled into bed, praying that everything that had happened had just been one freaky nightmare.

* * * *

It had been a very long time since Raphael had felt the elation of victory over an enemy. This was not because he had managed to avoid battle, or because he had lost his enjoyment of a good fight. It was because there had ceased, after a time, to seem to be any real point in it.

Tonight, however, he had protected his woman, and the sense of success and pride in his accomplishment had only been slightly leavened by the wounds he had sustained in his efforts. As the wounds healed and his strength began to return, his elation over his triumph had sent his blood to surging through his body, arousing his need to reaffirm his link with Isabel--his life companion, who had proven to him tonight that she was his in every sense of the word.

She had tried to protect him--just as an Elumi woman would have fought to protect her mate. He was so proud of her he could barely contain his pride, more so than he would have been if she *had* been Elumi, for she was so tiny and delicate, so fragile, and yet she had been brave, fearless in the face of death. She had not counted the cost to herself, not considered her lack of skill or strength in battling such a one as the warrior of Garyn.

He had adored her from the first, relished her beauty, her gentleness, her soft body and her glorious scent. Those things alone were enough to enslave his heart, but she was a far more wondrous creature than he had imagined. She was perfection. She was a goddess.

His goddess.

* * * *

A hand slid up her thigh, roaming around and up her ass cheeks to her lower back.

Izzy groaned and kicked backward, burying her face in the pillow against the bright morning light.

Not only was Raphael *not* human, but he didn't know how to follow simple directions.

"Unnnnhh. Go away," she growled, her voice muffled by the pillow.

A second hand followed the first, massaging her buttocks, her lower back, up her spinal column. The covers fell off, exposing her skin to the cool air-conditioning. Goosebumps skipped along her spine.

Heat fluttered low in her belly, forcing her mind to awaken.

"Fuck off," she groaned, attempting to roll away.

He caught her before she could escape, laying a leg across the backs of her thighs, an arm around her waist. He kissed the nape of her neck. "I would like to fuck you," he murmured.

Izzy craned her head back to look at him out of the corner of her eye. "That's so romantic."

"Thank you. I am growing accustomed to human speech."

She chortled.

She felt him smile against her skin just before his tongue swiped the back of her neck. He nipped her earlobe with his teeth, sending shockwaves of pleasure down her neck.

"I'm tired and want to get some sleep. I'm not in the mood, okay?" She was ... sort of ... but she wasn't about to let him know that. The man really was incorrigible.

"You will be." His voice was low, incredibly husky and deep. He rolled her onto her back, covering her lips with his.

She opened her mouth to cuss him out and then gasped when his tongue surged inside to plunder her depths. He caught her right arm, smoothing his palm up to her wrist to pin it to the bed.

His lips slid from hers, over her chin, down her throat. He nipped her, his teeth gently scraping her skin, soothing the abrasion with his warm, wet tongue.

This was getting out of hand. "Mmm. Oh. Stop that, Raphael. I mean it--" She broke off on a gasp as his mouth closed on her nipple, sucking it through her camisole until it stood in his mouth like a rigid point.

Izzy pushed at him with her free hand, looking at him from beneath heavy lids. She felt drugged by too little sleep and too much passion. "I said stop it. You're not going to change my mind."

He rested his head on her chest, looking up at her. His eyes glittered, almost luminescent--desire unmistakable. "Never has a woman resisted me before."

She swallowed. Wet heat made her womb clench with arousal. "Look, I just helped you get rid of a body. I've got ... things on my mind. I can't do this right now. It doesn't feel right."

He released her wrist, slowly. "I can make it feel better."

"All I want is sleep," she said, trying to convince herself as much as him.

He sighed and moved up beside her, curled his body around hers, and settled himself firmly in her bed.

Izzy gave up on fighting off contact, closed her eyes, and tried to ignore the presence of his erection digging into her backside. It seemed such a shame to waste it.

Chapter Five

Isabel swore he'd bruised her with that thing between his legs. She had a muscle cramp right at the base of her spine, just above her ass crack. She glared at Raphael as he wolfed down a pack of bacon, six eggs, four pieces of toast, and a pint of orange juice. She supposed he should have an appetite, what with all he'd done the night before. If he'd had his way, she'd be half dead now and unable to do more than lift a hand.

She'd had a hard time going to sleep last night--this morning.

Raphael was oddly endearing, both sexy and sweet. He'd cooked brunch for them both once she'd shown him how to work things, allowing her to sit back and watch him move around in the tiny kitchen. He served her first, making sure everything was to her liking before he sat down to eat.

She didn't know much about him, but she liked him. He was very cute, slightly awkward, but incredibly powerful and capable of things she couldn't even begin to understand. Which was, perhaps, her biggest problem with him.

She couldn't handle the whole Elumi/angel battle/war thing. From what she gathered, having any kind of relationship with him was going to be a problem in the long run. Never mind the fact that he didn't seem to have a job-- he had to kill ... people to stay alive.

His lips curled into a roguish smile as he put his hands behind his head and leaned back in his chair. "What is it you are thinking?"

"Stuff." She was thinking of how to broach the subject without hurting his feelings.

She massaged her aching head and finally got up and went into the living room. After a few moments, Raphael followed her, studying her frowningly. "What distresses you?"

Izzy stared at him in disbelief and finally shook her head. "Everything. Jesus! I helped you dispose of a body last night. I can't fucking believe I did that. I don't know what's worse, that I did it, or that it seemed reasonable to me at the time."

She looked at him helplessly. "This isn't your world, Raphael. We don't do things like that here--ok, well, granted there are bad people running around killing people, and there are soldiers fighting wars and getting killed and killing people, but--

"I like you--really, I do. I think you're sweet and cute and--but I can't deal with this. I don't want to be in the middle of your war, or whatever it is your people have got going on. I want--I need for you to leave. I just don't feel safe with you here knowing they'll come looking for you again."

He studied her, both hurt and anger glittering in his eyes. "It would not help you if I left. It would put you in more danger--because of the babe."

His anger fueled hers and the hurt she saw in his eyes only made her angrier still. She hadn't promised him a damned thing. Was it her fault he'd followed her home and thought he could just 'claim' her? "Well, if you ask me it was a really *stupid* time to decide to have a baby--right in the middle of some kind of war!"

"There is no 'good' time for me! It will always be this way for me! I can never go back. There will always be enemies who walk among humans and they will always be seeking a trophy that will gain them favor with their king and redemption so that they can return to Pearthen," he said angrily. "I will protect you. I am a skilled and seasoned warrior. I would not have considered taking you as my woman if I had doubted that I could protect you."

"That may be, but you had no damned right to drag me into this without even telling me what was going on! I should have had a choice. You didn't give me one. You just *decided* for me, decided to give me your baby without asking me if I wanted, decided to endanger my life without even letting me know I was in danger! I don't want to be planting bodies for the rest of my life! I want you to go. I'll take my chances on some of the others finding me. I just want you to leave--now."

He stared at her angrily for several moments and finally turned, stalking straight through the wall and vanishing.

* * * *

Pain and fury so blinded Raphael that he had no notion of where he was going, or any care. Stunned disbelief was not far behind the other two emotions, and he was so distraught that he very nearly lost his head.

Instincts honed of many years of fighting were all that spared him from instant death. As it was, the Garyn blindsided him, slamming into him from no where and pitching him against the wall of a tall building so hard it rattled the teeth in his head and crumbled brick and mortar, for he had not had the time or the presence of mind to morph.

The blow stunned him. He found himself falling, the Earth flying upward to meet him. With an effort, he threw off his shock and emotional distress and focused on the enemy bearing down upon him, executing a sharp climb at the last possible moment.

The Garyn, in close pursuit, was not able to do the same and slammed into a vehicle parked along the curb, crushing the top flat.

He was without his weapon and too disoriented for many moments to remember where he had hidden it. The memory surfaced as he saw the Garyn rise slowly, shake off his disorientation and shoot skyward once more.

Again, his distraction cost him. He would have managed to put far more distance between himself and his foe if he had had his wits about him. As it was, he had little lead when he dipped behind the top of a building and raced to retrieve his weapon in the building where he had sought shelter before--before Isabel, before he had come to the mistaken belief that he had found his life's companion.

Shaking that thought, he concentrated on eluding his enemy, struggling to reach the place where he had hidden his weapon before the Elumi could catch up to him.

He did not manage to shake pursuit, nor retrieve the weapon. Even as he entered the building and raced to retrieve his sword, the Garyn appeared before him, blocking his path.

Tightlipped with fury, Raphael halted abruptly, assumed a fighting stance and waited.

They circled one another, each looking for an opening. Raphael's goal was to reach the beam where his sword lay, however, and each time the Garyn swung at him, he leaped back and to one side, leading, until he had managed to circle his opponent and stood beneath the beam.

He stopped there, curling back his lips in a feral smile as he waited for the Garyn to attack. When the Elumi charged, Raphael managed to catch him beneath his armpits. Locking his hands behind his foe's back, he lifted man clear of the floor and swung around at the same moment, abruptly releasing him. The momentum sent his opponent flying backwards. The Garyn morphed, disappearing through the wall.

Raphael did not wait to see the results, however. The moment he regained his balance, he leapt for the beam, snatching his sword from it.

He'd barely touched down once more when the Garyn slammed into his mid section, carrying him across the room into the wall behind him before Raphael could completely morph. The concussion broke them apart.

Growling in fury now, Raphael leapt away, swinging his sword in a deadly arch that caught his foe across his middle. The blade bit, sliding over his ribs and burrowing into his belly, but the Garyn managed to leap backwards and avoided being skewered.

Regardless, Raphael's blow was a determining one. The Garyn was losing strength and blood too rapidly to prolong the fight. Uttering a challenging roar, he leapt at Raphael, hammering at him ferociously with his sword in an attempt to find victory before he grew too weakened to continue the fight.

Raphael found himself again fighting a defensive battle, meeting the blinding speed of the Garyn's blade each time, but he discovered that he, too, was growing weak, losing blood. They began to slip and slide through the gore on the floor, nicking each other over and over, but finding no clear opening to deal a decisive blow.

Finally, when both were so weak and winded they'd slowed, begun to have difficulty swinging their blades, the Garyn abruptly retreated. Gasping for breath, Raphael stood watching his foe's retreat, knowing he should follow and finish it, but too weak by now to care. His knees wobbled and finally gave way and he landed hard on the wooden floor.

Bemused, he looked down at himself, wondering why he was losing so much blood. The white glint of bone showed in his right thigh. He did not think that that was the problem, however, nor the gash along his arm. The worst damage seemed to be his belly.

Mopping the blood and sweat from his eyes the best he could with his hand, he clutched his belly and pushed himself to his feet. He almost blacked out when he leapt for the beam to retrieve his scabbard, but he could not afford to be caught without his weapon again, and he was afraid he would drop it and lose it if he didn't secure it. Once he had donned his scabbard and secured the weapon, though, he was so weak he wasn't certain he had the strength to leave.

He could not stay where he was. The Garyn might recover first and return to find him.

An almost overwhelming yearning filled him to return to Isabel, but he was not so lost to his responsibilities to his mate and child to seriously consider it. To give in to his need to be with her would be to endanger her and the child.

Besides, she did not want him.

After looking around the building a little vaguely for some time, he recalled the place that he had found for his family. It would be secure--if he could reach it--and he would be allowed to rest and heal in peace.

He was barely conscious by the time he managed to reach his sanctuary, the 'nest' he had been so busily preparing for his woman and child. Wavering on his feet, he stared at the large bed that he had planned to share with his Isabel, envisioning her curled up among the pillows he had taken such pains to collect and smiling up at him in greeting.

A smile curled his lips in return just about the time oblivion descended with the suddenness of a light switch.

* * * *

When he'd gone, Isabel stood in the middle of her apartment, thinking over the fight they'd just had, trying to ignore the sadness and the guilt that began to creep into her. She'd done the right thing. She knew she had, and she had been well within her rights to be so angry about what he'd done. He *hadn't* given her any choices.

Maybe, if he had told her at least a little she would've decided to be with him anyway. Maybe. Maybe not.

She supposed she could see his side of it. Selfish as it was, he could certainly have no hope of getting a female to let him within a mile of her if she knew everything going in.

He was lonely.

She'd seen it in his eyes--even from the first--that neediness that had nothing to do with sex and everything to do with desperation for human contact--or whatever. He couldn't go home and he wasn't supposed to have contact with humans.

He had to have been horribly lonely.

She shook that off. As awful as it made her feel, it wasn't her fault. Maybe he did and maybe he didn't deserve the punishment he'd gotten, but she certainly didn't deserve to suffer with him.

She had as much right to think of herself as he did, and if he'd spoken the truth, she had to think of the baby now, too. Making him leave wasn't going to be enough. If the angels or whatever they were could find her at the bar, they could certainly find her if she stayed in the city.

As badly as she hated it, it seemed to her that the only option to keep safe was to leave. She didn't like having to change her life, especially on the basis of what was supposed to have been only a one night stand, but pregnancy was always a risk when having sex. She'd just been caught this time into something far more complicated than she thought would happen.

Izzy touched her stomach, wondering what it would look like, how it would feel in her arms ... how she would ever figure out how to take care of it.

"Great. I'm already getting emotional." She felt positively weepy.

She straightened her spine and went to work packing up clothes and other essentials into a suitcase. It distracted her from thinking too deeply on anything more specific than what shoes she'd bring and how many pairs of underwear.

She loaded up her car with the suitcases and bags of food and then headed out of town. Her family owned a shack in the bayous. They hadn't been there since last summer, but it was very remote and hard to find. She'd always hated the place, as much for its pest problem as for its solitude, but the solitude was a huge bonus right now.

She couldn't imagine anyone other than family being able to find her there.

Two hours later, she parked the car at the family shack. It was worse than she remembered, but she was certain she'd get used to it.

A box of chocolates, a bag of Doritos, a quart of chocolate chip mint ice cream, and three days later, Isabel hadn't adjusted, and she'd used up all her edible "entertainment." Electricity that came on and went off at random intervals, no phone, no television, no internet, and only one dog-eared romance novel she'd already read three times over the years--why in the hell had she thought she could stand being out in the boonies?

More than anything, she had time. Time to mope around the shack and clean until it was more or less spotless. Time to dwell on all the mistakes she'd made in her life. Time to start fantasizing about baby names and wallpaper. And time to start missing the hell out of Raphael and to feel ultra guilty for leaving him without a word of where she was going.

What if she never saw him again?

Izzy worried her knuckle with her teeth, sitting on the legless, old couch with her legs curled up. She growled out loud and flopped onto her back, covering her face with an arm. She'd be nuts if she had to take a week of this.

She had to *do* something. As tempting as it was to simply dismiss everything she'd learned about Raphael and head back to the city as if nothing in her world had changed, she knew that would be a stupid move. Coming down had been smart, even if she hadn't completely thought it through. Going back would be the ultimate stupidity.

She needed a job, she decided. She had plenty of savings and money wasn't a serious issue--wouldn't be if she stayed in the cabin, because god knew the damned thing didn't take much to maintain when it was just a box with a lid on it--little electricity and nothing fun and expensive. Aside from food and a tank of gas now and then, she didn't have anything to spend money on.

She still needed something to keep from going stir crazy. Chances were whatever job she could land in the little town closest to the cabin would barely earn her enough to make gas money, but that wasn't the point. Keeping from going nuts was the point.

Grabbing her purse, she left the cabin and headed into town.

Chapter Six

Jobs were scarcer than hen's teeth. Isabel had tried every store, all--one--restaurant--even the gas station. Most of the places were run by a single employee--the owner. Giving up on that idea for the moment, she lingered in town searching for something she could use to occupy her time while she was hiding out at the cabin.

Raphael had said that, in time, the baby would develop enough that it would protect itself from discovery-- whatever that meant and she didn't really want to think about it a whole lot. Maybe, if she could just get through the next couple of weeks, she could go back to her apartment in the city?

She managed to round up some reading materials at the grocery store and the small used bookstore. When she'd deposited them in her car, she headed down the sidewalk to the feed store and picked out some seed.

The proprietor pointed out that it was past planting season, but she wasn't planning on harvesting any of it. The only part she cared about was having something to do.

When she'd combed every shop in town for small projects that had at least some appeal at the moment, she headed for the grocery store again to buy some edible entertainment.

She was going to get fat as hell if she kept dosing her depression with food, but the remoteness of the cabin made her feel threatened if her cupboards were even slightly empty--which was strange because when she'd lived in town there was almost never anything in any of her cabinets.

It was late by the time she'd finished screwing around and wasting her money on things she didn't really need. Dismayed that she hadn't noticed it was getting so late, she headed to her car, stowed the last of her purchases and headed out of town again.

The narrow road that led to the cabin wasn't made for speed. There were too many sharp twists and turns and huge potholes in the thing. By the time she got to the over grown track that led off from the road and back into the woods, it was already dark.

Feeling distinctly creeped out, and trying not to think about the fact that she was going to have to go into a pitch black cabin and feel around for her lamps, Izzy focused on keeping the car on the road and missing the trees that grew so close to the edge.

The cabin was black as pitch. The glow of the moon and stars lit the sky just enough to make a pale, eerie backdrop for the moss draped trees surrounding the cabin and add a little more creepiness to the scene.

Isabel studied the area for any sign of movement, working on dismissing the uneasiness she felt about getting out of the car and stumbling around in the dark. Most of the stuff she'd bought would be alright to leave, but she would have to make at least two trips to get her groceries inside.

Pushing the car door open finally, she used the light from the overhead to scan the ground between the car and porch steps for any sign of snakes. When she saw nothing slithering across the ground, she grabbed a bag and dashed for the steps. The door was still padlocked. She had to set the bag down and use both hands to get it unlocked. When she'd opened the door, she pushed it wide, trying to penetrate the darkness within. Dark shadows lay in darker shadows. She knew it was the furniture, but the hair lifted on her neck anyway. After studying over it for several minutes, she remembered there was a portable lamp on the small table near her favorite chair. Feeling her way across the room like a blind person, she managed to locate every piece of furniture in the room and bark her shins and toes on them before she fell over the footstool beside the chair she'd been trying to locate.

"Damn it! Shit!" Crawling up, she found the table and finally the light. Relief flooded her as light filled the room. Getting to her feet, she examined her bruises and then lifted the lamp higher and scanned the room.

A tall man stepped through the rear wall as she illuminated it and Isabel's heart braked to a halt in her chest.

It wasn't Raphael--the man was fair--and it was for certain it wasn't the Elumi floating in the bayou.

Letting out a shriek, Izzy hurled her lamp at the winged man's head and whirled to vacate the cabin. She'd almost made it to the door when he slammed into her from behind. The impact might have propelled her through the door and maybe even over the car except that his arm cinched around her waist at the same moment. Izzy doubled over the immovable object, her face slamming into her thigh.

The impact knocked the breath out of her. Stunned, she hung limply from the arm holding her, fighting to drag air into her lungs. It was just as well it hadn't occurred to her to try to use her weight against her assailant, because he didn't seem to be having any trouble at all holding her with one arm.

Turning, he kicked the door closed. After surveying the room, he moved to the couch and dropped her onto it. Isabel wilted onto her back, nursing her bruised stomach and paralyzed solar plexus. Finally, the pain began to subside and she was able to drag a deeper breath into her lungs.

Blinking back the tears of pain, she searched the room for the creature she knew had to be an Elumi of Pearthen.

"You stink of Marceenian."

The low growling voice jerked her head around.

He was standing in front of the door, his legs braced wide, his arms crossed over his chest.

Surprisingly enough, her electric lantern hadn't broken when she'd thrown it at the Elumi. It lay on its side on the floor near the back wall now, however, and shed little light within the room.

Izzy licked her lips. She didn't especially like the way the Elumi was studying her. His lips curled upward in something more akin to a sneer than a smile. "I would not shame my name by lying with a human--especially not one that had already lain with a Marceenian and carries his half breed babe in her belly."

Anger surged through Izzy, submerging her fear. She realized almost at once, though, that he was trying to make her mad. She wasn't certain why, maybe to test her to see if she would try to fight?

Swallowing her anger with an effort, Izzy pushed herself upright and drew her legs up to her chest, trying to keep from showing him how scared she was.

Her thoughts were chaotic and fear and pain didn't help her sort them any. It occurred to her, though, that he must have followed her from town. Nothing else made any sense, for she'd already been here several days. If he'd followed her from the city, she felt sure she would have seen him sooner.

So--he just happened to be in the neighborhood and caught the scent and decided to follow her?

Dropping his stance when she did nothing more than curl up on the couch, the Elumi moved away from the door. "I know that stench. It is that dog of a Marceenian, Raphael."

Startled, Izzy's eyes widened and she glanced at the man.

A smile curled his lips and she could've kicked herself. Now she didn't know if he'd just been fishing or if he'd known already.

Did it matter? It seemed fairly obvious what was going on. He didn't want her. He wanted Raphael.

She was bait.

She wanted to cover her face with her hands to hide the emotions she knew must be evident in her expression, but she didn't dare take her eyes off of him.

He crouched in front of her, studying her curiously. "Four days ago, I almost took his head. He has grown weak and slow and lazy since he was banished from Pearthen. He did not even have his weapon."

Four days? The day she made him leave? A wave of horror and nausea washed over Izzy. She fought it back with the reflection that the man could not have killed Raphael or he would not still be looking for him.

She felt like crying. She had been so mean to him, making him leave, and he'd been hurt, almost killed.

"He is utterly disgraced. I am amazed he was not executed for his failure to protect the ambassador instead of being exiled. But then, the king obviously was not particularly displeased since the ambassador who was slain was from Garyn."

It occurred to Izzy abruptly that luck had been with her. Her initial fear and pain had prevented her from putting up any sort of struggle, but it had also led him to believe she was no threat. As long as he believed that, he might taunt her, but he would not watch her nearly as closely.

She had no idea how she might use that to her advantage, but it was the only weapon she had.

"Did he tell you what he was doing while the ambassador, who was under his protection and a well respected statesman of my homeland, was being assassinated?"

Izzy stared at him blankly, though she knew the moment he said it what he was getting at. He'd changed tactics. Insulting Raphael hadn't made her mad enough to be stupid. He thought he would try jealousy.

"He was wooing a young Marceenian maid."

She'd been braced for that news and jealousy still seeped into her like poison--which was utterly stupid. It didn't matter what had happened before he'd met her. That was his life and his business--just as her past was her business. Besides, they really hadn't had anything but a one night stand.

It wasn't like they'd made any sort of commitment or anything.

Except that Raphael had seemed pretty convinced she was 'his' woman.

And she'd thought she was more interested in getting rid of him and his problems than being with him.

She wasn't, though, she realized. It didn't matter what she'd said to Raphael, or what lies she'd told herself. She'd been smitten with him right from the start and nothing that had happened since had cured her.

In fact, almost everything he'd done had helped him dig a little deeper under her skin. Maybe she was a fool, but she couldn't help it. The big, helpless, barbarian appealed to everything womanly inside her--passion, the need to be needed, the need to feel protected and cherished. It didn't hurt that he was also sweet, loving, and drop dead gorgeous.

Nine out of ten women would have been in love with him inside of ten minutes of meeting him, so either she wasn't a complete moron or she wasn't any brighter than the next woman.

"Do you think he will come for you? Or has he moved on to another female by now? Obviously, he has developed a taste for human flesh."

It took all Isabel could do to keep from glaring at him. She concentrated on staring at the far wall instead, resisting the urge to point out that *he* obviously thought that she meant something to Raphael and he would come. Otherwise, what use would she be as bait?

That thought frightened her, however. What if Raphael did come? He would be walking into a trap.

What if he *didn't* come?

Would the Elumi warrior just go away again?

She had a bad feeling he wouldn't.

By the time Isabel had been curled up on the couch for nearly an hour, she'd begun to be less scared than uncomfortable. "I need to use the bathroom," she said to the Elumi, who'd gone back to guarding the front door.

He tilted his head curiously and finally shrugged. "Do not run, little human. I would find it so entertaining to chase you, but I do not think that you would enjoy it nearly as much."

Chapter Seven

Izzy was more than a little stunned that he didn't follow her to the bathroom. She'd certainly hoped he would get the idea that she was too frightened, and/or too stupid to be any problem, but it was a little disconcerting all the same.

To fly or not to fly, she wondered while she attended her needs?

It might be better to lull him a little longer.

On the other hand, what if Raphael was even now coming after her? If she waited, he was going to walk into a trap. If she fled and she actually succeeded in getting away, she could warn Raphael.

There was that scent thing. Ordinarily, she would have put that down as an outright whopper, but he'd found her somehow.

Maybe he'd just seen her and followed her?

But how would he know about Raphael? And how would he know, as Raphael seemed to, that she was pregnant when *she* didn't know a damned thing?

He'd claimed he'd fought Raphael. He hadn't said anything about wounding him, but she had a hard time believing that two giants could hack at each other with those five foot swords and *not* wound each other.

Maybe the reason she hadn't seen anything of Raphael was because he was too hurt to come looking for her?

Not that she'd wanted him to and she certainly didn't want that now.

Sighing, she returned to the couch like a good little girl and curled up on it again, meek as could be. She was worried about Raphael in a whole new way, though, now, and it took all she could do to sit still. Next time, she decided. She would wait an hour or maybe two, and then she would ask again and she would crawl out the bathroom window and take off.

But to where?

She would be lost in the bayous inside of five minutes if she headed into it and she'd probably never find her way out. Besides, having to fight her way through swamp, snakes, and gators was scarier than dealing with the Elumi--especially the snakes. The alternative was to take off down the drive and she didn't think it would take him long to catch her.

She doubted very much that she could get into her car and start it up before he caught up to her.

Maybe she should wait until he fell asleep and brain him with something?

She began to study the cabin surreptitiously, searching for something she could use.

The iron frying pan her mother used for frying up catfish would probably spatter his brains all over the place if she managed to get a good lick in.

Her stomach roiled at the thought, but it was him or her--
or him or Raphael, so it was just going to have to be him.

She dozed off. She couldn't believe she fell asleep! She
jerked awake when she felt herself slipping sideways and
looked around a little frantically. The Elumi was still
stationed at the door, his gaze on her.

Damn it! Didn't they ever sleep!

Raphael had, so she knew they had to.

Straightening in her seat, she tried to shrug off the dulling
effect of too little sleep. She was just about to ask the
Elumi if she could go to the bathroom again when she
heard something that made her heart lurch painfully--the
flutter of great wings.

Her gaze jerked immediately to the Elumi. He'd tensed.
She knew then that he'd heard it, too, and that it wasn't just
a bird. The soft thud of a foot on the steps of the cabin
followed.

She'd left the car door open and groceries by the door! He
was bound to notice and realize something wasn't right.

She didn't hear any sort of hesitation as the tread moved
across the porch.

The Elumi stepped away from the door, his sword in his
hand now.

Izzy glanced frantically around. The only thing close to
hand was a paperback novel. That certainly wasn't going to
damage him. Maybe it would distract him, though.

When the footfalls stopped, Izzy grabbed the book and
hurled it at the Elumi, screaming for all she worth.

The Elumi whirled to look at her. At almost the same
moment, Raphael stepped through the wall behind the man-
-or it would've been behind him except that he'd turned
when Izzy screamed. Dismay filled her as he leapt away
from Raphael, whirling to face him.

"Go, Isabel!" Raphael roared, swinging his blade at his
enemy.

"Marceenian dog!" the Elumi growled, meeting Raphael's
blade with his own. The metal clanged together, ringing
loudly in the tiny cabin. Leaping from her seat, Izzy
charged into the kitchen and grabbed the iron frying pan.

It felt like it weighed a good twenty pounds.

When she reached the main room again it was just in time to see Raphael flying backwards. Instead of slamming into the wall, however, he disappeared through it.

Snarling, the Elumi charged after him, vanishing from sight just as Raphael had.

Izzy froze, listening to the clang of blades outside. She'd just dashed toward the front door when both Elumi, locked together, blades locked at the hilt, their teeth bared, flew through the middle of the cabin and out the other side.

Skidding to a halt, she changed directions and headed toward the back door. She'd already snatched it open when a crash from the vicinity of the main room brought her up short. Whirling, she saw Raphael slam into the floor with the other man on top of him.

Gritting her teeth, she drew the frying pan back like a bat and sailed into the living room. Uttering a growl, Raphael bucked the man off and rolled on top of his opponent just as Izzy swung the frying pan for all she was worth. She stopped. The pan didn't. The momentum and weigh carried it into Raphael's head.

Fortunately, it was a glancing blow. Unfortunately, it distracted Raphael. "Do not help!" he growled as the Elumi threw him off and instantly leapt on top of him.

Ignoring the order, Izzy leapt at the man while he was distracted with trying to choke the life out of Raphael. Drawing the frying pan back, she swung again, catching him up side of the head. The pan rang. The vibration went through the pan and into her hands, numbing them until she almost lost her grip on it.

The Elumi turned and glared at her.

Screaming, Izzy whacked him with the pan several more times, striking his shoulder once and his head twice.

Abruptly, his eyes rolled back in his head and he tumbled to one side.

Raphael sat up, looked at Isabel and then looked down at the fallen warrior. Abruptly, he leapt to his feet, grabbed the Elumi by the hair of his head and swung his sword.

Isabel whirled away, covering her face with her hands.

"It is done," Raphael said tiredly.

Isabel turned at the sound of his voice, peering at him between her parted fingertips.

He stared at her a long moment and dropped the sword to the floor. Striding toward her, he caught her upper arms and yanked her against his length, covering her mouth in a hard kiss and ravishing her mouth with tongue. Weak already with the shock and fear from the fight, Isabel melted against him, clutching his arms to steady herself.

Dizziness assailed her, darkness crowded close and fire poured through her, bringing every inch of her flesh tingling to life.

Reaching down, he grasped her thigh, guiding her leg around his waist. Izzy took the hint, looping her arms around his neck and curling her other leg around him, as well.

He broke the kiss, looked around and strode to the bedroom. Falling on the mattress with her, he caught her blouse, ripping it away and burrowing his face against her breasts.

Izzy groaned, threading her fingers through his dark, silky hair as he burned a trail of hot kisses from the valley between her breasts and caught one nipple between his teeth.

She arched upward as he sucked the tender nub, sending jolts of pleasure through her that made moisture gather in her sex.

She thrust her hands down his naked back to his buttocks, digging her nails into the firm cheeks to cup him against her achy sex. He groaned around her nipple, sucking her harder as he frantically disposed of her pants, pulling away just long enough to remove his own and free them from barriers of cloth.

She gasped when he covered her body and settled between her thighs, prodding her with the hot brand of his erection. She planted her feet on the bed, arching her hips upward to meet him. His thick length enticingly rubbed her clit, sending her into mindless need.

"I want you," she gasped. "Now."

"As you wish," he ground out, watching her with smoky eyes smoldering with insatiable desire. He rocked his hips, grinding himself against her bare cleft.

She bit her bottom lip, tightening her thighs around his hips. "Oh god, don't look at me that way. I'll cum right now," she said on a whimper. Pulses of pleasure shivered through her slit, ravaging her miniscule control with each teasing slide of his cock through her wet center.

He smiled with dark intent, sending goose bumps down her spine. His head descended, lips parted, breath heavy. She licked her lips, anticipating his taste and the hypnotic pull of his mouth.

Raphael covered her lips, stealing her breath away with his intensity. He ravished her mouth, sucking her tongue and lips as he shifted his hips and brought his cock to her entrance, thrusting inside with one smooth, deep stroke. He stretched her pussy to the limits, his length hot and hard and making her feel incredibly full.

Flaming tendrils of bliss licked at her insides, making her cunt quiver with impending release.

Whimpering, she tilted her hips, angling for deeper penetration as he worked inside her and out, driving harder, frantic to find ultimate satisfaction. He ground against her, nudging her womb, sending shockwaves of pleasure rocketing through her system.

She clung to his back, kissing him for all she was worth, riding toward the crest of bliss until it came upon her in a blinding flash. A moan tore from her throat. White hot pleasure erupted in her center, followed quickly by the jerking grind of his own orgasm. His seed burst inside her, and she trembled, her body shuddering, soaking up his semen and milking him for more.

He arched his back and cried out her name, his voice hoarse with pleasure. He collapsed on top of her, breathing heavily, kissing her face all over and smoothing her hair back from her damp forehead with gentle fingers.

He rolled suddenly, withdrawing with a sucking sound from her entrance. She was saturated, sticky--a mess. But satisfied beyond belief.

Izzy curled up against him as her heart rate and breathing slowly returned to normal.

Weak in the aftermath, so blissfully sated she felt like hot wax, Izzy lay with her eyes closed, smiling faintly. It occurred to her that they had a little problem in the living room. "You've corrupted me. There's a dead guy outside and I didn't even think about it until now. I shouldn't be so calm about it. I should be disgusted. This isn't exactly conducive to romance, you know."

"My warrior woman." Raphael chuckled. "Passion in battle and bed are easily one and the same."

She wasn't entirely sure that was right, but whatever. "I hope you never get passionate with one of the guys."

He looked affronted. "Never." He nuzzled her neck. "Twice you have fought for me. You can not deny you care for me, Isabel."

She stretched her neck closer. "Mmm. Guess not."

His head came up with a jerk. He looked a little startled. "You do?"

Izzy chuckled at the look. "I'm either mad or I'm mad about you, one of the two--and I'm not really sure which. I guess you've had me enthralled from the beginning."

His lips curled into a smile. "Then you will stay with me?"

Izzy lifted a hand to play with his hair. "Do I have a choice?" she asked teasingly.

He frowned, a look more of distress than anger. "Would you choose to stay?"

She met his gaze unflinchingly and cupped his cheek. "Yes, my love."

The End

Printed in the United States
36243LVS00002B/64-426